STILL WATERS

A Selection of Further Titles by Marilyn Todd

The High Priestess Iliona Greek Mysteries

BLIND EYE *
BLOOD MOON *
STILL WATERS *

The Claudia Seferius Roman Mysteries

I, CLAUDIA
VIRGIN TERRITORY
MAN EATER
WOLF WHISTLE
JAIL BAIT
BLACK SALAMANDER
DREAM BOAT *
DARK HORSE *
SECOND ACT *
WIDOW'S PIQUE *
STONE COLD *
SOUR GRAPES *
SCORPION RISING *

* *available from Severn House*

STILL WATERS

Marilyn Todd

This first world edition published 2010
in Great Britain and in the USA by
SEVERN HOUSE PUBLISHERS LTD of
9–15 High Street, Sutton, Surrey, England, SM1 1DF.
Trade paperback edition published
in Great Britain and the USA 2010 by
SEVERN HOUSE PUBLISHERS LTD

British Library Cataloguing in Publication Data

Todd, Marilyn.
  Still waters. – (The High Priestess Iliona Greek mysteries)
  1. Iliona (Fictitious character) – Fiction. 2. Women
  priests – Greece – Sparta (Extinct city) – Fiction.
  3. Secret service – Greece – Sparta (Extinct city) –
  Fiction. 4. Wrestlers – Death – Fiction. 5. Murder –
  Investigation – Fiction. 6. Detective and mystery stories.
  I. Title II. Series
  823.9'14-dc22

ISBN-13: 978-0-7278-6899-2   (cased)
ISBN-13: 978-1-84751-241-3   (trade paper)

For Linda and David. In-laws by marriage. Friends by choice.

All Severn House titles are printed on acid-free paper.

Severn House Publishers support The Forest Stewardship Council [FSC],
the leading international forest certification organisation. All our titles that
are printed on Greenpeace-approved FSC-certified paper carry the FSC logo.

Mixed Sources
Product group from well-managed
forests and other controlled sources
www.fsc.org Cert no. SA-COC-1565
© 1996 Forest Stewardship Council
FSC

Typeset by Palimpsest Book Production Ltd.,
Grangemouth, Stirlingshire, Scotland.
Printed and bound in Great Britain by
MPG Books Ltd., Bodmin, Cornwall.

ONE

Above him, the mountain peaks slept. The ravines, the gorges, the torrent beds were silent. Slumbering beneath a blanket of velvet. The man listened. Heard the wind hissing in the alders. The gurgle of water passing over the rocks. Even the distant hoot of an owl.

But no footsteps. No voice softly calling his name.

He waited.

The scent of mountain sage mingled with spicy wild basil and the fragrant pink oleanders that lined the river banks. Known to some as 'the Rose of the Brooks', most people referred to it by another name. 'Horse Killer', after leaves that were toxic enough to make a heart stop. Deadly beauty was a concept the man was familiar with. Mostly in human form.

The faint grey of dawn slanted through the clouds. It was time.

In the hills, quail were fattening up on insects and seeds, before migrating south for the winter. Mushrooms were sprouting across the forest floor and soon fog would be swirling round the oaks and the chestnut trees. The leaves were already beginning to turn. But for now the days were long, the air warm, and the autumn equinox that signalled the end to the campaigning season was still some days away. Would the end of this summer's fighting bring peace? Stupid question. There was always someone who wanted what other men owned, and in a continent where water, minerals and rich soil were precious, conflict was guaranteed.

In that respect, Sparta was blessed. This land boasted all three, with plenty to spare, and produced the best fighting force the world had ever seen. Which was just as well. With nine hundred city states scattered across three and a half thousand square miles, the smaller, weaker, more isolated kingdoms were easy prey for power-hungry predators. Thanks to the strength of Athens' navy and the mighty Spartan army, the tyrants were largely kept in check.

At what financial cost, though?

The sky turned from grey to yellow to copper to pink. Peaks came into focus. Some rounded and gentle, others jagged and sharp, some with crowns of snow that never melted away.

Birds started to sing in the thickets. Rabbits emerged from their warrens. The creatures of the night slunk back to their lairs. It was only when the sun peered over the mountain tops that the man knew Gregos would not be coming.

He unsheathed his dagger.

Gregos was never late.

Downstream, where the Eurotas widened and slowed, Iliona also watched the sun climb over the peaks. Unable to sleep, she'd watched dawn light up the lush grasses that grew round the temple precinct. Saw the fish rise in the river god's sacred pool. Waited while the sun warmed the wild rosemary and released its scent on the breeze. Where the bank was stony, deer came down to drink. An egret stalked the shallows with vigilant tread.

This was the quietest time of the day, a moment to be savoured – providing you could ignore the enormous piles of masonry and rubble, where the builders were installing a new watercourse, gymnasium and library. Had the temple not been standing proud among it all, you'd be forgiven for thinking the place had fallen victim to an earthquake. Holes here, channels there, the cypresses white with dust. Small wonder worshippers had tailed off.

'Up! Come on, come on, up, up, up!' The child's plea was both urgent and breathless. 'Don't stop, don't stop! Keep going.'

There was a gasp of frustration. A scrabbling that went on for several minutes, then silence. A few seconds later she heard the sound of anguished sobbing.

So much for the moment to herself.

Iliona followed the sound to a stand of willows overhanging the river, where a boy of seven, maybe eight, was hugging his arms to his belly and rocking back and forth on the ground.

'Shh.' She scooped his bony frame into her arms. 'Shh, it's all right.'

'No, it's not,' he gulped, swinging his head wildly from side to side. 'See?'

A dirty, bleeding finger pointed to a piece of white cloth caught in the treetops. There seemed to be a string trailing down.

'Your kite?'

'Yes. No.' His small, freckled face was swollen and red, his eyes brimming with hopelessness. 'I need to get it back, but it's too high.'

That explained the blood, the dirt and the frantic scrabbling.

Even the lowest branch was out of his reach. But the urgency? Judging by his rough haircut and hand-me-down tunic, he was a helot. Son of a serf, too poor to splash out on luxury toys; this was clearly a treasured possession.

'Suppose we pour a libation to the river god?' she suggested. 'Burn some incense, throw some rose petals into his waters?' She closed her eyes and pretended to sway in a trance. 'Beneath a nest of bronze and wood, wings will fall from the stars.'

The boy sniffed. 'What's that mean?'

She opened one eye. 'How do I know? I'm only the Oracle, who imparts the river god's riddles – no, wait. Suppose . . . suppose the nest of bronze and wood means the wind chimes in the plane grove? And suppose Eurotas is telling us that tonight, when the stars are out, a new kite will fall from the sky and land right beneath them?' She dropped to the boy's level. 'Why don't you come back at nightfall and see if it's true?'

'Can't.' Tears flooded his eyes. 'Need that one.'

'Why? Does it belong to somebody else? Have you borrowed it, perhaps, without asking?'

'No, it's mine, I made it.' He started rocking again, howling louder. 'It's a letter to Zeus,' he wailed. 'I wrote it myself. Tried to send it to Olympus, but it got caught in the branches—'

'Let's write him another.'

'No! No, it's got to be that one. It's my Mam's tunic, don't you see?' He didn't wait for an answer. 'I cut it off before they burned her, when no one was looking—'

Her heart dropped. 'Your mother's dead?'

'Aye, but if I send that letter to Zeus, he'll put it right. He'll tell Hades to send her back over the Styx—'

Iliona scooped the boy into her arms and hugged him tight. 'Darling, he can't,' she said gently. He smelled of parsley and cypress, poor people's funeral herbs, since they couldn't afford cinnamon and myrrh. 'She's a shade in the realm of the Underworld now, and even Almighty Zeus can't bring her home. Your Mam's gone for ever, sweetheart.'

She expected him to lash out in defiance, or collapse in a heap. He did neither. Pulling out of her arms, his body stopped wracking and wise eyes met hers.

'Maybe not,' he said slowly. 'But if I don't try, if I don't send that letter, my Mam'll never have the chance to come home.'

There was no arguing with the logic, which left Iliona only

one option. Reaching up, she grabbed the branch and swung herself up. Heard the stitches of her wound rip. Felt the hot gush of blood at the same time as the pain tore through her stomach. *Suddenly, she was back in the temple precinct . . . Too drained emotionally, too physically exhausted, to recognize the grievance in his eyes . . . She'd felt a blow. Looked down. Saw the knife in her side . . .*

'Can you reach?' a small voice asked from below.

She clutched at the willow branch, gasping for breath, sweat and blood drenching her tunic.

'Almost.'

After a while, the pain dulled to a furious ache. The bleeding eased up. What on earth was she thinking of? In an hour or two, there would be servants and workmen all over the temple. Let them get the bloody kite out of the branches. She lowered her foot, but when she looked down and saw the hope swelling in those tear-reddened eyes, she knew she could not fail him.

Ten minutes later, the High Priestess of Eurotas and a motherless boy released a piece of tattered shroud cloth to the heavens.

We all cope with death in our own way.

The head of Sparta's secret police certainly had his own way of dealing with death. Courage, endurance and discipline formed the backbone of every warrior society, but for the single most formidable fighting force of modern times, this wasn't enough. The code of the Spartan warrior decreed he must push himself to limits most other men could not endure. He schooled himself to survive prolonged periods of hunger and thirst, as well as extremes of temperature and other mental and physical deprivations. It was also drummed into him to be scrupulous, trustworthy, reliable, but, above all, detached.

The first three could be taught in the barracks, learned through training, or picked up as he went along. Objectivity was more complex. He might not tire on the battle ground, nor flinch from danger or pain. But was he able to look a man in the eye and despatch him to Hades?

To harden them up, warriors served for two years in the Krypteia, Sparta's notorious secret police. Sometimes they were tasked with hunting down and killing troublesome helots. A mission that relied heavily on camouflage and survival techniques, since most rebels plotted in secret. Other missions had them tracking down traitors, and the patience of the Krypteia was long. Years might pass before a spy, a turncoat, a deserter was found, though not for him the benefit of trial. He would just hear a footstep in an alley. See the bright flash of metal. Then know retribution had come.

As head of the Krypteia, Lysander monitored every warrior assigned to his organization. Which was why he worried when Gregos failed to meet the dawn appointment. Especially when it was of Gregos' making.

No one at the barracks had seen him.

'Thought he was escorting the gold train,' was the general consensus.

So had Lysander, until he received Gregos' note.

I know who. I know where. I know how.

Bend at dawn.

Not for nothing did the word 'cryptic' stem from Krypteia, and for anyone else, the last part of the message would be meaningless. But for Lysander, who had personally charged Gregos with the investigation, it was clear that his agent had finally identified the criminal(s). The bend in the river was the pre-arranged meet.

Still. If he was not at the barracks and had not kept the appointment, there was still one more possibility, and the most likely. Gregos had left the gold train in Macedonia and ridden south without stopping, other than to change his horse. Even for an experienced battalion commander, two hundred miles was one hell of a ride. Soldiers were also taught the art of deep sleep.

'Gregos.' Lysander hurled a pebble into the side of the old shepherd's hut, long since abandoned after a storm took off the roof. 'Wake up, you lazy bastard.'

In theory, all enlisted men were supposed to eat, sleep and drink at the barracks. In practice, they regularly sneaked home to their wives, their lovers, their own private spaces, and there was no punishment for disobeying the rules. Only for being found out.

But Gregos was an experienced soldier. Recently promoted from platoon leader, he was careful and crafty. Only the head of the secret police knew the location of his hideaway in the woods, and only then because Gregos had invited him there. Lysander remembered the night well. They drank, played dice, drank some more, then played darts. In the morning, the keg was empty, Lysander was broke, and neither men could speak for the pain in their heads. Every dart, though, was right on its target.

That had been over six months ago, and its crumbling walls were now almost obscured with ivy. The door had long gone, and Lysander could see rat droppings on the crude, tamped earth floor and patches of mildew on the stonework inside. Hardly homely. But shelter enough from sun, rain, women and the army. Every man needs some place to escape to.

'Gregos?'

As he drew closer, his nostrils were assaulted by a familiar smell. When he heard buzzing, Lysander broke into a run.

'Fuck.'

The mattress in the corner was a pool of congealed blood surrounded by red arcs that covered the walls and the floor. A haven for blowflies laying their eggs. He closed his eyes and exhaled very slowly, repeating the gesture two or three times. Then with a purse of his lips, he examined the scene. Followed the drag marks down to the river . . .

If they were lucky, he thought, he might at least be able to give his widow a body to bury, but river gods could be fickle. Like the deep, dark pool beside the Shrine of Eurotas, there was always the risk that if a body went in, the only thing it would see after that was the fishes.

No way had Gregos come out of this alive.

TWO

Two hundred miles to the north, in a place where lakes met mountains in a misty blue haze, a crowd gathered in the posting-station yard. The crowd was not large, since by its very nature the station was isolated, but the crowd sure as hell was keen. It's not every day an Olympic champion passes your way, and Nobilor was the most famous person any of them – merchant or servant, scribe or wandering minstrel – had, or probably would, ever see. More importantly from Lisyl's perspective, Nobilor was the finest wrestler ever to have lifted the laurel crown, and she couldn't believe her luck he was here.

'Did you know he was coming?' she asked Melisanne.

Her sister shook her silver-blonde mane. 'Madam didn't mention it, but then –' she glanced across at the station master's wife – 'Anthea rarely gives much away.'

'*I* knew.' Yvorna, the youngest of the three sisters, winked. 'I knew he was coming.'

'So that's why you're wearing that new tunic,' Melisanne said.

'Why didn't you tell us?' Lisyl was cross. She'd have put on a better tunic, too. A brighter shade than this dull, faded lilac. Pink maybe, or blue to match her eyes. To compensate, she tugged at the linen so it folded over her belt. She might be plump, but her ankles were pretty.

'She wants to make a play for him, that's why,' Melisanne said.

'What if I do?' Yvorna loosed her tumble of red curls in such a way that it couldn't help but catch the wrestler's attention. 'You two are both spoken for—'

'Yvorna, please!' Melisanne's eyes bulged in censure. 'Not in public.'

'What? You think anyone here's listening to us talk about you and old Hector, while Nobilor's in the yard?'

'Don't be such a bitch,' Lisyl hissed in her sister's ear. 'You know how Mel feels about him, and it's not her fault the station master is married.'

'No, it's not her fault, but it's about time she faced up to reality. He's never going to leave Anthea, Lis. Not in a million years.'

'Hector isn't old,' Melisanne protested vigorously.

He wasn't young either, though, Lisyl thought. A good twenty years separated him and her sister, but then age gaps were something Hector knew all about. His wife was nearly twenty years older than him.

'Feel my muscles, Nobilor!' a small lad cried, wriggling his way to the front. 'Feel them. See how strong I am!'

A massive paw covered the puny white bulges and nodded in solemn approval. 'Solid as rocks, son.'

'I'm training really hard,' the boy told him eagerly. 'I lift weights and punch sacks every day, so I can be just like you when I grow up!'

'You want to look like me?' Nobilor asked, and everyone laughed. Never handsome to start with, these days he looked like he'd come second with a meteor shower.

'All the men want to look like you,' Yvorna shouted, with a flighty toss of her curls. 'Your face is an institution, my lovely!'

Lisyl cringed, and beside her Melisanne blushed. Three sisters. Couldn't be more different if they tried. There was pale, blonde Melisanne, the oldest, the most ladylike, who held the family together. Plump, dark, sensible Lisyl. And buxom, red-headed, uninhibited Yvorna, bouncy, flouncy, swishing and swaying, the butterfly of the trio.

'You wouldn't want to live in an institution, sweetheart,' Nobilor flirted back. 'Anyway, I got married again, didn't you hear? The family will be along in a minute.'

Cheering wildly, the crowd rushed forward, clapping his shoulder and wishing him well. The only one who didn't, Lisyl noticed, was Cadur. Tall, lean, and with cheekbones you could slice bread on, he stood in the doorway of the stables, arms folded, his shoulder against the frame. When he saw her watching him, he held her eye for two seconds, no more, then turned inside.

'Come on, everyone.' A man with a neatly clipped beard that was rapidly greying clapped his hands. 'Back to work now.'

His olive skin betrayed origins east of the Aegean. Ephesus, Melisanne said. But Hector was living in Corinth when he met Anthea, where his family had been running taverns for three generations.

With a few groans and the odd grumble under the breath, the crowd returned to the drudgery of kneading bread, stoking boilers, brushing horses, scrubbing floors. Still. At least they'd seen their hero up close. There would be tons to talk about for the rest of the day. Especially with his mother, new bride and teenage daughter arriving shortly.

'How can you afford a new tunic on a serving girl's pay?' Melisanne demanded, dragging Yvorna behind a pillar.

'Not what you think, you dirty-minded cow!' Yvorna pulled loose of her grip. 'Dierdra gave it to me, if you must know.'

'Why?'

'Her admirers are always buying her gifts.' Yvorna twirled, letting the linen billow out. 'She can't possibly use everything she's given and says that's what friends are for. Sharing. Not that you'd know anything about *that*.'

'So you and she plotted together for you to throw your cap at Nobilor?' Melisanne snorted. 'You should be ashamed of yourselves.'

'I like the tunic,' Lisyl said sternly. 'Peach complements your auburn hair, Yvorna.' She gave it a playful tousle. 'Too bad he got married again, eh?'

'For goodness' sake! He was never going to fall for a serving wench,' Melisanne said. 'Those days are behind him.'

'Maybe I'll put these behind him,' Yvorna said, sticking her chest out. 'See if that changes his mind.'

'Don't be disgusting,' Melisanne snapped. 'You spend too much time hanging round that lump of mutton dressed up as lamb—'

'Well, that's where you're wrong. It's her who's—'

'—and masseuse, my eye. She's no more a qualified doctor than I am.'

'It's a post station, Mel! Her job's to rub the stiffness out of the riders, not heal the bloody sick.'

'And we all know where they get stiff.' Melisanne snorted. 'How many men did you say asked her to marry them?'

'More than asked you,' Yvorna retorted. 'So I suggest you stop telling me what to do with my life, until you've got your own "affairs" in order.'

'Don't make me throw a bucket of water over you two,' Lisyl warned. They were always sniping at one another, Mel and Yvorna. 'We should get back.'

Even so, she made no effort to return to her mountain of laundry, but headed for the stables. According to Hector, there were eight native strains of horses, but three times that number imported for breeding. Until today, though, she'd only ever seen three. The small messenger ponies, fine-boned and sure-footed, which they'd need to be for these rough, rutted tracks. And the Thessalian and Pineians, which were cavalry horses – and they didn't come this way very often. Now, suddenly, the yard was full of beautiful, elegant chariot horses! One a dark bay, the other a gold palomino, they must have cost Nobilor a fortune. Maybe tomorrow she'd pluck up enough courage to stroke one.

'Haven't seen Morin, have you?' she asked.

Other than Cadur, the stables were deserted, the ponies grazing out in the paddocks, the grooms off goodness knows where. Exercising them, combing them, rubbing them down, she supposed. The cycle of work never stopped.

'Nope.' He barely looked up from forking the hay. 'Can I give him a message?'

'I was just curious why an Olympic wrestler should bring a chariot, that was all.'

Through the thick, shiny fringe, his eyes were as dark as an adulterous liaison. 'Doesn't want to expose his family to the scrum of gawpers, I guess.'

The hay smelled fresh, there was the scent of leather in the air, while particles of grass and dust danced in the sunlight that streamed through the wide open doors.

'Yes, I see that.' If the rest of his party were only a few minutes behind, they must all have been travelling together until the last knockings. 'I meant, why bring a chariot in the first place?'

Bloody thing must have taken up a whole cart by itself.

'Racing's his hobby.' One shoulder shrugged. 'Pressure release, presumably.'

In theory, the Games were open to any freeborn Greek male, but competing took money, so most champions came from wealthy or aristocratic backgrounds. Nobilor came from the slums. He'd set off to Olympia with no money and even fewer expectations, yet came home sporting the champion's crown. Nineteen years after his glorious win, still no one had taken his title.

'Can't be easy,' Lisyl agreed. 'Every contest, he'll be that little bit slower, while the young bloods will be that little bit faster.'

'And hungry.' His mouth twisted. 'There's always someone looking to take down a legend.'

Morin insisted Cadur was surly, sly and not to be trusted. Lisyl watched the speed and intensity with which he worked, and supposed her boyfriend knew best. Cadur was certainly different. No one knew where he came from, he didn't mix with the men, and wouldn't use one word when none would do. Strange, then, that he and Yvorna rubbed along. Not in the same way as her and Morin, of course! No kissing, no cuddling, nothing like that. But for all Yvorna's banter and back-chat, she didn't have many friends apart from her sisters. That's because women misunderstood her and men only wanted one thing, but with Cadur it was different. They'd walk the lakeside together, her talking, him listening, and Lisyl couldn't really say why she wished that they didn't. She just . . . well, wished they didn't!

'Did Yvorna tell *you* that Nobilor would be coming?'

'Yep.'

'Dammit, why didn't she tell me? I wouldn't have told anyone!'

He stopped. Leaned on his pitchfork. 'You'd have told Morin.'

'That's different.' She tossed her head. 'We're getting married, and you don't keep secrets—'

'Cad, luv – oh, sorry.' The woman's voice was rough from too much wine and too little sleep, and the heavily plastered kohl round her eyes only emphasized that her age was closer to fifty than forty. 'Not interrupting, am I?'

The woman was looking at Cadur, not Lisyl.

'It's all right, Dierdra, I need to get back,' Lisyl said, and that was another funny thing. Cadur hadn't even looked Dierdra's way, his eyes stayed on her, and for no good reason she shivered. 'Tell Morin I was looking for him, eh?'

He nodded, and she could feel his eyes burning into her back as she picked her way past the stalls. Behind her, she heard the masseuse's throaty laugh.

'That Yvorna's a girl, isn't she? Did you hear what she said to Nobilor back there? *All the men want to look like you. Your face is an institution, my lovely.* Lord, she has a way with her, that one.'

'What can I do for you?' Cadur asked, but Lisyl was out of earshot and didn't catch her reply.

Scurrying back across the yard, milling with scribes and servants, water-bearers, heralds, merchants and barbers, the acid stench of horseflesh mingled with the smell of bread from the bakehouse and wood smoke from the blacksmith's forge. Late summer was traditionally a busy time on the roads. Students returning home from military school. Merchants wrapping up a late deal before snow closed the passes. Travellers in a hurry to catch the last ships. The usual bustle. Nothing out of the ordinary. And yet . . .

And yet . . .

Lisyl tutted. Don't be daft, what could possibly have changed in one stupid morning!

She gathered up the station master's tunics, and his wife's. The lake was clear and blue, so calm that the mountains reflected double and the clouds looked like candy on the surface. It was a known fact that anyone who fell in didn't drown, but was carried down to the palace of the Blue Goddess on the backs of sea eagles. Once inside, their youth was restored and they lived to a thousand, enjoying a life of unparalleled bliss.

For Lisyl, looking to get married next spring, life was already unparalleled bliss. So why then, for all the warmth of the

late-summer sunshine, were goose pimples running over her arms?
She looked at the flowers that swamped the lush meadows, the
butterflies feasting greedily on the thistles, the horses swishing their
tails as they chomped, the islands shimmering in the heat, and the
poppies, brighter than blood, that dotted the shoreline. She couldn't
put her finger on it, and she wasn't easily influenced. But as she
plunged the linens into the water, Lisyl had the strangest feeling
she was still being watched.

THREE

N o secret can ever be safe. Someone, somewhere, always
knows the truth. Or will eventually find out.
If you have a secret, keep it so.
Let not your friend your secret know.
The childhood rhyme played in Iliona's head.
For if that friend becomes your foe,
Shall all the world your secret know.
Drifting in and out of consciousness, faces floated before her.
Young, old, familiar, strange. Some smelled of scented oils from
the palace, others of temple incense, while the physician reeked
of the yarrow used to staunch the blood. But it seemed one face
glided in and out more than the rest. Blue-eyed and with blond,
shoulder-length hair, he wore a warrior's kilt, but she could not
understand. That nightmare was over. Closed, sealed, buried and
forgotten. All right, then, maybe not forgotten—
'Where do you think you're going?'
A hand pushed her back on the bed. The hand smelled of
yarrow.
'This temple doesn't run itself, Jocasta.' Iliona tried to ignore
the wave of pain that seemed determined to slice her in half.
'What happened?'
'You tell me. The temple guards found you unconscious on
the river bank, close to a small stand of willows.'
'Then I've wasted too much time already.' She swung her legs
out of bed, wondering who had filled them with lead. 'There's
a horrendous backlog of votive offerings. I've got groves to sanc-
tify, purifications to carry out—'

'You're staying put.'

'Excuse me, but I give the orders here.'

'Not in my infirmary, you don't.'

'Jocasta, this is my private bedchamber.'

'As long as I have a patient in that bed, it's an infirmary, and do you mind telling me just what the bloody hell you were doing, to burst those goddamn stitches?'

She thought of the rapturous look on the little boy's face, watching his letter float up to the heavens. 'Can't remember.'

'The hell you can't.' Jocasta hefted a wooden box on to the bedside table and lifted the lid. Inside, bronze forceps, probes and spatulas gleamed in neat, almost military lines, along with scissors, needles, saws and clamps. 'Now, lie still. I've re-stitched the wound, but I need to change the poultice.'

Iliona slumped back in defeat. 'The king came to see me, then?' That accounted for the scented oils from the palace.

'How he heard about this little episode I'll never know, but he was livid.' The physician cut away the bandage. 'Said it would never have happened, had you been treated at the palace like he wanted. You are his cousin, after all.'

'Second cousin,' she corrected, 'and I hope you repeated what I told him after I was stabbed. That the High Priestess of Eurotas wouldn't dream of asking others to put their lives in the hands of the temple physician if she herself did not.'

Jocasta peered through her raven-black fringe. 'Nothing to do with the little secret we share, then?' From the box she drew out an assortment of instruments, ranging from the fine and flexible to sharp-hooked retractors and tiny gold needles. 'That if there *was* to be any blabbing in your delirium, better to do it with me around, and not some total stranger?'

'You really think I was safeguarding my own interests?' Dammit, why did she always pick a fight? 'If what we did came out, it would mean exile and humiliation for me, that's true. But for you, it's public execution.'

Physician or not, Jocasta was a helot. Serfs, slaves, call them what you like, they were the lowest of the low, and the same rules of justice did not apply to them as freeborn citizens. In fact, justice didn't apply to the helot class, full stop.

'Drink this.' Jocasta held a phial to Iliona's lips. 'It'll numb you against what I'm about to do.'

'I don't want it.' Rebellion was the only dignity she had left.

Jocasta shrugged. 'Suit yourself.' With methodical precision, she proceeded to remove the poultice and probe the edges of the wound.

With methodical precision, Iliona fainted.

Jocasta must have slipped her a potion after all, because when Iliona opened her eyes, the sun was high and eagles rode the thermals above the bare spurs of Mount Parnon. The pain in her side had subsided to a throbbing ache, but the pain in her heart refused to budge.

Sounds drifted through the open window. The temple doves, cooing on the roof. Bronze wind chimes, clanking softly in the plane grove. A distant tramp-tramp-tramp of hobnail boots. She watched a lizard sunning itself on the window sill, lifting one foot then another on the baking stonework. The boots tramped closer, her door opened and a familiar scarlet tunic swung into view. Not blue eyes, she realized now, but grey. Grey as the sea in midwinter. His long hair wasn't blond, either, and was streaked with silver around the temples. Every day, she thought, he was turning that little bit closer into a wolf.

The visitor sniffed the air. 'Mouldy bread and garlic. My favourite.'

When he closed the door, the room seemed half the size.

'Lysander.'

'That's progress.' His voice was deep and full of gravel. 'You called me by another name earlier.'

Was it a hallucination, brought on by the drugs that killed the pain and dulled the senses, that made her mistake him for the son she gave away at birth, and who'd crashed into her life eighteen long years later?

Or her conscience making manifest her deepest, darkest secret?

'Sorry.' For calling him by another name? Or because her son was gone, and was never coming back . . . ? 'Apparently mouldy bread and garlic juice keeps wounds free of infection.'

He'd know that. She just couldn't think of anything else to say, and he seemed in no great hurry to start a conversation, ambling round her bedroom, examining the frescoes, fingering her perfume jars, running his hand over the curves of her alabaster water bowl as though it was a lover.

'I presume this is about my attacker?' she said, when the silence became too much. 'That you need me to give evidence in court?'

A statement sworn under oath sufficed in lesser charges. Not in cases of attempted murder, though.

One lazy eyebrow rose. 'What made you think this would go to trial?'

'Then perhaps you'd care to share with me the story that you've put around? Considering I'm at the centre of it.'

'Centre of what?' He waved a dismissive hand. 'As far as Sparta is concerned, this was merely a minor incident, blown out of all proportion by a hysterical crowd.'

'Minor?' She struggled to a sitting position. 'That maniac tried to kill me.'

'I think you'll find the official version reads that a disgruntled worshipper ran up and punched you on the temple steps—'

'I was stabbed!'

'Fist, knife, let's not split hairs. You fell. Hit your head on the flagstones, which accounted for the blood—'

'You bastard.'

Lysander bowed. 'At your service, ma'am. Though I think you'll agree it worked out for the best.' He ticked the points off on his fingers. 'The high priestess remains inviolable. The shrine retains its reputation as a refuge for sanctuary and safety. While a worthless piece of shit just –' he snapped his fingers – 'disappears.'

She hadn't considered the attack in a political light. But then, she didn't deal in death and deception for a living. 'What do you want?'

'You don't believe the Krypteia make social calls?'

'No.'

'Then you'd be right.' He poured a cup of wine without watering it. 'Your physician insists this will help rebuild your strength,' he said, swirling the dark red liquid around in the beaker. 'I personally feel that a nice relaxing break on a lakeside in the mountains would be far more beneficial.'

'What I need, Lysander, is to pronounce a few auspices, bless a couple of altars and then set some oracular riddles. Preferably in private.'

He held the cup to her lips, and even through the medicaments and poultice, she caught a hint of leather mixed with wood smoke.

'Privacy is a luxury reserved for the very rich and the very poor. You and I, my lady, are neither.'

She wished he wouldn't lump the two of them together. 'Then feel free to join me in my administrations. The Krypteia should be good at setting riddles.'

The wine was strong, but not half as strong as the hand that held the bowl.

'Do you know the Lake of Light?' he asked.

'Is that one of the riddles?'

Something twitched in his cheek. Indigestion, most like. 'I'm told the scenery is stunning and the climate quite impeccable. You will recuperate much faster there, I'm sure.'

'No doubt.' She was standing her ground on this one. 'But unless you're sacking me, the high priestess is needed here.'

'No one serves Eurotas better, my lady, and your presence at the temple is essential.' He set the cup down on the table. 'Were it open.'

'*What?*'

The head of the secret police resumed his pacing. 'Given the amount of construction work, the new watercourses, the various porticoes, bridges and steps, I felt certain you'd be worried a worshipper might trip over the rubble and hurt themselves, or fall down one of the trenches.'

'The hell you did. And in any case, you don't have the authority to close it.'

'Absolutely none.' He paused to admire a tapestry on the wall by the doorway. Odysseus resisting the lure of the Sirens. 'But the king, your cousin, has the authority. Once I'd explained how much easier it would be, not to mention quicker and more economical, for the works to be carried out when no one's around, he put his seal on the order straight away.'

Iliona stared at the hills, red-hot pokers jabbing at her insides that bore no connection to her injury. 'What about the Oracles? The temple physician who heals the sick? Our sacred obligation to keep the eternal flame burning in the tripod? If that goes out, I warn you, it will bring about the end of Sparta, we'll be ruined.'

'Ah, well, that's the funny thing.' He stroked his chin. 'There haven't been any Oracles since the stabbing and I haven't noticed that the world's stopped spinning, have you? A good physician can treat the sick anywhere, while both you and I know those coals have gone cold many, many times, yet Sparta remains strong and is, if anything, growing stronger.'

She should have known better than to try and fool him, and suddenly the wine tasted sour in her throat. It was, she decided, the flavour of defeat.

Lysander rested one foot on the bottom of her couch and folded his arms on his knee. 'What do you know about posting stations?'

Very little, she thought. Only that they were a novel concept, imported from Persia, intended to support a new network of communications being set up across the newly allied city states.

'Not half as swift or sophisticated as their Oriental counterparts,' he admitted, not waiting for her answer. 'But then our Greek courier service is still in the experimental stage, who knows if it'll even take off?'

Quite. What works in the wide open spaces of the Persian Empire wouldn't necessarily succeed in a hotchpotch of mountainous, landlocked, autonomous nations.

'But if the trials *are* abandoned, it won't be because of lack of cooperation from Sparta,' he said firmly. Adding that beacons were fine when long-distance warning signals were needed, or marking hazards for shipping, and runners were quite capable of carrying letters and conveying messages in situations where speed was not of the essence. 'When time is tight, though, nothing beats a fast horse.'

'Is that where you're sending me? To exile in some grubby little post house on the edge of nowhere?'

'Can't imagine why you think I'd want to exile you,' he rumbled, although they both knew he could list twenty reasons without stopping for breath. 'And this station is far from an outpost.'

Sited on a crossroads, one way heading north to south along the Amber Route, the other east to west linking the Aegean with the Adriatic, this particular posting station was a flagship for the newly united Greek nation.

'The potential for a nationwide courier service is enormous,' he added. 'But the system can only work if it's underpinned by first-class support, which in turn should generate a massive increase in trade.'

Iliona looked at the lines of old battle scars criss-crossing his bronze thighs, and a couple of fresher ones, too. 'Where do I fit in?'

'Well, now that's where it gets interesting. Suppose, for a

moment, Sparta's famous Oracle decides to visit the Lake of Light to recuperate? And suppose that, while she's there, the Oracle happens to foresee a brilliant future for this intrepid joint enterprise? Where would that leave Athens, do you think?'

You had to hand it to him, she thought grudgingly. Having finally defeated their common enemy, the Persians, a thousand city states were now basking in peace. Athens, the birthplace of this new democracy, had subjugated the island states of the Aegean with her massive naval strength, while Sparta kept the lid on peace on the mainland. But the alliance was uneasy. Why share half the power when you could have it all? was Athens' attitude. Her sights were set on an empire in which Sparta played no role, and she would stop at nothing to achieve it. So if blessings could be heaped upon the enormous amount of trade passing through the crossroads at the Lake of Light, the posting station would be forever associated with the Oracle of Sparta. Leaving Athens sidelined once again . . .

'Fine. If that's what you want, Lysander, I'll trek up there and bless this glorified tavern of yours—'

'This glorified tavern of *Greece's*.'

'—on one condition.'

'Hm.' He took his boot off the bed, brushed the coverlet and straightened it. The Krypteia never left any traces behind. 'Go on.'

'You tell me what this is really about.'

FOUR

Nobilor climbed into his chariot, wrapped the reins around his waist and pulled on a pair of translucent rawhide gloves.

From the corner of his eye, he could see his daughter slouched against a pillar, chewing on a strand of hair. Daphne worried him, she really did. At fifteen, she had (or so he was reliably informed) reached that Awkward Age, which apparently had nothing to do with her mother running off when she was three, but a lot to do with puberty and men. Chewing lips that had been ripped, torn, twisted and bitten, he was well aware that he couldn't watch Daphne every second of every day. But by thunder, he'd kill any man who laid a hand on his baby girl.

Knotting the reins to prevent himself from getting tangled up and dragged, his eyes searched the posting-station yard. No Calypso. Hardly surprising, he supposed. It was only a few minutes ago that he'd left his lovely bride, her long legs still tangled in the sheets and her blonde hair splayed across the pillows. He knew, before he'd even married her, that Calypso wasn't the type to grab a wrap and pin up her hair any old how to wave goodbye. But even so. His eyes continued to scour for her.

'That lazy cow not up to see you off?'

'Ma!' Nobilor stretched his groan into three syllables. 'Ma, please.'

'What? It's mid-morning.' Hermione planted her hands on her ample hips. 'Or are you worried she might hear me?' She lifted her chin so her voice would carry. 'Worried I might say something about that money-grubbing little bitch that might offend her?'

That did it. Doors and shutters sprang open in every direction.

'Now you've caused a scene,' he said.

His mother's reaction was to laugh. 'Calm down,' she cackled. 'It's not as though people don't know my opinion of the narcissistic little cow, now is it?'

The excitement was too much. Suddenly the enclosure was full of servants with an urgent need to fill their pails or empty out the slops. Many didn't even bother to pretend.

'Here. Dierdra.' Hermione beckoned over a woman whose dyed blonde hair had been tortured into ringlets more suited to a girl of Daphne's age. 'Didn't you tell me, while you were giving me that lovely rosemary rub, that there's a groom here who can saddle a horse in under two minutes?'

'I did.'

'Well, to be quite frank with you, dear, I don't believe it.'

'Ma,' Nobilor warned under his breath. 'Not now.'

'I don't believe any man can do it in less than three,' Hermione continued blithely. 'And if he told you that, then he's just bragging.'

Dierdra cupped her hands to her carmined mouth. 'Cadur?' At her shout, a young man emerged from the stables. One of the few workers who hadn't come to gawp. 'Lady wants a word, love.'

Cadur's walk appeared lazy, but Nobilor noticed he closed the distance as though he'd marched briskly, strength pulsing through every pace. But a strength, he decided, that was turned inwards, not outwards. The boy's eyes flashed hostile and dark.

'Ma'am?'

Hermione folded her arms over her chest. 'Your girlfriend here swears she's seen you saddle a horse in under two minutes. Is that true?'

Cadur lifted his gaze to the man in the chariot. 'Dierdra is my friend, not my lover,' he said in voice that only Nobilor and his mother could hear.

'Whatever you say, dear.' Hermione shot a wink at her son that said she knew otherwise. 'The point is, I say it can't be done, so suppose you prove one of us lovely ladies wrong. Billi, would you start the count, please?'

Cadur slanted a low, sideways glance at Daphne, still leaning against the pillar, but now chewing her nails instead of her hair. 'With all due respect, ma'am, I am not a performing monkey.'

'Then let's make it worth your while.' Hermione fished out a five-drachma piece, the equivalent of a week's wages for the groom.

'I don't think this is such a good idea, Ma.' Nobilor didn't like the way Cadur was looking at his daughter, but far worse was the way Daphne eyed him up.

'For heaven's sake, you're not still cross about them debts I ran up in Athens, are you? For the life of me, I can't imagine why. You've earned more money than any one of us can ever hope to spend.' She shot him a playful smile. 'Stop trying to begrudge your poor mother a good time, now she's old.'

'It's not the gambling and you're not old.' Something inside the big man was churning. 'But the mares are getting restless, Ma. Suppose we pursue this when I get back?'

'Fair enough.' The silver disappeared back inside the folds of her robe. 'But no cheating, you.' She wagged a podgy finger at the groom. 'No practising while he's gone—'

'I don't cheat,' Cadur said, taking a step towards her. His lips were tight with anger. 'And anybody who—'

To Nobilor's relief, any confrontations he might have been called upon to smooth over were nullified by a pony cantering into the yard. A thin-faced man wearing the official insignia of a warrant officer dismounted, brushing the dust from his tunic.

'Nice chariot,' he said, walking round it. 'Spokes made of polished cornel wood. Very nice indeed. Corners well, does she?'

'Not half.' Little more than a board with wheels either side and a wicker front frame, it was one of the lightest, and sleekest, racing machines Nobilor had ever owned.

'Only two horses, I notice.'

He was proud of his mares, too. Wild to train at the beginning, they were a cross between Thessalians and Persians, and it was their very boldness that made them good chariot horses. They were fast, intelligent and had stamina.

'I leave the bigger teams to the professionals.' He shot the official a self-deprecating grin. 'Can't afford to fall off and ruin my looks.'

The warrant officer did not see the joke, but then anyone who spent his life checking up on people wasn't hired for his sunny personality. It was a necessary evil, Nobilor supposed, validating the brands on the horses' flanks and making sure impostors weren't claiming to be couriers to get free mounts and accommodation. All the same, it didn't make for popularity.

'The name's Ballio,' he said, running a hand over the axle. 'Fast, is she?'

'Too fast, if you ask me,' Hermione cut in sharply. 'One of these days he'll run someone over, and *then* he'll be sorry.'

'Not as sorry as them,' Nobilor quipped back.

'Tch! You're just like your father, you.' She rolled her eyes. 'He never listened to me either, and look where it got him, poor bugger.' She turned to Ballio. 'My husband was a tiler, you know. Good one. In fact one of the best, but I kept telling him, *You're too old to be up on them roofs*. And did he listen? Not a word!'

'Ma.' Nobilor tugged at what was left of his remaining ear lobe. 'He died from pneumonia.'

'Don't tell me how your father died. I know how he died. I nursed him in my arms right up till the end. But the point I'm making,' a chubby finger jabbed him in the thigh, since she couldn't reach his arm, 'is that if it hadn't been for that illness, sooner or later your father would've come a cropper on those roofs and the fall would have killed him, that's for sure.'

She didn't see why everyone was laughing.

'Oh, Ma.' With a resigned shake of the head, Nobilor geed the mares into action.

An Olympic champion becomes a hero to rich and poor alike,

and there wasn't anywhere he could go without being recognized and mobbed. Which is why he rode. With the wind in his face and the world hurtling past, it was the one place he could be his own man. The one place he was free to forget . . .

With a crack of the whip, the mares broke into a canter, but despite the delay in the yard, there was still no sign of Calypso.

As he rode through the gateway, Nobilor cast a longing glance over his shoulder and wondered why it hurt more than having ribs broke that his wife wasn't there, waving him off.

Standing in the sacred plane grove by the river, her white robes billowing in the sticky breeze, Iliona acknowledged the soundness of the Krypteia's logic to close the temple during the construction work.

She lifted her eyes to the naked, jagged peaks of the twin mountain ranges that flanked the broad, fertile plain of Sparta. Another month would pass before the first snowfalls softened the harsh contours of the mountain tops, though dormice, bears and squirrels would already be laying down fat to see them through the winter. For people, the pattern was pretty much the same. With the harvest in, this was traditionally a time of quietude and plenty, a soft and gentle lull when even the poor had few worries on their plates. There was still work to do. There always was. Plump, purple grapes still dangled on the vines, olives ripened in the groves, neither the wheat nor the barley had been sown, and roofs and fences needed shoring up against the autumn gales.

But whether landowner or helot, carpenter or coinsmith, few had need of spiritual guidance right now. In a few weeks, of course, things would be different. The men would have been home from the wars for long enough for personalities to grate. The change in the weather would start affecting health. Things would be said and done during festivals that would be regretted. Then tensions would build up again, and people would turn to the river god for help, justice and advice. For the moment, though, their cares were few.

Listening to the wind chimes making sweet music in the trees, Iliona envied them their carefree existence. She inhaled the temple incense drifting on the air. Heard the distant bleating of sheep in the olive groves. She loved this land, this job, this temple with every fibre of her being. The slow burble of the river that carried hopes and dreams towards the delta and the sea. The big, fat frogs that croaked in the rushes. The satisfaction of knowing she was helping other people.

But lately . . .

She tucked a wisp of blonde hair back under her diadem. Lately, all she seemed to see was her son's eyes laughing up at her, and the face of her attacker, twisting up with hatred . . .

She ran her hand up and down the smooth trunk of the plane and thought, who knows. Maybe the Lake of Light would work its fabled magic and send the terrors back to hell?

'Opportunity to advance Sparta's political standing, my arse!' Beside her, Jocasta snorted. 'What's the real reason behind this madcap trip, did that murdering bastard say?'

Never trust a helot, Lysander said. *They chart rebellion.*

Who could blame them? Uprooted from their homeland, forced to work the fields with no rights, no assets, no dignity; small wonder insurgence bubbled just below the surface.

Take Jocasta with you to the posting station. She's less likely to cut your throat on unfamiliar territory.

'Unfortunately, that murdering bastard wouldn't be drawn,' she lied. 'It's not the Krypteia's habit to go round blabbing state secrets.'

Jocasta wouldn't cut Iliona's throat, and they shared some of the deepest, darkest secrets on the planet. Their destinies were, quite literally, written in blood. All the same—

'Then all I can say is, praise be to Zeus he isn't coming with us,' the physician retorted. 'He'd probably toss me over a cliff and say I slipped, the dirty, murdering scum.' She spat on the ground. 'If I was a man, I'd kill him.'

'Glad you take your medical oath seriously.' For the first time in a long while, Iliona felt like smiling. 'Now I suggest you go and pack before you spontaneously combust. With the temple shut, there's no reason for us to hang around.'

Or put another way, when the Krypteia said now, he meant now.

All the same, the high priestess remained on the river bank, watching dragonflies and butterflies, listening to the cry of the hawks and the warble of skylarks over the fields.

Twenty years ago, Greece was a diverse collection of city states connected by nothing more than a common language and religion. A weakness the Persian Empire sought to exploit in a mighty mass invasion, and had these city states not united against the enemy, it might well have succeeded. Instead, the Persians were routed, Greece was basking in a golden age of science, philosophy and art, and the economy was booming. Most of the lands were arid and barren, but the lush plain of Sparta put it in a unique position to export food, as well as horses, porphyry, fine art and iron – which was just as well. Peacekeeping ran expensive, and part of the trade for horses and iron included Macedonian copper and gold.

Any mule train carrying gold needs an escort, Lysander had told her. *I sent Lynx Squad, under the command of a man called Gregos, to guard the dust from the moment it was weighed into the sacks to the moment it was discharged in Sparta.*

The head of the secret police had made himself comfortable in the red, cushioned chair beside Iliona's bed, crossing his legs at the ankles and resting his elbows on its maple-wood arms. Too much gold to move in one go, he'd explained. Those precipitous, narrow mountain roads would stretch the army into too long a crocodile and make it easy pickings for bandits. Better to move the gold in four smaller caravans to avoid overstretching resources.

Despite all our precautions, the first caravan contained ten per cent ordinary rock dust, weighted with metal, when it reached its destination. Gregos and I went through it at length, and neither of us could see how, or when, the switch was made. But somebody, somewhere went to a lot of trouble to make those sacks look, and feel, like gold.

It could have been the Macedonians, ripping off purchasers at source, though in that case it would have made more sense to swap the last consignment, rather than the first.

Not all thieves are bright, of course, Lysander had rumbled, adding that it was also possible this had been a genuine mistake. *That somehow ballast got loaded, instead of gold.*

The second mule train scotched both theories. More rock and metal in place of gold dust. Ten per cent on the nail.

By this time, Gregos was on the alert, he said, *yet somehow the switch was still effected right under his nose.*

The Krypteia steepled his fingers as he stared at Iliona's bedroom ceiling. It was at this point, he explained, that he'd tasked his commander with the worst possible job for a soldier. Spying on his own men.

It could only be an inside job, and to say Gregos was unhappy is an understatement, but I know him. I know his family. They're good people, and I knew he'd come through for me. We all have to make sacrifices for our country.

Death comes with honour. Spying does not.

Vigilance, however distasteful, obviously paid off and Gregos figured it out. Unfortunately, somebody followed him, and silenced him before he had a chance to meet his superior officer.

Which means, Lysander said, *the thieves aren't just ruthless, they're clever, resourceful and extremely well organized.*

Iliona was beginning to see that. Lynx Squad comprised twelve crack troops, thirteen including Gregos, each accompanied by his personal helot acting as auxiliary troops, plus the pack master and any muleteers for the supplies. Too many people around to make the swap on the march, and in any case the gold would be too heavy for one, or even two men, to carry around on their person.

Macedonia to the north, she'd said. *The Lake of Light to the north, and a posting station that bisects two major trade routes.*

Exactly. Lysander's smile was as cold as a midwinter frost. *Up to that point,* he said, *the donkeys were only rested along the way. Here, the animals are changed.*

Meaning the sacks also needed to be redistributed, Iliona said, *where it would be very easy to store any substitute fillings close to the posting station, in readiness for a rapid changeover.*

And for the accomplice to stash the gold until it was safe to collect it.

He could change Lynx for another squad, he added, which would put paid to any more thefts. But it wouldn't tell him which of the men was involved.

For the same reason, I can't question them, either. If I do, I'll be alerting the thief, leaving all twelve under a cloud of suspicion.

Even if he nailed the bastard, he said, Spartan warriors were trained not to crack under interrogation. The accomplice, and the gold, would be lost in the wind.

In any case, none of Lynx Squad was in a position to leave the escort, he growled.

Whereas Gregos' killer had been free to follow him to Sparta, implying both access to horses and an ability to handle them well.

I need a diversion, Iliona. A legitimate excuse to bring a

Spartan contingent into the region without alerting attention.
The Oracle would kill two birds with one stone.
The second, presumably, being vengeance?
If you call blinding the traitors with pitch, then throwing them
into a pit while they're still alive vengeance, then yes. Lysander
stood up and cracked his knuckles. *I happen to call it justice,*
but that's just my opinion. Either way I am going to find them,
he said. *That gold belongs to peace, not to them.*

Driving at breakneck speed along the narrow tracks, Nobilor was
oblivious to everything except the reins in his right hand, the
whip in his left, and the vibration of the board beneath his feet.
    Oblivious to the lynx that snoozed in the clefts between the
rocks. To the waterfalls that cascaded down past chestnut trees
and pines. Oblivious to the lake below, a sheet of azure. According
to legend, the lake was the home of the Blue Goddess, Zabrina
of the Translucent Wave, whose circular shrine stayed warm to
the touch, even in winter, and whose throne was guarded by
dragons that laid eggs of pure gold.
    Nobilor was blind to beauty and legend.
    'Yah!' he shouted, cracking the whip. 'Yah! Yah!'
    Faster and faster his chariot flew, wheels rattling louder than
thunder. Hurtling round the narrow, rutted hairpin bends, there
was no time to take his eyes off the road, much less think.
    No time to dwell upon a marriage that had blossomed with
his Olympic success, then cracked under the strain, leaving him
with a three-year-old daughter to raise on his own.
    No time to worry about Daphne, whose hips and breasts
seemed to have rounded into womanhood overnight, bringing
men sniffing round like tomcats.
    As bay and palomino responded to the sting of the leather,
the past and the future merged into a present defined by horses'
manes flying in streamers and hooves that kicked up the dust.
Exactly how Nobilor liked it.
    Panting with exhilaration as much as exhaustion, he slowed
at the summit, steering the chariot into a clearing and guiding
the mares to a patch of lush meadow grass. Easing himself out
of the strappings, Nobilor shook his head in amazement. Who'd
have thought this ugly face would be decorating wine mugs? Or
that posh folk would be holding banquets in his honour? He ran
a huge paw over his forehead to mop off the sweat. If someone

had told him poets would one day be writing songs about him, he'd have laughed in their face. Other men are the subject of plays, not me, he'd have scoffed. Yet now look! Nearly two decades on, he was even more famous and still being challenged to contests. Not only challenged, but winning them, too.

'Aye.' He patted the flanks of his chomping mares. 'Everyone loves a winner, don't they?'

It was inevitable that, over the years, he'd have several teeth knocked out, an ear ripped right off, and more fingers broken than he could count. His ribs got cracked with tedious regularity, his nose smashed too, and, on one memorable occasion, in Corinth, he'd been crowned with the bone sticking white and shining through the skin of his left arm – and all because the rules of wrestling were simple. There were none.

Three falls on any part of the body to be declared the winner, no holds barred. He'd heard of men dying from accidental throttling or, like boxers, days after, from the effects of strong blows to the stomach. Nobilor shook his head. If folk only knew how many potions he had to swallow, how many ointments needed rubbed in. Not just at the time, but it hurt like buggery for ages afterwards, and after each contest took that little longer to heal.

But the money compensated. And he had, not to put too fine a point on it, been staggered at the way women who wouldn't normally have looked twice threw themselves at him left, right and centre. And still were, he chuckled, thinking of busty, red-headed Yvorna. Still bloody were, that was the miracle of it. And admit it, he'd never have met Calypso if he hadn't been famous.

Oh, Calypso. His throat tightened. Calypso, Calypso, Calypso. As beautiful as her husband was ugly. As delicate as he was knotted . . .

'C'mon, girls,' he said hoarsely. 'Time to go.'

But Nobilor made no attempt to drag the mares away from their succulent clumps. Not yet, he thought. Not just yet. Instead he walked round the chariot, testing the tension on the reins, checking the bag of chalk dust that would stop the straps from slipping in his hands, examining the buckles on the harnesses.

'Hello, hello, what's this?'

He leaned down to peer more closely at the axle pin on the offside wheel. Maintenance was a task he entrusted to others, but even so. It didn't look right, that pin. Not right at all.

'Sloppy,' he muttered. 'They shouldn't have left it like that.'

Still. If it was dangerous, someone at the posting station would have fixed it before he'd ridden off. Nobilor pushed it out of his mind.

Above him, the sun was shining in a cloudless sky, kites mewed and crickets rasped in the trees. The colours of the leaves were changing to a kaleidoscope of ambers and rusts. Red apples shone, ripe and round. A feast for the wasps. Nuts split and scattered over the forest floor for jays to eat and squirrels to bury.

All in all, not a bad day, he thought. He'd woken late. Made love to Calypso, then eaten a hearty breakfast of ham and cold chicken before making love to his wife a second time. Now here he was, doing what he loved most. Racing his chariot, with the sun on his back, the wind in his hair, and his knuckles white from the strain. He straightened up from the axle, knowing that whatever tomorrow might hold, whatever uncertainties he was required to face, he would cope. He was a big man with a big future. Hadn't he always risen to whatever challenge was waiting?

'Sorry, girls,' he told the mares, and felt bad when they rolled their eyes in longing at the juicy blades of grass. 'It really is time to go.'

Daphne, though . . . He worried about his baby, by the gods he did. It had been tough raising her on his own, and sure his Ma pitched in and he'd had slaves to take care of his girl. But at the end of the day, the onus fell on him and him alone. His kid. His responsibility. But at fifteen, his baby was growing up fast. He worried about her more than ever before—

'Yah! Yah, yah!'

Nobilor cracked the whip, and with the world ripping past, his worries about Daphne disappeared. He felt the horses' excitement in the thunder of their hooves. Saw it in the pricking of their ears, as chariot, driver and horseflesh fused into the one racing machine. Faster they raced, down the narrow track, past pines and chestnuts, larch and laurel. The scenery blurred. The lake swelled as they made their descent. Became broader, brighter and bluer.

Then—

One minute Nobilor was leaning into the bend. The next the chariot was flying through space.

Down.

And down.

And down . . .

The faces of three women flashed before him. His mother, his daughter, his bride. He tried to speak. To call out their names. But no sound could pass his throat.

Nobilor's last thoughts, before the blackness engulfed him, were, *not such a big man after all, in a crisis . . .*

Long after the sound of tearing branches had given way to the trill of warblers and the horses finally stopped screaming, a figure stood at the spot where the chariot had careered into the ravine.

Nodding in satisfaction of a job well done.

FIVE

'**L**ysander's quite right.' Jocasta threw herself down on Iliona's voluminous feather-filled bed. 'Sparta *will* be the first name to spring to mind after your visit.'

For all the wrong reasons, though. Iliona groaned.

From a distance, the posting station could pass for any aristocrat's villa anywhere in Greece. Same blood-red terracotta roof tiles. Same columned entrance court, where fountains danced and fragrant resins burned, and where topiaries lined a statue-filled garden to one side. The difference lay in the scale of the construction, including a stable block that made Hercules' clearing of the Augean look like child's play.

And of course few noblemen saw squads of Nordic kilt-wearers milling around their yard or Thessalian merchants checking the straps of their saddlebags, much less Germanic leggings throwing themselves over a gelding. They wouldn't have exhausted runners coming in, refreshed couriers setting out, wagons and carts being hitched and unhitched. Or altars to Zeus *and* Apollo, as well as a statue of Hecate who protected crossroads, and a bronze pillar with Hermes' bust on the top, since he was the patron of merchants and travellers. Iliona also spotted at least two pairs of almond eyes that belied very different, and far more outlandish, beliefs.

'There has to be a way out of this,' she moaned. 'After all, it *was* an accident.'

'An accident that just happened to befall the most famous

person ever to pass through,' Jocasta reminded her. 'And the superstitious mountain folk, who already believe crossroads are haunted by witches, can now add cursed to the list.' She folded her arms behind her head. 'Cursed by the Oracle of Sparta.'

Iliona groaned even louder.

And to think it started off so promisingly, too.

'Welcome to Phaos, my lady.' A man with olive skin, neatly clipped beard and pleasant if somewhat lined features bowed when they rode through the archway. 'What an unexpected honour.'

Iliona swallowed her smile. The Krypteia were hardly likely to give the gold thieves warning. 'This is not an official visit.' She'd needed to make that clear. 'More a personal retreat.'

'Then you have chosen well.' His name was Hector, he explained. He was master of this posting station, and was there ever a lovelier location to be based at? 'I doubt the gods on Mount Olympus enjoy such beauty and purity of air.'

I'm told the scenery is stunning and the climate quite impeccable. You will recuperate much faster there, I'm sure.

'What attracts me, Hector, is not so much the elemental beauty of the place.'

Though heaven knows, lakes and mountains always made for an idyllic combination, especially where the landscape offered such spectacular diversity. On this side of the lake, the hillsides were densely wooded, a riot of red and yellow autumn colours. On the far side, the spurs were sparse and down to scrub, and where some shorelines were rocky, others were marshy, while more still comprised long, white sandy beaches that were just itching to be walked in bare feet. The islands in the middle beckoned, rugged, mysterious, breathtaking, inviting.

With a lake surface of some hundred and seventy square miles, she supposed there were bound to be topographical differences. What surprised her was the amount. Where some of the mountains slipped sensuously into the water, others plunged straight down, where it was said that the strange patterns in the cliff faces were sculpted by Titans, long before the gods had been born.

The only consistency in this kaleidoscope of landscape was Zabrina's watery kingdom. Cobalt blue and transparent to ten fathoms, the Lake of Light certainly lived up to its reputation.

'It isn't even the intoxicating scent of raspberries and sweet myrrh on the air,' she added lightly. 'It's that brand-new bath house, Hector, that I've had my eye on from the top of the hill.'

She looked longingly at the rotunda's tiled roof and central chimney. Swore she saw the statues in its colonnaded entrance crooking their fingers to beckon her in.

'Then I regret your eye will need to retain that image for a little longer, my lady.' Hector steadied the reins while she dismounted. 'The afternoons are reserved for gentlemen only. I can, of course, have a tub delivered to your bedchamber, but if you want the full treatment – the steam bath, the plunge pool, the massage – I'm afraid you will have to wait until morning.'

Out on the lake, swans and pelicans were mirrored in the crystal cobalt waters. Oh, to be a swan . . .

'In fact, you've picked a bad time, full stop,' he was saying. 'The Festival of the Axe God has left me perilously short-handed.'

She'd thought it strange there were hardly any servants about.

'Still, what can you do?' Hector had shrugged. 'It's their religion. I can't stop the locals from attending.'

At that point, Jocasta paused from shaking off what seemed like half of Greece. 'You don't employ slave labour, then?'

Trust her.

'Only what the state obliges me to, ma'am. In my experience, staff work better when they have a financial incentive.' He'd turned back to Iliona. 'I usually keep a much larger skeleton staff on during the festivals, but after Nobilor's accident, I felt it better to give everyone a chance to let off steam—'

'Nobilor the wrestler?'

'The very same.'

'What kind of accident?' Jocasta asked, grabbing her medical box. 'Where can I find him?'

'At the bottom of a ravine,' growled a uniformed official, striding out from the doorway. He placed his fist to his breast in salute.

'Nobilor enjoyed driving chariots at full speed,' Hector explained. 'Unhappily, these mountain tracks aren't built for sport and our celebrated champion took the bend a little too fast.'

'Or rather didn't,' the thin-faced official corrected.

Iliona grimaced. 'We commented on a gap in the trees when we passed,' she told the two men. 'The branches were torn and twigs snapped, but the vegetation was blackened from smoke. In fact, the stench of burning made our horses shy.'

The two men exchanged glances.

'It is a sad day, my lady, when Greece is reduced to rolling barrels of blazing tar down a hillside to cremate its heroes in situ,' Hector said grimly.

'You *left* him there?'

A twist of the lip expressed better than words the impossibility of retrieving Nobilor's body. 'The ravine left me no option.'

What did she expect station managers to look like, she wondered. Had she stopped to think about it, she'd have pictured a round, jolly man with twinkling eyes and quite possibly roving hands, too. Hector looked like life had excavated his face with a pickaxe, though for a man in his forties, his belt showed no sign of straining. Either way, though, he didn't look the type who went round burning the corpses of heroes where they had fallen.

Then again, who the hell did?

'His mother's suggestion,' said the thin-faced official. 'Not to put too fine a point on it, my lady, but after three days of aborted attempts to retrieve the body, she was worried the smell—'

'Quite so.' Hector stepped forward as a means of changing the subject. 'Cadur? See to our guests' horses, would you, while I check which of the staterooms is free.'

There was an economy of movement about the unsmiling young man who answered the summons, and either high priestesses passed this way all the time or Cadur was simply not interested. Either way, his dark eyes didn't lift from unbuckling bridles.

'Ah, just the person I was looking for!' Hector sprinted over to a handsome, grey-haired woman in an expensive green tunic, whose ear studs glittered in the sunlight. In her arms was a bale of neatly folded linen, and there was a familiarity between the pair as they conversed.

'His mother?' she asked.

Something flashed behind Cadur's eyes. 'His wife.'

The word 'ma'am' came as an afterthought. She'd need to watch this one, she thought.

'Fancy purebreds you have here,' Ballio said approvingly. He had already noted their brand on his wax tablet. The inverted tripod of Poseidon, the Earth Shaker. 'Not the ox horns one normally associates with the River God, Eurotas, though.'

His knowledge and professionalism had impressed her. 'Like I said, officer, this is not an official visit. These horses are from my own stud.'

'*Your* stud?' His lips pinched in a cross between admiration and surprise.

'Land ownership by women is an abomination in the sight of the gods,' intoned a low voice from the shadows. 'It flies in the face of natural succession and is an offence to the natural order.'

Iliona turned to the tall, thin individual dressed in the elaborate white robes of a priest. His eyes were pale green and bulging, reminding her of overcooked gooseberries, and on his head he wore a small bronze crown of roses, almond flowers and holly leaves. He also looked like he chewed wasps just for the fun of it.

'Sparta does indeed impose different laws to the rest of Greece regarding women,' she said, smoothing her robes so he couldn't miss the slit that revealed her thigh. Another uniquely Spartan characteristic. 'But female independence is well established among the gods.'

'You would do well not to compare yourself to the Olympians, madam. Arrogance does not become you.'

Perhaps baiting him wasn't the best solution.

'What's your name?' she asked.

'Sandor.' A skeletal finger pointed to a circular shrine set high on the cliff top. 'I serve the Blue Goddess. Zabrina of the Translucent Wave.'

Hence the bronze crown. Roses for worship. Almond blossoms to celebrate the end of the ice on the lake, since the almond tree is always the first into flower. Holly, of course, represented resurrection and eternity. For all those souls who perished out there.

'Well, Sandor, we seem to have got off on the wrong foot, and if I'm treading on any of those misunderstood toes, I apologize. However, I am not here in any official capacity—'

'You have cursed this posting station.'

Two hundred miles astride her black stallion, Hades, hadn't improved the wound in Iliona's side. Now it was starting to hurt.

'That is nonsense,' she said evenly. 'I've only just arrived.'

'Having made magic before you left,' he agreed.

That was all the trigger she'd needed.

'I'm sorry if my presence is a breach of your chauvinist principles, Sandor, but where I come from, we live by mathematics and science, where rational thought outweighs superstition, and rituals are carried out to maintain order and calm. The Oracle of Sparta doesn't "make magic" – and she certainly doesn't curse a posting station at the expense of a much-loved hero.'

Ballio, she noticed, was tapping his stylus against his wax tablet as though he was making notes. Cadur was busy unbuckling saddles, and if she didn't know better, she'd have thought he was deaf. While Jocasta was leaning against a pillar with the sort of grin on her face that Iliona had an urge to slap off.

'So you have no powers?' Sandor asked.

'Of course I have powers.' Just not the type he was suggesting. 'I simply don't go around cursing things.'

'But you could, if you wanted?'

'*If* I wanted, then yes.'

'Therefore you do make magic.'

'Fine, Sandor. If that's what you want to call it, then I make magic.'

'A minute ago you said you couldn't.'

'A minute ago I didn't want to put a curse on you.'

'So you do make magic and you do curse things?' His lip curled in a sneer. 'First you swagger, then you lie, until finally the Oracle shows her true colours. Nobilor was alive before you left Sparta, but thanks to your witchery, his new bride's a widow, his daughter is fatherless, and his bones cannot be laid to rest, nor can his spirit.' The overcooked gooseberries pushed themselves into her face. 'I don't know what you hoped to achieve, but Zabrina is no match for your mischief. Make no mistake, priestess. You will rue the day you came to Phaos.'

The only good thing to come out of that exchange, Iliona decided, was that it would really piss off the Krypteia – and there was not one damn thing he could do about it. He'd got exactly what he'd set out to achieve. From now on, the crossroads and posting station would indeed be associated with the Oracle of Sparta, and though the moral of the story was *be careful what you wish for*, Iliona thought it might also work to her own advantage.

The Krypteia might not be so eager to employ her services in the future.

SIX

The Axe God was busy shaping the Tree of Life when Iliona approached the clearing. Jocasta needed to stretch her legs after so much riding, she said, and made Iliona promise to rest while she was gone. Iliona had given the physician her word, but didn't define what she meant by 'rest'.

With their protective powers, poplars were the traditional tree of the autumn equinox, and today the Divine Woodsman was busy hewing niches in its trunk. Dancers dressed in flowing red robes, the poplar's sacred colour, were twirling to the sound of Pan-pipes, while a drummer beat time to each thwack of the double-headed axe. Any suggestion that this was a solemn undertaking was banished by the toasting of each niche with foaming mugs of a local drink made from fermented barley. Iliona felt it would be discourteous not to join in.

'Hello, I'm Dierdra.' A woman upon whom life's knocks had been well and truly etched appeared at her side. 'I'm a masseuse at the bath house, and I thought I'd introduce myself, since I'll probably be pummelling your poor stiff muscles in the morning.'

Her voice was deep and throaty, and, looking at her, Iliona thought she would not be out of place adorning the kerbs of the agora or touting by the docks. The heavy kohl around her eyes only added to the impression, as did the excess flounces on her frock and froth of ringlets in her hair. But closer inspection revealed this was nothing more than overkill. That here was a woman clinging desperately to her youth, without realizing that it emphasized her age. A case where less would very definitely be more.

'You've no idea how much I'm looking forward to that, Dierdra.'

'Oh, yes I do.' The masseuse chuckled. 'Everyone comes to me the first time, thinking they're crippled for life. But when they leave my table, they're as lithe as a snake and— *Oi! Find someone else's jugs to ogle, you pervert!*'

Along with everyone else, Iliona spun round, but Dierdra's bellow had done the trick. Whoever the pervert was, he'd made himself invisible, though who could blame the poor man for gawping? Critical side of forty or not, she'd retained her figure, if not her looks, with breasts that would have most women crying rivers for, regardless of age.

'Heard about your run-in with Sandor.' Dierdra adjusted the diaphanous mantle that covered her curls, because no freeborn woman dared to venture outdoors bareheaded, especially on ceremonial occasions.

'News travels fast,' Iliona murmured.

'Gossip's the lifeblood of this posting station. Without it, half this lot wouldn't have anything to say to each other from one week to the next, though between you and me, milady, I'm not sure I can stick another season of noses poking where they don't belong. It don't half get on my wick. Oops. Sorry.' She pulled an apologetic smile. 'Rude of me to moan.'

'Not at all.' Iliona thought of Nobilor. 'It does everyone good to let off steam.'

'Well, now, that's sweet of you to say so. Anyway, lovey, I wanted to give you this.' She unpinned a silver brooch in the shape of an owl, with coral for eyes. 'Cross between a welcome gift and a good-luck charm, if you like.'

'I can't possibly—'

'Course you can.' Dierdra pinned it where Iliona's mantle crossed her shoulder. 'With that Sandor spitting his poison, you'll need an amulet, and honestly, I've that many jewels I don't know what to do with them all. I mean, it's not like I can wear them to work, now is it?'

'That's very kind of you, but . . . well, this may sound a silly question, but why buy so much?'

'On what they pay me here? Do me a favour.' Dierdra rolled her heavily kohled eyes. 'I just attract marriage proposals, me, and quite honestly, it's embarrassing at times. The way they cling, you know? What starts off as a gentlemanly admirer can turn out a proper pest in the end.'

'I thought all men were pests to start with,' she quipped.

Dierdra tutted. 'Pests or bastards, it's rare to find a good 'un.'

Iliona wouldn't know, she'd never found one, and the best thing to come out of her marriage had been divorce. 'Well, you know the saying, Dierdra. Good men are ugly, and handsome boys are bad. But if by some miracle they are handsome as well as good, then they're married, while if they're ugly and good, they'll be broke.'

Bleached ringlets joggled up and down with laughter. 'Now *I'll* give you a tip. Treat your men like wine, luv, and you'll never go far wrong.'

'Wine?'

Dierdra clinked her beaker against Iliona's. 'First you walk all over them, then you keep them in the dark. Then with a bit of luck they'll mature into something you'll enjoy having dinner with.'

'Ooh, what's so funny?' asked a high-pitched, little-girl voice. 'Do share the joke, Dierdra. You're always such a riot.'

Pushing through the crowd, like a butterfly emerging from its chrysalis, came the most perfect specimen of femininity that Iliona had ever seen.

'My lady.' Dierdra bobbed a curtsey. 'Meet Calypso.' She paused for effect. 'Nobilor's widow.'

Studying the flawless complexion, enormous blue eyes and legs that went up to the clouds, she decided it wasn't so much the shock of discovering that Nobilor's second wife was so beautiful. It was that she was so fragile.

'Be a darling.' Calypso passed Iliona a fur cushion that was the same hue as her strawberry-blonde hair. 'Hold this while I fish a stone out of my sandal.'

'Delighted – ouch!'

Dammit, the cushion had just sunk its teeth into her finger.

'Oh, now, Pookie, what has Mummy told you?' Calypso lifted the dog out of Iliona's hands and held it level with her giant saucer eyes. 'Naughty boy, snapping like that. What do we say?'

She turned him round to face Iliona and waggled his little paw.

'Pookie says sorry,' she twittered in a sing-song voice that was only slightly exaggerated from her own. 'Iliona forgive Pookie-Wookie? Pretty please?'

'Iliona forgive Pookie-Wookie.' Sucking on the blood, she vowed the next time she got that little sod on his own, so help her, he'd have no bloody teeth left to bite with. 'Pookie?'

'Nobi named him that when he was just an itsy-witsy-liddle puppy.' Calypso plumped a kiss between the dog's minuscule ears. 'He kept pooking all over his feet, see?'

'Got to go.' Dierdra nodded towards a buxom redhead with a froth of tumbling curls wielding a giant pitcher of beer. 'Yvorna.' She clucked her tongue. 'Wonder what she needs my advice for this time? Anyway, mind you come to the bath house first thing in the morning,' she warned Iliona. 'The quicker we work on those muscles, the better. *Yes, yes, I'm coming!*' She chuckled. 'I don't know, youth today! Not an ounce of patience between them.'

Looking at the redhead, flirting with every man whose goblet she topped up, Iliona didn't imagine Yvorna needing anyone's advice, much less taking it. But appearances can be deceptive. We all put on a face for the public, it's only a case of how often.

'Shall we sit down?' Calypso pointed to a fallen log. 'It's in the shade, and Pookie gets so restless in this heat.'

Iliona looked at the teeth marks in her finger. 'Poor poppet.'

The irony was lost. 'I know I should be wearing black for mourning, and doing all that loose hair and ashes stuff, but I look such a fright in dark colours,' Calypso trilled. 'You must think that's terrible.'

'Actually, pink suits you.'

'It *does*, doesn't it?' Big blue eyes lit up in joy. 'Nobi always called us Pinkie and Pookie. Don't you think that's absolutely darling?'

Following Calypso trip-trip-tripping across the clearing as though her knees were tied together, Iliona tried to reconcile the Olympic bruiser with this shallow lovely. He must have been knocking forty when he married her, and by all accounts hardly a sculptor's model in his heyday.

But there were enormous pressures in being a trophy wife.

On both sides.

'I'm sorry about your husband. The accident must have been a terrible shock.'

'If you don't mind, I'd rather not talk about that. It's simply too ghastly . . . Hermione!' She broke off with a squeal. 'What are you doing here?'

'Begrudge a grief-stricken woman a break, do you?' Nobilor's mother betrayed her slum origins by fanning her neck with her mourning robe. 'Or do you think I'm too old to watch young folk enjoying themselves?'

'You said you were staying behind to look after Daphne.'

'So that's it.' Hermione plonked her knees squarely apart as she sandwiched Iliona between her bulk and Calypso on the tree trunk. 'You came here to get away from me!'

'More like *you* came to spy on *me*.'

'With my Billi in that terrible makeshift grave just four short days ago, I wouldn't have thought there was any need to spy on you. But it just goes to prove. You always were a sneaky cat.'

The blonde wrinkled her pretty little nose. 'If my Nobi was here, he wouldn't stand by while you—'

'Drink up, girls.' Yvorna, Dierdra's young red-headed friend, rapped her knuckles on each of their goblets in turn. 'Otherwise your throats'll be too dry to cheer the little squirrels when the Axe God lifts them up to hang their dollies in the branches.'

She pointed to half a dozen tots dressed from head to foot in fur, clutching knitted dolls in their sticky little fists.

'They're adorable,' Iliona said.

'Not so adorable once you know the history,' Yvorna said with a wink. 'I mean, it's not called the Tree of Life for nothing, is it? In the old days, those dollies were very much alive and kicking.'

Iliona took a harder look at the woollen offerings. 'You mean hanged?'

'I do mean hanged.'

'Have a care,' Hermione snapped, as Yvorna accidentally spilled beer over her skirt. 'I'm not overrun with mourning clothes, you know, and this embroidery didn't come cheap.'

The redhead simply laughed. 'Didn't you know it's good luck? Pour a libation to the Axe God, my lovely, and pray for his enormous chopper in your bed!' Her tasselled skirts swished as she turned away. 'Bottoms up, girls.'

'Don't listen, Pookie, that's so vulgar.' Calypso covered the little lapdog's ears. 'You have to make allowances,' she confided to Iliona. 'The shock of losing both parents turned her a bit wild.'

'Bit?' Hermione snorted in the finest tradition of a truffle hound. 'That little alley cat goes through more men than that dog of yours goes through boiled frogs.'

'Not lately,' Calypso protested, not making it clear whether she meant Yvorna's appetites or Pookie's. 'I heard for a fact she's in love.'

'Love? That strumpet was over my Billi like a rash until we arrived.'

'Girls don't stop flirting just because they're in love, y'know.'

'Oh, and what would you know about love? After the way you sank your hooks into my boy—'

Iliona left the women to their sniping and wondered what it must have been like for Nobilor, caught between the two. Another reason why he drove chariots at full speed round mountain bends, presumably, though surely he must have foreseen the difficulties of mixing his forthright, unsophisticated mother with his dainty, superficial bride? Then again, if he'd fallen heavily for Calypso, he might have been too dazzled to think through the repercussions.

With a fanfare of trumpets, the dancing girls scampered off and the music harmonized to harps and lyres. The cue for the Divine Woodsman to start positioning his sacred objects in the niches. Wooden bulls symbolizing strength. Ravens to represent the souls of the dead, cockerels for fertility, wagon wheels for change, cranes for loyalty, pigs for tolerance. Finally, he embedded his axe deep into the grey pitted bark, consecrating it to the Tree of Life as an emblem of power, the symbol of creation, the tool from which all things in the forest are shaped.

To her surprise – and relief – Sandor had not put in an appearance at the festivities. *Spitting poison*, Dierdra called it, and Iliona fingered the brooch the masseuse had given her. Men on the road, a long way from home, would quickly feel isolated and friendless, and it was easy to see how attachments were made. A warm wit, a rich laugh, healing hands. The perfect antidote to a traveller's loneliness, and she was reminded of Odysseus, who spent seven years with the beautiful Circe on his way home from Troy. Arrogant to the end, Odysseus blamed Circe, branding her a sorceress who cast spells and caused him delay. Well, Dierdra was no temptress, but the Blue Goddess was, and the spell cast by this beautiful lake would be strong. Sooner or later, though, reality would strike. Deals still needed to be concluded, merchandise delivered, payments collected or made, and reluctantly the travellers would pack up and move on. Yet amid this ebb and flow of lonely wanderers, there was a core that never changed. Almost a family in the way they had been thrown together, the workforce relied on one another for everything from food to friendship, from gossip to moral support. It was inevitable that affections would bloom in this tight-knit community, but so would jealousies, envy and rancour.

Had Sandor been one of Dierdra's admirers?

Gossip's the lifeblood of this posting station, she said.

Iliona didn't doubt it. But with gossip comes rumour, dripping malice into the ears of the gullible under the pretext of friendship . . .

Her gaze turned to Ballio, hovering tight-lipped at the fringe with not so much as a cup in his hand. She watched his eyes narrow to slits as the masseuse pushed through the crowd to greet Cadur, planting a kiss on each of the groom's chiselled cheekbones. Somehow Iliona didn't see Ballio showering Dierdra with jewels. More one of those *noses poking where they don't belong* that would eventually grind you down and make you want to move on, like Dierdra for instance. Or else wear your nerves to a frazzle, inciting tempers – and worse – to explode.

At the blast of a horn, the dancers returned, dressed this time in long white tunics overlaid with panels of smoky-green gauze. In their hair they wore chaplets of sow thistle and cranes-bill, and their faces had been painted with white lead. Linking hands in a circle, they began to sway round the Tree of Life to the haunting sounds of a flute.

'Their costumes represent the leaves of the poplar,' a cultured female explained in her ear. 'White on the underside, but you can see that the green on the top is closer to grey, where the leaves were scorched by Hades' smoke.' She smiled. 'If you believe in such tales.'

Anthea. Hector's wife, where up close the wrinkles were even more pronounced. And those weren't laughter lines round her eyes and mouth, either, despite the lightness of her tone.

'I believe in telling such tales to the children who come to my temple,' Iliona replied. 'You should see their little faces light up, when I mimic Hercules snatching three-headed Cerberus from the Underworld, wearing his crown of poplar for protection.'

'Children. Yes.' The tone became wistful. 'They love stories.'

A woman who had never had any herself, she realized. The lines came from sadness, and regret.

Anthea sighed. 'Little ones rarely pass through the station.'

'You seem to have a plentiful supply locally.'

Playing hopscotch, tag, blind man's buff or leapfrog in the clearing.

'We do, but even that's difficult to juggle. One has to be so careful, with the two neighbouring states constantly tearing each other's throats out.'

'Uh . . . ?'

'You didn't know?'

Anthea explained. For centuries, the mountain and lowland peoples had been in conflict. The highlanders, the Enkani, known

as the Eagles, were hardy huntsmen, while the people of Phaos
were primarily herdsmen, potters, boat-builders and fishermen.
The contrast could not have been greater.

'In theory, the two should enjoy good trade agreements,' she
insisted. 'Instead, each believes their own skills and lifestyles to
be superior, and that the other tribe is lower than scum.'

War had been a routine part of their culture until the estab-
lishment of the trade routes and subsequent founding of the
posting station, where a permanent military presence in the town
of Phaos put paid to most of the skirmishes.

'But not, sadly, to any ill feeling,' she added. 'The Bulls,
that's the lowlanders, claimed victory, because this complex
was sited next to the lake, but that was purely a practical decision based on grazing for the horses, access to water, and a
flat site for building. The trade routes obviously cross the mountains as well, so we, at the station, take great pains to remain
impartial.'

Eagles and Bulls tearing each other's throats out. A detail
Lysander had conveniently forgotten to mention.

'Sandor,' Iliona said. 'Which side is he on?'

'Theoretically, he remains neutral, since both tribes revere
the Blue Goddess.' Anthea applauded the dancers. 'But he
resents the impact of trade in his jurisdiction, claiming the
increase in traffic is an insult to Zabrina, who relies on quiet
and calm. It's no secret that Sandor would like to see this enterprise fail.'

Not superstition, then. Politics.

And if he could scupper this flagship of the newly united
Greek nation, it would put pressure on the system as a whole.
Iliona watched the flautist tapping his wooden clogs to keep
time, and thought, it would only take half a dozen key posting
stations to go out of business for this newfangled communications
network to collapse. After all, the whole point of experiments
was that they could easily be abandoned. A trial stage is just
that.

'How are you enjoying the Dance of the Virgins, my lady?'
Hector's smile was broad and contented. He brought with him
a pronounced smell of oil of bay. 'These days we pay homage
to the dolls that hang in the branches, but it's not so far back
that maidens like those were sacrificed in their place.'

'It's a lot further back still since those girls were virgins,' his wife snapped. 'Half of them will lift their skirts for three copper chalkoi, the rest lift them for free.'

'It's a posting station,' Hector said patiently. 'Wherever men need to unwind, there will be girls willing to help them.'

'On which subject, either you have a word with Yvorna or I will.' She gave the pleats of her robe a vigorous shake, and Iliona noticed the green linen matched exactly the hue of her eyes. 'We can't have her back-chatting the customers, Hector. She plays practical jokes on them, and all sorts.'

'Have they complained?'

'That's not the point.'

'I beg to differ,' he said. 'She's vivacious and people appreciate that.'

'You mean men do.'

'Ninety-nine per cent of our trade comes from men, now let's not bicker over a servant girl, Anthea.' He applauded as the dancers wrapped up their performance. 'The sun's setting, it'll soon be time for the feast. You will join us, my lady?'

'I'd love to, but I think I will freshen up first.'

'If there's anything you need, let me know,' Hector said, bowing, and as they walked away, Iliona could hear Anthea asking him where on earth he had been, the Illyrian envoy was looking all over for him, the porter needed a word in his lodge, the horse doctor had a query over one of the mules, it was extremely irresponsible of the station master to abandon his duties without telling anyone where he was going. Her voice wasn't a whine, but the question had a passive, pleading air to it. Then Iliona remembered the contented smile on Hector's face when he'd joined them, and the pungent smell of oil of bay. Put the three together, and you have the suspicions of a woman who fears her husband is having an affair, using unguent to mask the scent of her rival.

Gossip's the lifeblood of this posting station.

Wasn't it just. Already, in the space of just a few hours, Iliona found herself sucked into this incestuous whirlpool of suspicion and doubt – and the trouble with blood is that it is so easily spilled.

One man had already paid for stolen gold with his life, while another plunged head first over a precipice.

In the branches, the woollen dolls swayed.

SEVEN

The gold mines lay in eastern Macedonia, in mountains shaped like a hand on its edge. The peaks were serrated, bare, unforgiving and grey, often covered by snow until early summer. But the lower slopes were swathed in chestnut trees and planes, a haven for roe deer and rabbits, with clearings peppered by spikes of furry verbascum, where birdsong rang clear and rivers ran clean.

But bears and wolves also prowled through the forest.

And not every predator walked on four legs.

Lysander stood at the mouth of one of the mines that riddled the hills, watching, without blinking, the poor wretches who split the rock. The lucky ones were those assigned to the opencast trenches that ran diagonally up the hill. Not so lucky were those forced to scramble along badly lit tunnels that disappeared hundreds of cubits into the rock face, tracking the rich veins of ore. Either prisoners of war or kidnapped by pirates then sold on at auction, the slaves came from as far afield as Caria, Syria, Colchis and Lydia. Friendless, frightened – but strong.

Lysander followed the progress of the gold, watching as Gregos must have watched. Once the rock had been hacked out and brought to the surface, teams wielding iron hammers pounded the stone until the pieces were reduced to a size suitable for the hundreds of crushing mills. He watched the slaves pushing, three to the spoke, as the chips were ground between a pair of flat, circular stones. Eventually, the rock became dust, at which point it was ready to have the gold filtered out, and this was done in the river. Using first fingers and then sponges, it was effectively panned, the gold remaining behind because of its weight.

Such a grindingly slow, labour-intensive business, involving four, four and a half thousand men, required close supervision and eyes like a hawk. The guards were hard, the slaves were shackled. Life expectancy was short.

The head of the secret police chewed his lip.

Talking of figures . . .

Each of the four caravans was tasked with transporting

twenty-five thousand drachmas' worth of gold in special double-lined sacks. A hundred thousand drachmas in total. Stealing ten per cent was bold and audacious, especially considering a skilled artisan would only expect to earn five hundred a year.

The thieves certainly made sure it was worth their while.

Lysander wondered how quickly their values would change after spending a little time in his company.

Access to the women's quarters was via a staircase of polished oak, with staterooms at the end of a corridor lined with gaily painted doors and lit by sconces burning scented oils. Hector clearly believed that relaxation after an arduous journey should begin with the first step.

'My name's Melisanne, ma'am.'

The girl was tall and slender, with silver-blonde hair and a serious face. Her hands, in fact all of her, were spotlessly clean, her saffron tunic was impeccably draped, the border round the hem set at exactly the same parallel level all the way round. The word conscientious was all but tattooed on her forehead.

'I'm Madam Anthea's personal maid, but she's assigned me to you during your stay, as a mark of esteem and respect.'

Respect?

Or to spy on the Spartan priestess?

'That is most generous of Madam Anthea, Melisanne. Please tell her I'm very grateful.'

In the morning, once the pack animals had been discharged, Iliona would be able to show her appreciation with the gifts she had brought. Whether a posting station demanded the same contributions one would normally take to another person's house was moot, but it didn't seem right to arrive empty-handed. Hospitality was hospitality, no matter the terms.

Also, a donation to Zabrina of the Translucent Wave might not go amiss, either.

'The master hopes you find your quarters pleasing, milady. He said to tell you that if Eurotas can cope with a chamber that's well clear of the kitchens, that overlooks the gardens on one side, the lake on the other, and with the bath house just a short hop away, then he might be in business.'

Iliona laughed. 'Tell Hector that Eurotas has a feeling he will always be in business.' She remembered the cleanliness of the water in the horse troughs, and the neatly swept yard.

'The master very much wants this new venture to turn a good profit.'

'I didn't realize there was such a thing as a bad one.'

Melisanne didn't smile. 'But you do find the room pleasing, milady?' she asked, Iliona's response obviously not clear enough.

Ditto Hector's rhetorical joke.

'I shall be very comfortable here, Melisanne.'

With no experience of posting stations, Iliona had been prepared for a clean, but nonetheless small chamber furnished with cheap, but nonetheless cheerful sticks of furniture. Not tables and footstools of fine polished chestnut. Not thickly upholstered chairs and deep wicker chests. And especially not couches spread with damasked linen that had been fragranced with gentian.

'I hope you like the way I laid your things out, milady. I've put your robes in one chest, your shawls in another, and lined your sandals under the couch. Your perfumes and cosmetics are on the table behind you, along with your mirrors and combs. The water in the bowl's fresh, the room has been aired, and there's a feather fan on the pillow in case you get hot in the night.' She bobbed. 'Can I help you undress and wash, ma'am?'

'I can manage, thanks.'

'Really? I mean—' She turned pink with embarrassment. 'Should I re-pin your hair now, milady?'

'Spartan women are bred to be independent, Melisanne. I would no more ask you to wash and dress me than you would ask me, but I appreciate the offer. Thank you.'

The girl's eyes bulged at the idea of the rich, pampered women who usually passed through being left to tint their own cheeks with mulberry juice, apply hot curling irons to their own hair or, horror of horrors, pluck their eyebrows themselves. 'So . . . what can I do?'

'Go and enjoy the festivities,' Iliona said firmly. 'If Anthea asks, tell her I sent you, but I'm sure you'll be better employed there than hanging around here, waiting on me.' She cocked her head on one side. 'Pretty girl like you, I'm sure you have a young man you want to meet up with.'

The blush spread down her neck to her chest. 'I do have a man, ma'am, but I am unable to join him at the feast.'

'Ah. He's an Eagle, is he?'

'That's my sister's fiancé. Morin.' He was a highlander, she explained. 'Works in the stables, always pestering Lisyl to give up her virginity, but she won't. She's a good girl, is Lisyl. Honours the true Phaos principle, to remain pure until the night of her wedding. Not like my other sister.' Her lip twisted. 'Yvorna just doesn't care, that's the trouble.'

'Carefree is not a bad trait when you're young.' Iliona was only twelve or thirteen years older than Melisanne, but suddenly she felt old enough to be the girl's mother. 'Anyway, she's in love, isn't she? That'll soon calm her down.'

'In love? Yvorna? Well, I must say that's news to me.' Melisanne didn't seem to notice that the priestess had only been here a few hours, yet was already aware of events. 'Mind you, that girl would rather drink vinegar than tell me her secrets, and I'm her sister, for heaven's sake.'

'Perhaps that's why.'

She sighed. 'When our parents died, we promised to look out for one another. Needless to say, Lisyl and I kept our end of the bargain, but Yvorna? She always pleases herself, no matter what, and I tell you, milady, she'd rather confide in that weird stable . . . Oh no! Don't tell me she's fallen for Cadur?'

'He is an exceptionally good-looking young man.'

Melisanne gave a toss of her silver-blonde mane. 'I don't trust him. He creeps down to Dierdra's cottage at night, I've seen him. Hard worker, but doesn't speak, doesn't mix. Even Hector has no idea where he's from—' She stopped short. 'I meant the master, of course.'

Iliona thought, the man who keeps himself to himself usually has something to hide.

'Of course.'

With the heat of the day past, she flung open the shutters, admitting sunshine, birdsong and a stunning view of the lake, where storks and ibis dotted the trees and swallows dipped low over the water. The view on the other side was no less enchanting, overlooking a paved garden where neatly clipped laurels rubbed shoulders with giant cardoons, fountains splashed, and statues stood watch over flower tubs brimming with heliotrope and lilies. Heavy, perfumed and full. A woman's touch, she decided. Small and compact, the garden oozed the same grace and discretion as Anthea herself, with its rows of herbs lining the paths and roses scrambling up the pillars along the portico, their hips bright scarlet and shining. Against one of the columns, a girl of fifteen stood frowning and chewing her nails.

'Who's that?'

'Daphne.' The maid neatly rearranged the combs on the table and lined up the pots of cosmetics. 'Nobilor's daughter.'

Oh dear. Another factor in the wrestler's difficult equation, and Iliona wondered where she fitted in.

'Thank you, Melisanne, I've taken up enough of your time.'

The girl didn't move. Clearly, she needed things spelling out.

'Off you go.'

Still nothing.

'Is something the matter?'

'No, ma'am. I mean, yes, ma'am.'

Shifting her weight from foot to foot, with her eyes fixed on a knot in the flooring, this was a completely different Melisanne to the earlier competent, confident servant.

'This curse of yours, milady.' She swallowed. 'Does it affect everyone?'

'I beg your pardon?'

'I mean, is it a general curse on the trade and the future of the new courier system?' She was twisting her hands like she was wringing out linen. 'Or something that applies to everybody who works here?'

Iliona looked at the incense vases balanced on their stone pedestals, the bronze candelabrum glinting in the sun, the animal-skin rugs spread over the polished oak floor. 'There is no curse, Melisanne. Not on the posting station, the traffic, the trade or the people.'

'The priest says—'

'Priests can be mistaken.'

'As you are the mouthpiece of Eurotas, milady, so Sandor speaks for the Blue Goddess, and Zabrina is gentle. She never lies.'

So this was to be a battle of divine powers, was it?

'A mistake is not a lie,' she said patiently. 'It is a genuine error, and we are all guilty of those. But if it puts your mind at rest, Melisanne, I'd be happy to put myself in a trance and tell your fortune. Tomorrow, if that would suit you?'

'Would you, ma'am?' Her eyes lit up, but with relief rather than gratitude. 'Oh, thank you. Thank you so much!'

'My pleasure.' Hundreds of people were employed at this station, and if Iliona had to win them over one at a time, then so be it. She rubbed the aching wound in her side, and thought, some rest! 'Now off you go and enjoy the festivities. You can tell me about it in the morning.'

Alone in her chamber, she approached the niche in the wall and, from the silver phial in the shape of a dolphin, poured a libation of wine. In theory, her prayers should have been to Zeus, for his sense of honour, justice and good faith. She smiled, wondering what the Krypteia would make of her offering prayers to Athene, patron and protector of the arch-enemy Athens. He'd argue treason. She'd argue that Athene was also a leader of armies, and no army was stronger than Sparta's. That wasn't why she'd chosen the virgin goddess of warfare.

She unpinned the brooch Dierdra had given her and laid it on the tiny stone altar, a focal point for her prayers. Was it coincidence that it was shaped like an owl? Iliona was no great believer in fate. She believed everyone was responsible for forging their own future, and that destiny lay in your own hands. Treason again? The High Priestess of Eurotas denying the very River God she was supposed to serve? Possibly. But did it matter how the pieces went together, providing the mechanism was sound?

Which is where the Goddess of Wisdom came in. Iliona used tricks and illusion every day to help people overcome their problems, qualities Athene was familiar with. She was a schemer, a strategist, a manipulator of men, and had she been a boxer, Athene would have hidden metal nuggets inside her leather knuckle protectors. Whilst Iliona wouldn't necessarily stoop to such tactics, she couldn't deny that murder ran in her blood. Her father had slowly and systematically sent the preceding king mad, dripping poison into his wine under the aegis of friendship, until the poor man slashed himself to death outside the temple. And she, too, had killed in cold blood, and whilst in both cases the ends justified the means, it didn't mean she slept at night.

Three times Iliona poured the libation, then anointed the tiny altar with oil of cloves. Invoking Athene, she prayed for the goddess's insight. With just a smidgen of conniving thrown in.

Changing into a gown of rose pink trimmed with silver, as far removed from her official robes as she could get, her mind turned to Gregos' murder. Snooping wasn't part of her brief. Retrieving the gold was Lysander's problem. All the same, it wouldn't hurt to have a wander round the stables at some stage, she mused. If the gold was being switched at the posting station, as he suspected, it was unlikely the rocks would be stored far from the swap site, which ruled out the paddocks, the vegetable plots and the hay fields. Equally, lugging heavy sacks out of the accommodation block would attract too much attention, whereas deep piles of hay made for perfect cover. Especially when few animals needed to be housed indoors this time of year.

She twisted her hair into a simple bun, securing it with ornate, bejewelled pins. The frescoes on the wall were yet another surprise. The quality of the artwork was quite astonishing for such an isolated outpost, and the pictures set just the right tone for travellers a long way from home. Soft. Restful. Reassuring. Iliona threaded earrings through her ear lobes, from which dangled tiny gold bunches of grapes, then slipped on various bracelets of shining electrum. On the west wall, Orpheus was busy taming wild wolves with his lyre. Opposite, Aphrodite rose prettily from the foam, while a pastoral scene, showing Helios's cattle grazing in the light of his setting rays, covered the wall to the south. Truly, they were works of art—

Wait a moment.

She laid down the choker she was about to pin round her neck and took a closer look at the pictures.

'Well, well, well.'

Wild beasts from the mountains being brought to heel. A goddess rising out of the water. Grazing cattle . . . The people of Phaos were known as the Bulls. Herdsmen and fishermen, whose sole aim in life was to subjugate the wild highland huntsmen.

We, at the station, take great pains to remain impartial.

Like hell they did. The symbolism couldn't be clearer, which prompted the question: was this Hector's doing? Anthea's?

Or both?

'What did she say? Is the curse permanent?'

'I'll need to look for another job after this.'

'Where? You won't find one round here.'

'There's Phaos.'

'The city? That's on the other side of the lake!'

'Who cares how far it is,' someone else piped up. 'If there's work, I'm taking it, mate.'

'What work? If the posting station closes, the town'll die too.'

'So are we all cursed, or what?' the wheelwright wanted to know. 'My wife's expecting a baby and I don't want it born with two heads.'

'Why? Don't you want it to take after you?' Yvorna retorted.

Sniggers rippled round the jetty where the servants had gathered. Out on the translucent water, fishing boats dotted the surface like ink spots, in search of sponges, crabs and eels, while waterfowl bobbed round the reed beds and pelicans on the islands grunted and preened.

'This is no joking matter, young lady.' The porter wagged his fat finger. 'We've had a curse laid on us by the Spartan priestess—'

'Priestess, my arse,' sneered a water-bearer. 'If she's not here in an official capacity, that makes her a witch.'

'Well, you'd know all about that, seeing as you're married to one,' said Yvorna, and this time the laughter was open.

'You never take anything seriously,' a gardener murmured without criticism.

'What's to take seriously about this?' Yvorna threw up her hands. 'My sister told you what the Oracle said. Sandor's mistaken. There is no bloody curse.'

'Then how come Nobilor's dead?' one of the cooks asked.

'Yes, how come?'

The mood swung to hostile again.

'A whole churn of milk went rancid in the night. You tell me that's coincidence!'

'One of the chickens stopped laying.'

'I slipped getting out of bed this morning.'

'You lot! Honestly, I can't believe my ears.' Yvorna tipped her head back and laughed. 'Chickens often stop laying, you big dollops, just as milk always turns sour in the heat, and you, you clumsy oaf, you're always tripping over things.'

'What about me, then? I didn't have this headache yesterday.'

'You weren't drunk yesterday.'

'Are you siding with her, then? The bitch who put a curse on us?'

'Morin, you pick on someone your own size!' Lisyl waded into the argument with a mock punch at her big, burly betrothed. Chatting to Melisanne in the clearing, she'd arrived late and only caught the last part of the exchange. 'Leave my baby sister alone.'

'Do you mind? I'm quite capable of looking after myself, thank you very much.'

'See! The curse has them fighting each other,' a chambermaid said. 'Sister pitted against sister, it's civil war—'

'Civil warts more like.' Yvorna stuck her tongue out. 'On your bum, so you can't sleep or sit down.'

'Are you cursing *me* now?'

'With the black blood of bat and venom of snake—'

'Don't joke about this, Yvorna. I'm scared stiff my kids—'

'Who said she's joking?' The water-bearer again. 'Maybe the witch cursed Melisanne, who cursed her sister in turn—'

'Oh, for heaven's sake, either we're all doomed or we're not,' Lisyl said, 'and Melisanne quite clearly says that we're not.'

'So you're under the spell, too?'

'Hey.' The crowd parted as a young man with chiselled cheekbones pushed his way to the front. 'If any of you have a problem, take it to Hector. Lisyl and Yvorna are your friends. They don't deserve to be put on public trial.'

'Absolutely.' Dierdra forged through to stand beside Cadur. 'You should be ashamed of yourselves, bullying these poor girls, or do any of you want to call me names, too?'

'Course not.'

'Sorry.'

'We're just worried.'

The crowd thinned out as they headed back to the clearing, where the Axe God was quenching his thirst with a pitcher of ale.

'That's the trouble,' Lisyl said, nodding in his direction. 'They've all drunk too much.'

'Or not enough,' Yvorna added wryly. 'Anyway, thanks for sticking up for us, Cadur.' She planted a smacker of a kiss on his cheek. 'No one else was going to.' She glowered at Morin. 'Quite the opposite, in some cases.'

Lisyl was also watching her boyfriend. Taller and broader than most, and with dark curly hair, he hadn't moved from the spot.

'Yes, thank you, Cadur. Dierdra.'

She gave the older woman a hug and then, as an afterthought, embraced Cadur. He smelled of fresh hay and pine, and his muscles were harder than iron.

'No problem,' he rasped.

He seemed uneasy being hugged, but with Morin showering daggers on her, Lisyl hung on for all she was worth, then kissed both his cheeks and hugged him again, even tighter. Take that, she thought, for calling my sister names!

'Come on.' Yvorna linked one arm through Cadur's, the other through Lisyl's. 'The feast should be starting up soon.'

With Morin linking his arm through his fiancée's and Dierdra hooking up with Yvorna, they walked in a line back to the clearing, where flutes and drums drowned out the laughter.

From beneath the Tree of Life, Melisanne watched them approach. At first glance, she thought, you'd think this was a happy band of friends rejoining the festivities, not a care in the world between them.

But Nobilor was dead and the posting station was cursed.

Regardless of what Iliona had said.

EIGHT

I n the hills, where Jocasta was gathering herbs, there was a sense of change in the air. It whispered through the drying of the leaves, the rustle of squirrels hoarding hazelnuts for the winter, dormice weaving nests to keep them warm through the long months of hibernation. Soon the collage of colours that ranged from flame to rust red, amber to sulphur, would change to a grey leafless monotone and wolves would howl.

But for now, on the cusp of the autumn equinox, this was a season of bounty. Of ripening berries, finely spun spiders' webs, clucking pheasants and fairy rings. As well as plenty of herbs to collect!

Vervain, clary, boxberry, hawthorn, fennel, and not forgetting horehound, whose flowering stems were excellent in combating digestive disorders. There were also sloes to pick, and broom, not to mention her old friend thorn-apple, which, though toxic and needing to be used with caution, offered outstanding painkilling and narcotic properties. What surprised her most about the plant was that smoking the leaves actually eased asthma attacks. You wouldn't credit such a thing, but like they say, what doesn't kill you makes you stronger.

When she left Sparta, she hadn't set out to treat anyone other than Iliona, whose wound had stood up astonishingly well to the journey. But as she'd passed through the yard, Jocasta noticed a groom with boils, a maid with leg ulcers and a gardener limping with what looked like sciatica. With so many people employed in and around the station, there'd be menstrual disorders, ear aches, insomnia, migraines and fibroids – and she'd seen at least one lazy eye.

There would be several competent physicians in the town of Phaos who could take care of such ailments, but that was on the far side of the lake. A long way to trek just for a poultice. In any case, physicians don't come cheap and, judging from their faded, worn tunics, the workers at the station didn't earn a fortune. Of course, the horse doctors would be more than capable of healing them, but with the vast volume of traffic passing through, the veterinarians were rushed off their feet.

One of the first changes Iliona made when she took over as high priestess at the Temple of Eurotas was to bring in a physician and treat the patients for free. The king, her cousin, had turned puce when she told him, but by that time it was already a done deal.

The rich won't stop hiring their own doctors, she'd told him. *They'll want him to call on them, not the other way round, and in any case they wouldn't be seen dead consulting a helot.*

Helot? The king almost needed an undertaker, never mind a physician. *You never said anything about—*

The point is, she'd said firmly, *the nobility's customary endowments of silver and gold will be put to much better use subsidizing a healing room than sitting around in the treasury, gathering dust.*

The Oracle would set the poor riddles, telling them to leave chaplets of flowers on the river bank, or toss bread rolls shaped like fish into the water, as a means of repaying the god.

Rather ironic, when you stop and think about it. Slaves were fed, clothed, even physicked for free, Jocasta mused. Yet if you were freeborn and doing the same job of washing rich men's sweaty feet or combing their hair over their bald spots, cleaning their floors or scrubbing bathtubs, you weren't half as well off financially. And you probably didn't have to work as hard, either. The whole point of being wealthy was to flaunt what you had – and nothing screams rich like an overstaffed household.

Then again, who in their right mind would swap freedom for comfort?

Plucking leaves, berries, stamens and flowers, Jocasta placed them carefully in separate sections of her satchel. Even though she, as a helot, was caught in the same trap, enjoying a far higher standard of living than she could ever expect as a free-woman, she would not let the good life cloud her vision. Freedom for her people remained top of her list.

One day.

One day, my friends, the helots will be free.

One day we will return to our homeland . . .

Rutting bucks contested supremacy in the valley with loud grunts and clacking of antlers. An adder slithered off its stone and disappeared in the dark, damp leaf litter, searching out prey with its tongue. Magpies chattered noisily in the treetops. With the sun starting to sink, Jocasta reluctantly wound her way down the hillside, nibbling raspberries as she followed the track. Her first task would be to classify her herbs, then cleanse and re-dress Iliona's wound. The stab had been shallow – as weak at the attacker himself – and hadn't, thank heavens, penetrated the muscle. But Zeus alone knew what she'd been up to, to split it open again. Luckily for Iliona, she was young, she was fit, she was healthy. An afternoon's rest would go a long way towards healing the wound. Zeus willing, the patient had even taken a snooze.

Crossing a small brook by means of a tree trunk which had fallen over the water, Jocasta thought she heard footsteps. She stopped, and decided it was probably a badger snuffling around. Maybe a rabbit darting into its hole. All the same, she clapped her hands in case it was a marauding bear. Bears run at the first sound of noise.

Further downstream, the river opened up into a small pool overhung with willows and pungent with the smell of soft moss. With the bath house off limits until morning, she'd have happily made do with a good flannel wash, but there was nothing quite like submersion and this was too inviting for words. She assessed the sun dipping down through the leaves and decided there was still enough time for a plunge. She slipped out of her clothes and into the water. Cool, refreshing and sweet to the taste. She surrendered to its luxury, floating her long black hair on the surface like duckweed.

'Pff.'

She blew the water out of her mouth as she came up for air. That felt good. Better than good, and watching scores of painted lady butterflies heading south on migration, their flickering orange and black flight mirrored in the crystal-clear water, she decided that the water nymph who lived here was blessed.

She sank again, wondering where the best place would be to dig up some of the dark purple crocuses that were unique to this region. Said to have bloomed where Medea spilled the elixir of life. Jocasta could well believe it. Medea was a sorceress and the crocus was a highly potent poison, though in the right hands it went a long way to alleviate gout pain. But this local bulb had a reputation for easing the symptoms of fever accompanied by joint, chest and stomach pain. Something to follow up on tomorrow.

Surfacing, she caught movement from the corner of her eye. Shadows, surely? Bears don't stalk the weeping willows. All the same, Jocasta was a helot, and when you're plotting rebellion and the death of the king, you can't afford to take risks. You remain constantly alert, watching and listening. Attuned to the nuances of nature.

The pool was too shallow to dive, so she splashed and played as if she was alone. If there was anyone spying, she intended to retain the advantage.

Helots are good actors, as well.

After a few minutes of apparently idle bathing, she emerged close to where the willows had moved, arching her arms out in the uninhibited manner of one who thinks they're alone.

'Is this good?'

Faster than lightning, she'd spun round, brought him down in a headlock, driving her heel into his groin.

'I mean, I'm naked. Leaning over you. Isn't this what you wanted?'

He wore priest's robes, white, getting browner with each agonizing roll in the dirt. The bronze crown had slipped over his forehead.

'Are those grunts of passion I hear, Sandor?'

'Aargh.'

'Not good enough, I'm afraid. I like my men to scream.'

She balled her fist and rammed it into his kidney.

'*Aaargh.*'

'Louder.' She repeated the action. 'Oh, much better.'

She left him retching his guts up beside the pool. That'll teach him, she thought, to go spying on women.

And telling everyone the place had been cursed.

NINE

D aphne was still alone in the garden when Iliona set off to rejoin the festivities. The sun was slipping towards the Isles of the Blessed, reddening the sky and casting long shadows over the earth.

'That's not what people mean by a balanced diet,' she said gently.

All afternoon, the girl had been alternating between chewing her nails and sucking her hair. The only thing that hadn't altered was her scowl.

'What do you care?'

As an unmarried woman, she could still wear her hair down, and it shone chestnut in the dipping sun. From this angle, it appeared to be her only good feature. Slouching did nothing to improve what Iliona hoped, fingers crossed, was still puppy fat, and frowns are rarely attractive.

'You've cursed us all and you're proud of the fact. You don't care that you've ruined my life.'

Holy Hera, not another one.

Iliona looked round the garden. The lavender lining the path, clumps of basil and rue, stately lilies and rambling roses. There were statues of Apollo the Prophet, Demeter the Gentle, and Hermes, who protected travellers and trade. But Hermes also summoned the dying. Laying his golden staff of finality across their eyes.

'I know this is a really tough time for you, Daphne—'

'You don't know anything! We were fine until you came on the scene and now look. You've ruined everything with your horrible curse!'

With that, she ran into the building, kicking up her heels behind like a small, spoiled child. Which, of course, she probably was.

'Do you want me to talk to her?' a voice asked from the shadows.

'Cadur.' Where the hell did he spring from? He made no move to apologize or even repeat his offer. The ball, she realized, was still in her court. 'I – um – well, why not?' It couldn't hurt.

'I just want to make it clear to her that there is no curse, before the situation gets out of hand.'

Dark eyes glittered through the glossy fringe. 'The old ways die hard. Both the Eagles and the Bulls believe dragons still live in the mountains and that shape-shifters walk after dark.'

'And you? What do you believe, Cadur?'

'I believe your black stallion could use another rub down.'

'I'm sure he could.' Iliona wasn't so easily deflected. 'But Daphne is a very modern young lady. She won't believe in dragons.'

'Of course not.'

'That's a very emphatic response. It sounds as if you know her well.'

'No, but she'd like it very much if I did.'

Not cramped by modesty, then? She watched him indolently stroll back through the archway, following the direction Daphne had taken. There was an air of intelligence about this young man, and something else, too, that she couldn't quite put her finger on. Again, she wondered how long Cadur had been in the garden, and what he had been doing there. Was he watching Daphne? Watching her? Or waiting for somebody else?

'Oh, hello!' Surprise lit Yvorna's face as she emerged from the storage cellar, but for the first time there was no broad smile on display and it looked for all the world as though she'd been crying. 'Not at the feast, then?'

'On my way now, as it happens.'

'Me, too.' She closed the door to the store room rather too quickly. 'I'm famished.'

'Is everything all right?' Iliona asked, as Yvorna surreptitiously wiped her eyes.

'Bloody onions, that's all.'

'Not a lover's tiff?'

Yvorna shot her an old-fashioned look. 'The last thing you want to listen to around here are rumours, milady. Half this lot believe everything they're told, the other half make it up as they go along.'

Was that a denial? Or a polite way of saying mind your own business? Girls who are constantly in the spotlight wouldn't necessarily want to flaunt their private life, too. Some things need to remain just that. Private.

In the clearing, trestle tables had been laid out, piled with fresh goat's and ewe's cheeses, bread, olives, sardines, and *koran*, a silver-scaled fish unique to this lake, not unlike trout in appearance, but whose flesh was white in the summer, red in the winter, and just beginning to turn pink at the moment. Washed down with foaming beer and chunks of crusty, dark bread, the meal was delicious, and in between chatting to the Illyrian envoy, listening to an advocate from Athens brag about the length of his speeches and having her ear bent by a hypochondriac cloth merchant on his way home to Corinth, she quietly observed the key players in the posting station's ongoing drama.

Beneath the Tree of Life, with its dangling woollen dolls and carved offerings tucked into the niches, the Master and his wife ate in silence. With his beard neatly clipped and an air of natural authority, Hector certainly seemed the right choice for the job, but what made the authorities choose a tavern-keeper over other contenders? As lanterns were lit, one by one, round the glade, Anthea's gold ear studs glittered, as did her cloak pins and the pendants that hung round her neck. Her robe was expensive, as you'd expect, but there was an air of sophistication about the way it was draped, the style of her hair, even her posture that convinced her that Anthea's background was noble. Iliona helped herself to another sardine, and thought, the aristocracy never, ever diluted their bloodlines. So what would make Anthea break the taboo and marry, quite literally in this case, below her station? Despite standing with their shoulders almost touching, the chasm between husband and wife was deeper than Hades. A cloud of sadness hung over them both.

As with earlier ceremonials, Ballio made no effort to join the group, but lingered on the sidelines, still watching intently as if making mental notes. Dierdra stood by an unsmiling Cadur's side, tapping her foot to the flautist's merry tune, and drinking more than was probably good for her. Melisanne was talking to a couple of serving girls under a poplar a little way off. From their gestures, the conversation seemed to revolve around manicure techniques. Somehow, Iliona didn't see Melisanne smuggling gold.

'It's Daphne I feel sorry for,' she heard someone say.

Leaving the Illyrian envoy to the cloth merchant's comprehensive list of digestive complaints, she slipped round the back of a laurel to eavesdrop on the group.

'No one'll want to marry the kid now. Zeus, that girl's ugly.'

'Plain,' Yvorna corrected.

'And what if she *does* take after her father?' Lisyl piped up. 'I'd be as proud as punch, me. Nobilor was a legend.'

'Aye, but uglier than a box full of worms.'

'Who cares how ugly an heiress is?' someone else said. 'Suitors'll be queuing from here to the coast.'

'Not if Calypso inherits.'

'She can't, mate.'

No man in the family, the group were reminded, and in the absence of male heirs, the law is quite clear. His fortune reverts to the mother.

'Unless Nobilor specifically made a will leaving it all to his wife, in which case Calypso won't give a damn about some spotty kid finding a husband.'

'She'll be too busy spending the money.'

'Aye, well, we'll know soon enough. I heard Hector telling Ballio the banker's due any day now—'

'Not a moment too soon for Hermione, I'll wager. Being stuck out here with a daughter-in-law she can't stomach—'

'Not as much as she hates that bloody dog!'

'There you go,' said Lisyl's big, burly fiancé, Morin. 'Talking about Daphne again.'

Iliona wandered down to the lake, where white water lilies shimmered like ghosts in the moon's radiance, and the lights of Phaos twinkled like glow worms on the far side. Bats skimmed the water, while the scent of yellow trumpet flowers and marsh parsley freshened the air.

Many questions had been thrown up in even this short space of time, not least why the accommodation at the posting station was so luxurious, and who was responsible for those controversial frescoes. But that conversation just now provided one answer, anyway. Until now, Iliona had blithely assumed the bereaved family was hanging on at the station in the hope of somehow retrieving Nobilor's remains. Instead, they were waiting for the money.

Because without knowing which way his fortune would go, neither Hermione nor Calypso was able to leave.

Trapped in a hell between avarice and grief, with a fifteen-year-old in the middle . . .

Iliona didn't blame Nobilor for racing chariots flat out. On the open road, with the wind in his face and the scenery blurring, the pressures of juggling a leggy new bride with a

domineering mother, a brooding teenage daughter, god knows
how many aches and pains after twenty years of fighting, and
the strain of retaining his title as he grew older would disap-
pear. At the reins of his chariot, he'd be free.

And now he was.

The champion had discovered, in the cruellest possible way,
that a man's reactions are not as quick in his forties as they are
in his twenties, nor is his strength, his eyesight or his judgment
as keen. All the same. She watched a hawk moth searching the
flowers for nectar. It was a horrible way to end a glittering career.
Rotting at the foot of a gorge, because no one can get down to
recover your body and give it the burial it deserved . . .

*You've cursed us all and you're proud of the fact. You don't
care that you've ruined my life.*

My life, not ours. Iliona looked up at the mountains and sighed.
Was Daphne aware that her future hung in the balance? That
everything hinged on what news the banker brought with him?

Certainly if Cadur had managed to speak with her, it hadn't
taken him long. He'd arrived at the feast shortly after Iliona,
when Yvorna immediately went running up to whisper something in his ear, and for a moment, Iliona thought the young man
was going to smile. Then Dierdra came over and Yvorna ran off
again, but only after giving Cadur's cheek an affectionate pinch.
Whatever made her cry in the store room, she seemed to have
got over it. But then girls like Yvorna become skilful at covering
up—

'These horses of yours.'

'Dammit, Ballio, you made me jump out of my skin!'

'Beg your pardon, ma'am. Didn't mean to startle you.'

So why creep up on me, she wondered?

'Just wanted to compliment you on your fine specimens of
horseflesh. Indeed, majestic is not too strong a word.'

'Thank you.' She forced a smile. 'I breed them for the cavalry,
mostly.'

'Profitable venture?'

In the moonlight, his official insignia glinted, and for the first
time she noticed he had a tooth missing on the lower right side.

'I suppose it's the same in Sparta,' he said, when no answer
was forthcoming. 'Only rich men can afford to join the cavalry,
because although the state says they'll pay for the horses, they
don't bloody mean it. What they mean is they'll give you a loan

that has to be repaid when the animal dies, and if you don't have the money you're in deep bloody shit, pardon my Phrygian.'

What was or wasn't the same was none of his business, any more than the profitability of her breeding horses. All the same, she couldn't help but wonder what made him so bitter.

'Yes. Well. Best be getting back.' Ballio saluted and turned. 'Ma'am.'

How to make a posting station, Iliona mused, watching him go.

Take a handful of mismatched Greeks who, thanks to a rigid class system, only have each another for company. Add two clans that have been at one another's throats from time immemorial, then mix in an irregular supply of itinerant workers, seeing how Hector didn't employ slave labour.

Finally, simmer gently in an isolated outpost and hope to the gods the pot doesn't boil over.

She stared at the mountains reflected in the stillness of the lake that was home to the Blue Goddess, Zabrina.

Keeping secrets around here must be a nightmare, she thought. Those who kept them would need to guard them with their life.

Rising from beyond the lake, the Evening Star, who closed the gates of darkness on the sun, prepared to take her vigil in the sky. Rubbing the sleep of daylight from her eyes, she suddenly noticed the revels being held in honour of the Axe God. Laughter, trumpets, singing, drums. It all sounded very jolly.

As she climbed higher in the heavens, she looked down on the celebrants eating, drinking, singing, dancing, and felt a twinge of jealousy that she would never be honoured in such a devout and forthright manner. But the twinge, as always, quickly passed. Her job was to prevent the Hound of Doom from devouring the constellations and bringing chaos to the world, for everybody knew that if the chain broke loose, the universe would end. That made the Evening Star every bit as important as the god that hewed the Tree of Life – even if her role wasn't so robustly acknowledged!

Having said that, she couldn't resist watching the party for a little longer. So many people, she thought wistfully. Male and female, young and old, and all those carefree children! Being a goddess, and thus able to see into human hearts, the Evening Star knew the future of every one of the revellers. She knew who would find love, who would encounter tragedy, who would grow rich, or sick, or bitter.

None of which, of course, was her concern, so with a resigned cluck of her celestial tongue, she returned to scanning the sky for hostile canine traces.

Even though more than one among the revellers was a killer. And more than one a victim.

TEN

Through the open window, the haze that clung to the mountains shimmered violet over the lake. Ospreys skimmed in search of fish, swallows dived, horses grazed in meadows brimming with ox-eye daisies and orchids. Iliona opened one eye, then immediately closed it again. Any beverage made from fermented barley was bound to make its impact felt, she realized that. Especially when quality had been sacrificed very firmly in favour of quantity. And when you added on the countless toasts, the late-summer heat, an aching wound in her side and two hundred rough and dusty miles, waking up to twenty woodpeckers drumming inside your skull was pretty much inevitable. What she hadn't bargained for was a tongue that had somehow grown a thick scale of armour. Oh, yes. Someone had also crept in and scoured her eyes with salt during the night.

It took a moment before she realized that one of the woodpeckers was tapping its foot against the side of her couch.

'Good morning.'

The foot was bronzed and muscular, and belonged to a wolf. Iliona peered to see if he had a bag of salt in his hand.

'It may be morning, Lysander, but I assure you it's not good.'

'Damn right.' Something moved in the back of his throat and it sure as hell wasn't phlegm. 'That has to be a record, doesn't it? Sabotaging your country's reputation in under an hour.'

Bad news always travels the fastest, and any hopes that Iliona had harboured about rectifying the situation before he arrived vanished into thin air. 'How did you get into the women's quarters?'

'Same way I'll get out.' His smile was cold. 'Without being seen.'

In other words, he could kill her right now and no one would ever know what had happened.

'Are you sending me home in disgrace?'

'It strikes me that you're perfectly capable of disgracing yourself without help from me. But at least your incompetence means the gold thieves won't suspect you're on to them and, if anything, it's bought me more time.' He leaned back in the chair, folding his arms over his chest. 'Although I'd appreciate your not making a habit of cursing our allies. One world record is enough.'

Only the Krypteia could twist disaster to his advantage.

She struggled to sit up, but the woodpeckers turned into steaming hot hammers, while tongs tried to prise her brain out through the roof of her skull. 'How did you get on at the gold mines?'

'Hm.' He handed her a beaker full of viscous purple gunk. 'Drink this.'

'What is it?'

'Sour milk with blackberries. It will make you feel better.'

'I don't want to feel better. I want to die.'

A muscle twitched at the side of his mouth. 'That can be arranged, too.'

She hoped that was his idea of a joke, but his head was turned away as he reached for a spoon, and anyway what did it matter? His face never betrayed emotion.

Probably because he didn't have any to betray.

'Apparently you eat it with this.' He handed her the spoon. 'And before you ask, I haven't laced it with hemlock.'

Until then, the question had not crossed her mind.

'Do you need help?' he asked, as the beaker suddenly shook in her hand.

'Lysander, I would rather drink the hemlock.'

'If it's any consolation, you look like you already have.'

'That bad?'

'That bad.'

He stood up and began to pace the bedroom, while she took a tentative mouthful of slime. Strangely, it tasted quite good, but even so. Any significance in the symbolism of the paintings he could damn well work out for himself.

'My trip to the mines proved one thing, anyway,' he said, spiking his long warrior hair with both hands. 'The Macedonians aren't swindling us.'

She thought of the mines. Of the men forced to work them. Once, as a child travelling with her ambassador father, she'd visited Laurion, south of Athens, where the silver mines were. Her father forbade her to go near the place, it was a veritable plague spot, he warned. But children are inquisitive, Iliona perhaps more than most, and while her father was fawning and flattering, or whatever it is that diplomats do, she gave her servants the slip. What had she expected? A chain gang, obviously. But one in which the men sang to keep the rhythm going, like the helots in the fields, who sang the Reaping Song, the Sowing Song, the Threshing Song, and so on. There was no joy in the Laurion silver mines. The plague her father had warned her about wasn't the usual bogeyman story, that might be vampyres this week or harpies the next. This threat was real.

At the mines, slaves toiled in squalid conditions, surrounded by dirt and debris, with inadequate shelter and disgusting food. For hours they were forced to crawl on their hands and knees through dark tunnels to hack out the silver, and those on the surface fared little better. Wheezing over the smelting pots, the whip cracking on their backs. Iliona sensed the disease and depression. Knew then, young as she was, that their life expectancy was low.

That visit to Laurion laid the cornerstone for her policies at Eurotas many years later.

'Call me stupid,' she said, 'but wouldn't it have been easier to bring the gold to Sparta by sea?'

If she remembered correctly, the only thing that separated the mountains, where the gold mines were located, from the Aegean was ten miles of marshy delta. Don't tell me there wasn't some kind of track running through that!

'Much easier,' Lysander rumbled. 'But that would have alerted Athens to what we were up to, given their navy patrols the region for pirates.'

Politics again. Everything came down to bloody politics. 'What happened to a unified Greece, where everyone's on the same side?'

'The only side Athens is on is her own.'

He was right, of course. The hangover meant Iliona wasn't thinking too clearly, but with Athens hell bent on establishing an empire of her own, she wouldn't hesitate to exploit any weakness in her power-sharing partner's defences. No doubt maintaining a navy of that magnitude was causing her financial headaches, too, but the cost of keeping peace across the interior was crippling Sparta. Iliona polished off the last remnants of the soured milk. On the one hand, hoplites were wealthy enough to buy their own armour and weapons, as indeed were the cavalry, and aristocrats were expected to contribute heavily to the war chest. On the other hand, supply trains ran expensive, as did full-time education and training, and the sheer diversity and dispersion of the various campaigns was proving an imbalance on the Treasury's resources. With the north Aegean a close ally of Athens, there was no chance of sneaking the gold out by sea. Better to risk theft than reveal state secrets.

'So having satisfied yourself that the switch wasn't made at the source, what's your next move?'

'This.' He swung a bronzed leg out of the window.

Two floors up, yet she didn't even hear the thud when he landed.

The obvious place to prepare tinctures, ointments, poultices and salves was the posting station's kitchens, with its raft of facilities. Jocasta moved a small table into the corner, laid out her balances and scoops, her pestles and mortars, and if the staff thought it was odd, her boiling and brewing, toiling and stewing, no one said so much as a word. Even the chief steward didn't challenge her movements, but then again, she'd always found that if you act with authority, people accept it without question. She simply told the overseer what she was doing and got on with preparing her infusions and mixing her pastilles. Confidence gave it conviction.

'Gargle with this,' she told an Athenian student whose throat was sore from too much singing last night. 'Do it once every half-hour and you'll be crowing like a rooster by nightfall.'

In no time, word had spread round the yard. She could hardly roll pills without interruption.

'Give this to your wife.' It was a standard infusion of fennel, dill and borage seeds, to which she'd added goat's rue. 'If that doesn't stimulate the flow of breast milk, tell her to come and see me herself.'

In between mixing lubricants, astringents, caustics and desiccants, she prescribed calendula compresses for a linen merchant's inflamed varicose veins, artemisia to expel a courier's tapeworms, and oils to eliminate head lice for the Illyrian envoy's chief scribe. Mostly, though, the patients were locals, queuing to have their stomach pains eased and their headaches relieved. Overindulgence came with a price tag, but Jocasta had neither sympathy nor contempt for their condition. As a physician, she remained apart and objective. Her concern as always was treatment, not cause.

Though as she decanted her drugs into silver, horn or copper flasks, depending on which was the most suitable, she couldn't help wondering how swollen the priest's testicles were when he woke up this morning.

Bigger than footballs, with luck.

It wasn't Sparta, of course. None of the libraries and galleries or wide, sweeping gateways that Iliona was used to, and in place of towering marble statues these were life-sized and, let's be honest, not particularly well sculpted, either. Equally, however, there were no pickpockets on the prowl, no hawkers or vendors constantly tugging your sleeve and, most blissfully of all, none of the beggars that normally swarmed around the edges, trying to separate bathers from their change with their pitiful whines. She looked at the sign nailed to the door, proudly proclaiming *Water changed every day,* and realized why it was ladies first.

'Would you prefer the sweat room and plunge, or the strigil and soak?' the attendant enquired, helping her out of her clothes.

Yesterday she'd have given her right arm for the steam bath. Relaxing in that circular, vaulted, windowless chamber she'd seen from the top of the hill, while two hundred miles of dust sweated quietly out of her system. But yesterday she hadn't drunk several goblets of beer and her head wasn't being crushed by a millstone.

'Think of me as a dried lentil,' she said. 'Let me steep.'

Nothing was ever simple, of course. Before she could numb herself to oblivion, the attendant insisted on wetting her skin, then rubbing her from head to foot with a mitt of coarse linen. Jocasta would approve.

It will aid circulation and help the wound to heal quicker.

Quite possibly, but it also made Iliona's skin soft to the touch, and you can't complain about that. Like a child, she let the attendant lead her to the next room, where her body was smeared with a mixture of olive oil and ash, then gently scraped off with light strokes of the strigil, lifting any dirt and grime with it.

*To Oizys, daughter of Darkness and Night: I will give you anything
you desire – anything – to stop my head pounding.* The goddess
who brings pain can surely take it away, but it seemed Oizys had
been exceptionally busy last night and was probably dead to the
world from her exertions. She certainly wasn't answering Iliona's
prayers.

'There you go, my lady. Now for the pool!'

No doubt the Krypteia would consider hot water effeminate,
preferring to roll naked in ice than have himself grouped among
cissies. Even Aristophanes condemned bath houses as 'wicked
and dissolute', blasting those who frequented them as 'lazy and
idle'. Well, to each his own was Iliona's attitude. The lentil set
about steeping until it started to wrinkle.

'Ooh, I say, you're up early,' a little-girl voice trilled.

For once, the clacking wasn't inside her head. It was the sound
of Calypso's wooden soled sandals trip-trip-tripping across the hot
tiles to prevent her feet from burning. Emerging from the swirling
steam like Aphrodite from the foam, she tossed her towel on the
floor, settled Pookie on top of it, then swung her long legs into
the pool.

'Everyone else seems to have terrible hangovers this morning.'
She smiled brightly. 'Looks like it's just you and me who took
it easy last night.'

'Mmm.'

'Well, you have to, don't you? Axe God yesterday, Eagles'
feast tonight, the equinox tomorrow. No end this time of year.'

Eagles' feast . . . Equinox . . .

'Tonight?' Iliona whimpered.

'Up in the hills. Everyone's invited – except the lowlanders,
of course. So silly, this partisan divide. Why can't people live
and make do?'

Her sentiments exactly, because one hangover was quite
enough thank you, and she quietly cursed Dionysus for inventing
the vine, then Demeter for allowing mortals to let barley ferment.

'Anyway, the Feast starts after sundown. Something to do with
the first crescent of the new Hunter's Moon, I'm no good when
it comes to remembering details.'

Or much else, Iliona thought, and hard as she tried, she still
detected no signs of grief in this gorgeous young widow. Maybe
Calypso knew Nobilor had drawn up a will in her favour? Indeed,
maybe that was why she'd married him in the first place?

Knowing that, sooner or later, her rich, famous husband would come a cropper racing his chariot?

'Where was he headed?' she asked.

'Delphi.' Her strawberry-blonde hair barely changed colour in the water. 'Another title-fight challenge, with the King of Somewhere or Other putting up his champion for Nobi to wrestle and hoping he'd come out covered in glory.'

'Delphi? Sounds like there was a lot riding on this fight.'

'Gosh, no. He was always called out in the most prestigious locations . . . Oh, Pookie, don't chew the towel, darling, or Mummy will be vewy, vewy cross.'

Pookie didn't give a wat's arse. He continued to destroy the linen with a series of soft, throaty growls. For a second, Iliona was tempted to jerk the towel while Calypso wasn't looking and see whether Pookie could swim.

'Was he nervous, or worried, at all?'

'No, no, he just likes chewing . . . Oh, you mean Nobi.' Even looking sheepish, she was lovely. 'You're thinking he might have been worked up at another big fight and got careless, but my Nobi was well used to that sort of thing. He'd have won hands down, he always did. Mind, the backbiting that went on behind the scenes was nobody's business. Talk about jealous.'

'Other competitors resenting his success?'

'Put it this way, Nobi said there's no such thing as a good loser. They'd spike his drinks, spread vicious rumours, you name it, they tried it – and they say women are bitchy!' Calypso slipped elegantly under the water. 'I'm just glad he went out a winner,' she said, when she surfaced. 'We're so proud of our baby, aren't we, Pookiekins?'

Interesting that not everyone liked a winner, and as slaves dipped leather buckets in the pool and took them away, full, while others ferried in brass cauldrons of hot water to keep the temperature constant, a nasty little thought began to germinate. One that said, sometimes accidents aren't necessarily accidents. They're just made to look like one—

'Who knew your husband raced to unwind?'

'Who didn't, you mean. Nobi was well known for . . . Oh, not you again!'

'I have the right to a soak, same as everyone else.'

Hermione displaced so much water that Calypso's dog jumped off the towel, yapping and drenched to the skin.

'Your trouble, is that you always think your needs take preference—'

'You have no idea what my needs are, Hermione, but if you think I'm staying here while you pee in the water, you're wrong. You'd be wise to out while you can, Iliona. I'd rather take my chance with a crocodile than wallow in here with a hippo.' With prettily pursed lips, she grabbed her sneezing lump of dripping fur and stomped off.

'Don't worry, love.' Hermione winked. 'I only tell her that so she'll bugger off and leave me in peace. I'm fully house-trained, really.'

'You followed her on purpose and bullied her out of the way.'

'No fooling you, is there?' Hermione chuckled. 'Mind, they said you could hear through the ears of the deaf and see through the eyes of the blind.'

They also said she could count the grains of sand on the seashore and measure the drops in the ocean. Iliona saw it more as a case of sound judgement.

'How's Daphne?'

'She's fifteen, who knows? They bottle everything up at that age.'

One would hesitate to call Nobilor a mummy's boy, but he was rumoured to bow to Hermione's wisdom on domestic matters, and it was common knowledge that he'd relied on her totally after his first marriage broke down.

'It couldn't have been easy for any of you, when Nobilor married Calypso.'

Who must have had a huge impact on him, for the champion to marry a woman his mother hated.

'Tch.' She washed off the ashes sprinkled over her head for mourning. 'Let me tell you, I had her measure right from the very outset.' Hermione sniffed. 'Money-grubbing little cow wasn't going to oust me from my own hearth, now then.'

That would have made for an interesting atmosphere. The mother openly hostile to the new bride, while Calypso worked towards easing a domineering old bag out of the picture. Once again, Iliona wondered where Daphne's loyalties lay.

'*Me* money-grubbing?' Calypso came back for her towel, which Iliona now saw had been elaborately embroidered. The widow's own handiwork? Somehow she didn't see those dainty, manicured hands twirling a needle. 'I've never seen anyone throw gold around like you!'

'Listen, I'm doing the economy a kindness by not hoarding, and if you don't believe me, you just ask the high priestess.' Hermione turned to Iliona. 'Spartans aren't allowed to stockpile their money. The state turns it into lead bars, am I right?'

'Bloody heavy they are, too.'

Not strictly true. In practice, the nobility accrued massive amounts of silver and gold, but they stockpiled their wealth in the form of statues and other fine artefacts. It was to prevent the middle and lower classes, the perioikoi and helots, from getting rich, that gold as a currency had been abolished. With wealth comes power, with power comes change and the government didn't like change. By introducing an exchange system based on cubit-long iron spits, the lower orders were kept in their place.

That way, the state only had oppression to fear . . .

'See?' Hermione looked smug. 'And anyway, it's not all about me. Someone has to take care of Daphne, now she's a young woman with marriageable prospects.'

'Nobi always said you spoiled her.'

'He never did! My Billi said I was a brick, rallying round when her mother walked out when she was a toddler!'

'He said there were hundreds of times when he'd come home and could hardly see you for a mountain of tunics, sandals and jewels. And when he mentioned it, you'd just laugh and tell him to *stop nagging and pour your old mum a glass of wine,* you were knackered.'

'Well, I was.' Hermione wagged a fat finger. 'I don't find it as easy to spend money as you. You've obviously been prac-tising a lot longer.'

'Bitch.' Calypso's sandals clip-clopped back across the tiles in a pique.

Those legs, Iliona thought wistfully. Went up to Olympus and beyond.

'I was a good influence on my son,' Hermione insisted. 'I told him, the first thing you do, now you've won that laurel crown, is buy a villa in the posh end of Thebes. *I was thinking more of a place in the country, Ma,* he said, but I mean, really. The sticks?' She made the prospect of a rural idyll sound dirty. '*Trust me, Billi,* I told him, *in this business people have precious short memories.*'

That summer, she'd pointed out, he was dining with aristocrats, city elders, anyone who was anybody, in fact. And well-heeled though they were, and no matter how much power these men held, it was Nobilor they envied.

'*Yes,* you, *son,* I told him, when his jaw dropped. *You're popular in a way those rich folk can never dream of,* and I was right. I appreciate you're one of them, my lady, but you tell me, what politician was ever carried shoulder-high through the streets? Exactly. And name one single banker who was cheered to the rafters whenever his name cropped up. *Out of sight is out of mind, Billi. Unless you stay in the thick of it,* I warned him, *you'll be forgotten by this time next year.*'

'Wise words,' Iliona said.

'I'm not so sure.' The bluster went out of her with astonishing speed. 'Maybe if he'd had his place in the country . . .' Hermione beckoned the attendants forward to give her a hand out of the pool. 'Excuse me, love. Not . . . not feeling too well.'

Grief is a terrible thing. Iliona watched her waddle away. Everyone travels the journey differently, but the destination is the same.

It's the ordeal of endurance that takes us all by surprise.

ELEVEN

Lisyl pushed Morin away, she wasn't in the mood, she really, really wasn't. Late up to begin with, there was tons of catching up to do and, as with all these celebrations, folk get careless when the drink is flowing freely. There was always masses of extra washing the next morning.

'Come on, Lis. I'm only talking about a kiss and a cuddle.'

'I can't. Look at all these cloaks and mantles, Morin. I'm way behind, we're a laundress short, with Phyllis off sick three days running, and you can't pound quality garments on the rocks like ordinary work clothes.' She fingered the gold thread round the edge of Iliona's gown. 'Stuff like this takes time.'

'We'd best hurry, then.' With a lunge, he threw her backwards into a pile of soft hay and dived on top of her. 'Cor, you smell good.'

'Morin!' Lisyl was furious. A minute ago, her workload had been huge. Now she'd have to pick blades of grass and seed heads out of the laundry as well! 'Look what you've done!'

'I'm looking at what I'm about to do,' he said, showering her with kisses. 'Oh, Lisyl. My big, plump—'

'For goodness' sake, give it a rest.' She pushed his hand off her breast. 'I only came down to the stables to—'

'Drive me wild with desire.' The hand shot up her skirt.

'—tell you I might be delayed tonight.' What was he, an octopus? As soon as she shoved him away from one part of her body, he was all over another bit. 'Are you listening to me?'

'You're going to be late, of course I'm bloody listening. Now stop yakking and let me . . . Oh, for gods' sake, what the fuck's up with you today?' He pinned down the arm that was pushing him off. 'I'm warning you, when we're wed, I'm not putting up with this nonsense. A man has his needs, and it's about time you and me—'

'Don't start that again. You know how I feel—'

'You feel damn good right now, I know that.'

'Stop it!' She struggled to break free, feeling stupid that tears were stinging her eyes. 'I'm late, I've got loads of work on—'

'You've got too many bloody clothes on.'

'Morin, please.' Every time they had a kiss and cuddle these days, it turned into a wrestling match.

'Aye, that's the word. Please. You want to *please* me . . .' Mouth and hands roved over her exposed flesh. '*Please* will I touch you . . .'

To her shame, Lisyl's body didn't respond, and he mistook her squirms for wriggles of pleasure. 'You won't regret this,' he whispered. 'It'll be the best thing that's ever happened, you wait. Open up a world of pleasure beyond your imagination. Husband and wife. Me and you—'

'All right, all right. But not now. Not here, Morin.'

He sat up. 'You mean that?'

'I do.' She covered herself up, her cheeks flaming. 'But I'm serious. When I surrender my virginity, it needs to be somewhere special.'

'A special place for a special occasion for my special girl,' he said proudly. 'Leave it to me, and I swear it'll be an experience you'll remember the rest of your life.' He helped her to her feet and gave her a kiss. 'I love you, Lis. Honest I do.'

'I know you do, you ugly great lump!' She kissed him back. 'And I love you, too, only for goodness' sake, will you please let me get back to work!'

'Tonight? When you say late, you'll definitely come, though? I mean, I've told my whole family you're attending the Feast of the Eagles, and I don't want to look stupid.'

'You could never look that, love.' She put her arms round his big, hard middle and squeezed. 'Wild horses couldn't keep me from meeting your clan.'

She bundled up her laundry, now grubbier than ever, and ran off, picking bits of straw out of her hair. Morin looked at the pitchfork, thought for a minute, then decided to quench his thirst first. With long strides he set off for the well, whistling as he went.

Behind the last stall at the end of the stable block, a figure slowly rose to its feet.

TWELVE

Iliona was faced with two choices. Either have her long-awaited massage and forego the Eagles' Feast in order to have a good snoop while there was just a skeleton crew on tonight, or forego the massage in favour of a poke around now. Either way, the afternoon was out. With men, who made up the majority of the guests, flitting back and forth between the bath house and the accommodation block, visiting the barber's, lifting weights or throwing javelins in the gymnasium, a woman would stand out like the proverbial sore thumb.

So, then. Tempting as it was to have Dierdra pummel her aches and knead away her pains, it made sense to shelve her pleasure until tomorrow morning. Especially when few people were interested in anything other than themselves at the moment! The only two she'd need to watch out for were Ballio, and the priest who served the Blue Goddess. Surely, that wasn't beyond her?

Leaving the bath house, her hair still slightly damp, she noticed a very tall, very broad young man striding out of the stables, with dark, curly hair and a smug grin on his face. She watched him head for the well, douse himself with water from the bucket, then engage in chit-chat with half a dozen bleary-eyed grooms. Their body language suggested much time would be spent comparing hangovers. What better opportunity to investigate the stables?

She took a casual stroll round the yard, glancing towards the lake, where a score of laundresses on their knees scrubbed clothes with rather less enthusiasm than usual, rinsing them, wringing them, then laying them out on the stones to dry off. Melisanne's pretty, dark-haired sister scampered down to join them, her hair tousled and her tunic askew. Another one suffering the Axe God's wrath? Iliona wondered. Or could her boyfriend's grin have any bearing on Lisyl's dishevelment?

Outside the porter's lodge, several servant girls were cooing over the guard dog's new puppies, scribes penned letters from dictation under the awnings and moneylenders weighed coins with deft hands. Further out, in the yard, the Illyrian envoy was preparing to leave with his entourage, as was the hypochondriac merchant, while a courier wearing the King of Thrace's colours was benefiting from a quick change of horse and a runner adjusted his sandal straps before setting off. Hector was placing food on the altars to Zeus and Apollo, an itinerant minstrel strummed his tortoiseshell lyre and servants rumbled amphorae over the cobbles.

No one noticed the high priestess slip into the stables.

After the clamour of the yard, the clang of the blacksmith's anvil and the thud of the wheelwright's hammer, the silence was stunning. Maybe the odd rustle of a mouse through the hay, the occasional lazy drone of a wasp, the creak of timbers up in the hayloft. Otherwise nothing. Complete, dry, dust-sprinkled silence. Why wasn't everyone nursing their hangovers in here?

The stable block was vast. Three, four, possibly even five times larger than her own stud, but then hers didn't cater for scores of donkeys, oxen and mules. She scratched her head. If the rocks were indeed hidden in here, the expression needles and haystacks was not wide of the mark, and counting the grains of sand on the seashore would be a piece of cake in comparison. Then again. With donkeys carrying the gold on to Sparta, it was always possible that the thieves might be pulling a double bluff and hiding the stolen gold inside the saddle blankets. She could do worse than start her search there.

Not dissimilar to the mattresses that poor people slept on, saddle blankets were made of wool and stuffed with sweet-smelling dried grass, although few helots slept with leather belly-straps round them! Once the blanket was secure and the animal made comfortable, the load could be added, and asses were capable of hauling quite heavy weights. However, for long, arduous journeys over the mountains, the load per beast was rarely onerous, dismissing any theory of the gold being divvied up in Sparta within seconds.

For one thing, had it been stuffed inside the saddle blankets, the pack-master would have noticed chafing on the animals' backs and reported it. And even if the pack-master was the thief (though as a helot, it was unlikely he'd have either the resources or the social network to plan such a crime) any animals tasked with additional loads would tire faster and stand out a mile. As would any change in the shape of the blanket. Pack animals were chosen for the straightness of their spines, since a bent back would create a tendency for the load to slip, despite strappings round their chest and rump. A man-made hump might as well have a sign hung on it: 'Look Here'. There was no way the gold had been hidden on, in, or under the saddle.

Iliona was back to square one.

Though at least it lent substance to Lysander's theory that the interception was here, at the station. Feeling very much at home among the acid stench of horses, she systematically prodded the stalls with a pitchfork. Again, she thought, needles and haystacks . . .

'Looking for anything in particular, my lady?'

'Hector.' A professional smile covered some rather unprofessional butterflies. 'Just being nosey, I'm afraid. These stables aren't anything like my own.'

'Lucky you.' He let out a soft snort. 'Not knowing whether you have too many or too few animals at any one time. Never knowing if you'll be catering for changing them two, five, eight times a day – or then again none at all.'

Until now, and despite the lines on his face, Hector hadn't struck her as the worrying kind, although she was well aware that conscientious men are often kept awake at night by their problems. She wondered how well Anthea slept.

'Trade is an unpredictable mistress, Hector.'

He shot her a sharp glance, though whether that was from seeing the High Priestess of Eurotas wielding a pitchfork in his stables or the result of a guilty conscience, she couldn't tell.

'Unlike politics,' he replied sourly. 'Which never stops.'

'The new courier service is proving popular, then?'

'Not without teething troubles, my lady.'

'I'm sure the joint heads of state understand that, being still in its infancy, it's hardly an exact science.'

'To say we're learning is an understatement,' he muttered, then bowed. 'Sorry. My problems are not your problems, I have no desire to burden you. How rude of me.' He rubbed his hands briskly to change the subject. 'I'd be happy to give you a guided tour, if you like, though when it comes to this side of the business, my wife is the horsy one. Best if she showed you round. Expert to expert and all that.'

'I look forward to it.'

Out in the paddocks, Yvorna was tugging Cadur's sleeve with what could only be described as a sense of urgency. She didn't appear to be urging him to follow her at all. The gesture seemed more by way of emphasis on what she was saying, though for his part, Cadur was shrugging his shoulders, as if to say there was nothing he could do. Yvorna obviously thought otherwise and the way Cadur rubbed his face with his free hand suggested she was winning the battle. Not defeat, exactly, Iliona decided. More that he was conceding to give extra consideration to what she was asking. Iliona could almost hear him agreeing to try, but that he couldn't promise.

'I presume you'll be attending the Feast of the Eagles,' Hector was saying. 'It takes place close to the summit of Sentry Mountain at midnight, so I will have your stallion saddled and ready from dusk.'

'Thank you.'

He offered his arm. She accepted.

'They're celebrating the first moon of the hunting season, but quite honestly, the way the mountain men and lowlanders face each other off can be quite childish. Both sides play up their festivities, timing them so they *almost* clash, but not quite. The aim is to outdo one another, and they need each other's yardstick for that.' He smiled. 'There is a lot of posturing still.'

Iliona thought of the frescoes on her wall. 'I'll bet.'

He steered her to the far end of the block, where the stables led into open-fronted sheds which housed various wagons and carts, most of which were still loaded with timber, hemp, roof tiles and granite. A couple of them were full of amphorae of olive oil, carefully padded with straw, and one piled with grains of wheat.

'Not the most common form of transport,' Hector said. 'They're too slow and too cumbersome, and only any good on the flat.

But heavy vehicles are also proving more popular these days, simply for the loads they can carry, and already there is talk of enlarging these sheds.'

'If the roads were in better condition, wagons might catch on more.'

'I don't know what it's like in your neck of the woods, my lady, but the roads are well nigh impassable here in the winter. Carts would get stuck in the mud, ruts would twist the wheels off. Personally, I can't see any need for expansion. I'm convinced the novelty will quickly wear off.'

Iliona had stopped listening a while back. 'Would Nobilor's chariot have been stowed under cover?'

'Most definitely. The hot sun is no friend to painted wood-work, my lady. It dries the grease on the axle pins and fades the colours. Every vehicle that passes through this station is garaged in the lean-to.'

'Who has access to this area?'

From the corner of her eye, she noticed Melisanne set a single straw at right-angles on the table, then retreat silently indoors.

'Huh? Oh. Uh . . . everyone who works in the yard has access to the sheds. The field hands often take their meal breaks in the shade, and it's a popular spot for the staff to congregate, because they can talk without the master nagging at them. They think I don't know, but I do. I know everything that goes on in this station.' He smiled. 'Why do you ask?'

This wasn't the time to start airing theories that his chariot might have been sabotaged. 'I was thinking of Nobilor's privacy issues,' she said lightly. 'Even here, it seems, the poor man would have been mobbed.'

'Fame has its consequences,' Hector murmured, 'but anonymity carries a far higher price. Is there a problem, Ballio?'

The thin nose of the warrant officer peered from behind one of the wagons. 'Just admiring the coachworks.' He tapped the wooden side with his knuckles. 'Made by a good craftsman, this. Look at the axle. Those joints. Marvellous workmanship. Superb.'

'I'm sure.' Hector picked up the straw lying at right-angles on the table. 'Well, if you'll excuse me, my lady, I need to see what kind of a mess the Illyrian envoy's party have left behind.' He seemed unaware that he was sniffing the straw. 'Six men, far from home, who aren't exactly teetotal. Repercussions are quick to manifest themselves.'

Not a physical mess. More a psychological muddle. And these men had only stayed for three nights . . .

'Like the lilies that beautify the Blue Goddess's aspect,' a low voice intoned, 'indiscretions will also rise to the surface.'

Hector's face reddened. 'Quite so,' he told Sandor. 'But like the alder sacred to Zabrina, whose bark yields a red dye, whose flowers yield green, and from whose twigs comes a rich brown pigment, there is strength in diversity.'

'I disagree,' the priest said. 'That which is divided always grows weaker. Is that not so, my lady?'

He wasn't asking her opinion, he was picking a fight. To agree with Hector would give Sandor ammunition, while to side with him would be to drive a wedge between her and her host.

'When you take coals from a fire and distribute them evenly, the heat from them withers and dies, just as when you saw a spoke out of a wheel, the vehicle becomes destabilized.' She watched his gooseberry eyes glow with satisfaction. 'But when a clump of chives becomes congested in the herb garden, the plant becomes healthier for being divided,' she said. 'And I can assure you that when a jug of wine is divided between friends, that friendship most definitely grows stronger.'

'Spoken with true wisdom,' Hector said, bowing. 'Now about that Illyrian envoy.'

She watched him saunter back through the stables, chewing the straw Melisanne had left on the table. Ballio could have been carved out of stone.

'Will you gentlemen be attending the feast tonight?' she asked cheerfully.

'Men of Phaos aren't welcome, ma'am.' The warrant officer patted his insignia.

'Those who serve Zabrina must support all factions,' Sandor said. 'The Goddess is as impartial as she is gentle.'

'Yet you did not attend the Festival of the Axe God?'

'Regrettably, I had other business to attend to,' he replied through gritted teeth.

'Important business indeed, for it to take precedence over showing impartiality to both factions.'

'Be careful,' he warned in a whisper that only Iliona could hear. 'Be very, very careful. Even the strongest oak can fall in a gale.'

'Then we must give thanks to your Blue Goddess that the

, winds are set to stay fair.' She smiled sweetly. 'Perhaps you would help me choose an appropriate offering?'

Out on the wide open plains of Macedonia, dotted by cornel and broom and low-branching gnarled oaks, the commander of the gold train watched for bandits. Unaware of what really happened to his predecessor, he was under the impression that Gregos had been thrown from his horse and had broken a leg, giving him the chance of promotion he'd been waiting for. He vowed to himself that he would not be found wanting on this mission and scanned the horizon like a hawk.

Quite frankly, robbers would be foolish to tackle so many armed men in such an exposed position. The helots were first-rate archers, every one. Also ten donkeys – five to carry the gold and five to spell them – plus mules to transport their daily supplies would make for excellent defence cover for the detail. But the new commander was keen to acquit himself and kept a careful eye out as they crossed the windswept mountain pastures and rushing rivers.

Nothing moved, but he, like the rest of the team, remained on the alert. Their careers depended on the safety of this caravan. Each would lay down his life to protect the gold.

At least, this is what the new commander believed.

'Careful? If anyone needs to be careful, it's that dirty little pervert.' Angry scissors cut through Iliona's bandage. 'The bastard was spying on me while I was naked in the pool.'

'Sandor? Are you sure?'

'Trust me, I know a depraved piece of shit when I see it, and for once his eyes had a reason to bulge.' Nothing like a nice, hard kick in the balls to make them pop. 'Was he limping?'

'He didn't seem too comfortable.'

'Good. At least it's put paid to his peeping for a while.' No fun, when the equipment's out of order. 'Bite on this.' Jocasta pushed a twig between the patient's teeth and proceeded to wash the wound with a mix of vinegar and water. 'You're doing well,' she said, 'there's no putrefaction, but I don't understand why the skin's not healing faster. Are you sure you rested while I was gone yesterday?'

'Quite sure.'

Must be the altitude, Jocasta supposed. Might be the water . . .

'What are my chances of dissuading you from riding your horse to the Feast of the Eagles?'

'None whatsoever.'

'Then I'll need to double the strength of the medicaments.'

In a small bowl, she set to blending thyme oil, yarrow and a creamy juice from the plane tree.

'According to one of the couriers,' she said slowly, 'Athens has just put a woman on trial for practising medicine.'

It was rare for Jocasta to give credence to hearsay, for Rumour is a dangerous friend. Uninvited, he comes and goes at any hour of his choosing, changing his form at every turn, and the worst part is, you never hear him approach. Only a vague whispering, like the sound of waves breaking on a distant seashore, signals his departure, and though he claims to see everything that goes on in heaven and on earth, his words flit like bees loaded with pollen, the false mixed with the true. As he trickles his tales into indiscriminate ears, the story grows bigger every time it is told ...

This was different, though. She could not afford to dismiss such a rumour. Not when the implications for herself were so grave.

'*Practising medicine while female* isn't a crime provided you're employed at the temple,' Iliona assured her. 'Your healing skills are bestowed on you by the River God, Eurotas. That's all you ever need to say.'

Jocasta wasn't so sure. Citizens at least have the law to protect them. As a helot, she'd be thrown to the wolves.

'I'm not at the temple.'

'You're still under its protection, and mine, and in any case you haven't cut off your hair and pretended to be a man in order to set up your own medical practice.'

'In other words, the real crime is cross-dressing, and the fact that lives are saved counts for nothing?'

'Athens is nothing if not conscientious when it comes to imposing her chauvinist principles.'

Wasn't that a fact, Jocasta thought. The men exerted total control over their women, from the day they were born until their wedding, when they were passed, like chattels, to their husbands. Widowed mothers, spinster sisters, even aged grandmothers were under their thumb, confined to the house unless attending a religious festival.

'The only time Athenian women take any real role is at funerals,' Iliona said, 'and even then, they're not permitted to cry.' She paused. 'As if they'd want to.'

'It's the double standards I can't cope with,' Jocasta retorted. 'Athens sets herself up as the role model for modern society, citing her architects, scientists, mathematicians and navy. Yet Athenians treat their hunting dogs better than they do their own wives, while brothels have sprung up like weeds.'

'Well, you know what they say in the Parthenon. *If children could be born without women, the world would be a far better place.*'

'An Athenian courier was actually bragging yesterday about how there's only one female virtue, and that's silence. Then had the gall to come to my table in search of a cure for his piles.' She agitated the contents of her terracotta bowl. 'He wanted virtue. He got it. Dashing to the latrines eight times in the night must have felt terribly virtuous, just as he'd have been imbued with a sense of extreme righteousness, riding the next twenty-five miles with a burr under his saddle. Lie still, please. I can't apply paste while you're laughing.'

'Discrimination is universal, Jocasta. It is only ever a question of who and how much.'

Too true, though it was invariably the poor who bore the brunt. She took a small phial from her box and removed the stopper, releasing a strong smell not unlike fresh turpentine. She poured half the contents into the mixture and thought this was a perfect example. The tree which it came from grew in the arid, mountainous deserts of Judah, and was unique in having two barks, through which a gummy grey juice seeped in the summer. Collected mainly for perfume, where the oil was separated from the resin in a process involving great secrecy, this rare aromatic was beneficial for coughs and sore throats when made into a syrup – at least for those who could afford it. But by boiling the sap in wine, and thus preventing it from solidifying, it also healed wounds and eased pain when applied externally. Jocasta had never seen any reason, when she submitted her budget, to explain why the cost of her medicines was so high. In her view, the poor deserved the same chance as anyone else, but at least with this wound the high priestess was reaping the benefits of that exorbitant bill.

'This talk about marriage makes me think of Daphne,' Iliona said. 'How she must be feeling, now Nobilor is no longer around to choose her husband for her.'

'Relieved, wouldn't you think? Fifteen-year-old girls auctioned off to men in their thirties, forties, fifties and upwards? Barbaric,' Jocasta spat. 'Half the time the poor bitches haven't even met these creeps until the dowry's been settled, and once they're married, that's final. They're stuck, even if the bastards knock seven bells out of them and are screwing around.'

'Whereas it's a man's patriotic duty to divorce a barren or adulterous wife, yes I know. It's why I'm glad I'm a Spartan, where we girls have a full say in our futures.' Iliona leaned on her side so the rest of the fragrant, glutinous balm could be applied. 'We're the only ones in Greece who can walk out of a marriage without loss of status or assets.'

She was right, of course, it wasn't just the Athenians, and Jocasta wasn't born yesterday. Her people were no different from the rest when it came to chauvinism, and if helots reclaimed their homeland tomorrow, the irony of it was, the men would instantly reimpose the old laws in which they'd retain full sexual liberty – while women would be kept at home in a state of complete subjugation.

'I'll say one thing for this posting station,' she said. 'Bigotry isn't tolerated. They even employed a female groom, can you believe that?'

'Employed?' Iliona asked. 'As in past tense?'

'If the other grooms didn't maul her, Sandor probably made her life hell with his pontificating about women being the source of all misery, only ever any use serving as maids, cooks and nurses.' She snorted. 'It's a bugger, isn't it, being a strong, independent woman in a man's world? Even you, for all your money and privileged background.'

'I never expected helping deserters escape or rescuing rejected babies from execution to be a stroll in the park.'

Jocasta didn't mean that. Iliona risked her life for what she believed in and, because the cause was justified, she was happy to put hers on the line alongside. But those were clandestine affairs. Secrets shared only between themselves. Jocasta was thinking more of the way the High Priestess was constantly battling for the rights of the poor who came to the temple, countermanding royal edicts in the process, defying the Elders, challenging political directives and standing up to the Krypteia. Now if this happened in a country where women were equal, what must it be like for the rest of Greece?

What would it be like if we helots went home . . . ?

She bandaged the wound and thought, one step at a time. Freedom first. We can thrash out the inequalities later.

Zeus never promised the road of life would be smooth. Or that she'd have to pave it herself.

'Was it Hector's idea to hire a female groom?' Iliona asked. 'Or Anthea's, do you know?'

In theory, the station master was in charge, but his wife had noble blood in her veins and from what little Jocasta had seen, Anthea didn't appear to be a victim of masculine suppression. She tied off the bandage. 'Perhaps she was simply the best man for the job? Now then. I want you to rest again this afternoon. Will you do that, or do I have to forego my trip to stand over you?'

'I shall be telling Melisanne's fortune,' Iliona replied. 'I hardly think I'm going to split my sides laughing over that.'

'Facetiousness won't make this heal faster, my girl. Just remember you were stabbed and that these things take time.' She waved a bronze scalpel menacingly. 'You've already pushed my patience and this wound to its limits.'

'What trip?'

Fine. Change the subject. Just don't come running to me when the bloody thing festers. 'For one thing, I want to collect a sack of those big brown shiny nuts – you must have seen them. They're like chestnuts, in that they split and scatter over the forest floor, except these fall out of prickly green capsules and are poisonous to everything except horses, squirrels and deer.'

'Tell me when you've got your sackful, so I can stop eating anything I haven't prepared myself.'

'You won't say that when your varicose veins are thicker than hawsers and you're crying out for a compress made from the juice.' She pushed her hair back from her face. 'I thought I'd try my hand at growing a couple of these trees in our new temple garden. The flowers appear like candles in spring, very early as well, and I want to dig up some of the local lilies to take home. The ones with yellow turbans that peel backwards and have nice, bright orange stamens.'

'What new temple garden?'

'Didn't I say?' With everything else, it must have slipped her mind. 'The area between the new gymnasium and the library is still rough ground at present. I thought we could brighten it up with a selection of exotic plants from our travels.'

'Define we.'

Jocasta stashed her instruments back in the case, stoppered the phials and stowed them away, too. 'You don't expect me to do it all by myself, do you?' She snapped the lid shut and grinned. 'After all, I'm only a poor feeble woman.'

She'd already drafted out a diagram on a roll of parchment.

'In less than a year, the garden should start to take shape. In four or five, it'll be the talk of Sparta, if not the whole of the Peloponnese.'

It was only later, when she was back in her own room, that she realized that rebels can't afford to put down roots, whether botanical or any other kind. She took out the parchment, opened it out. Then held it against a flame until it was nothing but ash.

Fifty feet below the gold thief's feet, water lilies glimmered like opals in a sea of mirror-calm turquoise. Ospreys skimmed the surface for fish. An easy job, when visibility was ten fathoms, sometimes more. Squirming prey was carried off in thick yellow deadly claws, while ravens cawed from the crags, bees droned in the furry verbascum and crickets pulsed in the long grass. A more peaceful and pleasant place to hole up could not be imagined. Or more apt.

Most scholars were of the opinion that Jason's fabled Golden Fleece was just that. A cloak of pure gold, created from lining the river bed with fleeces to trap the alluvial gold that washed down from the Caucasus every spring. A practice that was still in operation today. Therefore, to these scholars, the Argonauts would have sailed through the Hellespont and hugged the southern shores of the Black Sea until they reached Colchis, where the sacred fleece was guarded by a monster that never slept.

But there was another school of thought circulating at the moment, which proposed that the name Colchis was in fact a corruption of Kolikis, a Baltic stronghold sited at the northern-most tip of the Amber Route, right on the edge of the Ocean that was the end of the world. If so, then the Golden Fleece would have represented the ultimate symbol of status and wealth. A sheepskin studded top to bottom with amber, so many beads that it would have looked, and weighed, like gold.

Was Jason a gold-digger, or a merchant? A raider, or a trader? Did it matter?

Either way, he'd had to overcome obstacles to reach his goal, from yoking fire-breathing oxen to a plough to sowing dragon's teeth that sprang up as an army of warriors, even to slaying the many-headed monster that guarded the fleece. Gargantuan tasks which Jason could not possibly have achieved on his own, proof that even heroes need help. In his case, his accomplice was a beautiful enchantress, whose weapons were poison, soporifics and guile. But once his labours were won and he'd got what he came for, he no longer had need of her help, it was time to get rid of the accomplice. The glory was his, and his alone. It was Jason who went down in history. Not her . . .

The thief wasn't looking for glory or fame. Just the money.

And the last gold train would be passing the Lake of Light very soon.

THIRTEEN

'**I**'ve never had my fortune told before,' Melisanne said, glancing at the smoking tripod in the middle of the floor. 'They're always passing through, these soothsayers, fortune-tellers and seers. I just never had the – the—'

'Money?'

'Courage,' she said awkwardly.

Iliona closed the door and led her to a wicker chair awash with fat, feather-filled cushions. 'Knowing the future can certainly be a double-edged sword, but you have my oath, there is absolutely nothing to worry about.'

Taking her cue from the Oracle at Delphi, her predictions were so vague and ambiguous they couldn't frighten a mouse – and whatever her faults, Melisanne was no mouse. For all her deference as a servant, she was confident, capable, conscientious and loyal, and she'd had to grow up fast after the death of her parents. Equally, though, despite the whole gamut of human nature passing these crossroads, she'd never ventured beyond the mountain passes. This lake was her world and it remained closed, tight-knit and superstitious. Was it any surprise the poor girl was nervous?

'Let me put your mind at rest by telling you what's going to happen.'

If she was to undo this wretched curse, she needed Melisanne's undivided support. In order to achieve it, she needed her trust.

'I'm going to put myself in a trance,' she said, throwing herbs into the tripod. Chamomile, bay and caraway seeds. 'Then I shall call upon the gods to guide me into the Mysteries. Do not be afraid. Nothing can harm you. But when I speak, it will not be my voice you are hearing. It will be the gods speaking to you.'

Well, almost. Iliona wasn't wearing long sleeves for nothing.

'Make yourself comfortable. Breathe deeply. Relax.'

With a combination of fragrant herbs and comfy cushions, that wouldn't be difficult. It was only ever a question of judging when the subject was sufficiently primed, and in this case Sandor had done the hard work for her. Thanks to his scaremongering, the whole workforce believed in the high priestess's powers. She smiled. This tripod was nothing more than a bog-standard cauldron that lived under the couch and was filled with hot coals in winter to warm the room. But Melisanne would remember it as being a sacred vessel, covered with magical symbols. Suggestion is a powerful tool.

'In the name of the four winds, plus heaven and earth, and the Ocean that girdles the world,' Iliona chanted, 'I call on sweet Hestia of the Hearth to speak to me.'

Generally, people consulted fortune-tellers for one of six reasons. They wanted to know the outcome on matters of love, money, profession, health, travel or war. Melisanne's case was different. Iliona had offered to read her future, not the other way round, ruling out any possibility of invoking Dike to bequeath justice, Ananke to secure obligation or the Muses to bring musical and other artistic talents. Also, Hope was misleading, Fate too capricious and Aphrodite far too specific. Hestia, though, protected the very heart of the home. She stood for security, happiness and family values. A gentle goddess, just right for Melisanne.

'Come to me, Hestia, sister of All-Knowing Zeus.'

She swayed, prayed and chanted some more. A trick that had fooled princes and paupers, nobles and merchants. Sceptics don't seek answers from oracles.

'Speak to this girl through the mouth of the High Priestess of Eurotas.'

Squeezing a small air cushion strapped under her arm, Iliona blew the smoke across the room without moving her hands. Melisanne gasped.

'I answer your summons, Iliona of Sparta.'

Too busy watching the smoke, Melisanne didn't notice the bronze tube that slid down the other sleeve to disguise her voice. In her mind, the priestess knelt slumped in a trance.

'But know thee that as I blow the breath of life into thee and offer thee guidance, cross me and my wrath will be felt the length and breadth of this lake.'

A little terror never went astray.

'I will turn flowing rivers back towards their source.' Her voice resonated through the tube. 'I will stop the stars in their tracks, tear up the forests by their roots and make the very earth groan beneath thy feet. But give to me an offering of almond cakes with honey, and I will calm the angry seas and quell the storms.'

Melisanne quickly threw the small cake on the fire. The fire sighed.

'I am looking deep into your heart, mortal child. I see you are kind, thoughtful, compassionate and considerate, but when someone breaks your trust, you feel anger. I also see that you are honourable, honest and courteous in your manner, yet often you are critical of yourself, is that not so?'

The silver mane nodded in wonder.

'And though you put on a public face of discipline and self-control, there are times when you are deeply, yes, yes, *deeply* troubled. Indeed, there have been occasions when you have had grave doubts as to whether you've made the right decision.'

Blue eyes widened. 'You're reading my soul,' she whispered.

'It is a good soul,' the goddess assured her.

In fact, it was everybody's soul, since Iliona rattled out the same phrases for every prediction. The usual premise of having 'considerable potential that has not been unleashed and which could, with the right help, be turned to advantage'. She would categorize them as 'independent thinkers who didn't take another's word for something without satisfactory proof'. And of course her old friend, those 'fine aspirations which, at times, can be slightly unrealistic'. Ambiguous enough to apply to everybody. One size fits all, that was the key, but it convinced gullible subjects that the deity she'd summoned knew everything about them and they could place their trust in her words.

'Looking backwards, I see water,' the tube droned, because having read Melisanne's character, the goddess needed to establish that her past was as transparent as the Lake of Light on her doorstep.

'Water and a small child. The water is troubled. There is an accident—'

'Lisyl! When she was five, she nearly drowned while she was playing down in the reeds!'

Three children, a large lake, not a huge leap of faith.

'I see a man in the past, too. A relative. He is clutching his chest, as he is consumed by the blackness within.' No clues forthcoming. Iliona pressed on. 'An uncle, a cousin—' Oh, come on, Melisanne. Everyone's family suffers a sudden heart stoppage or, if not, an agonizing tumour, ulcerated lungs, the list just went on and on . . . 'A grandfather, perhaps?'

'My father's brother died of the apoplexy,' Melisanne whispered, 'and his father, my grandfather, suffered weeks of agony before his stomach ulcers finally killed him.'

Of course he did. And finally . . .

'In the flames of the Oracle, I see your future. I see love, warm and spreading, like the sun in a hayfield. I see hard work that is not always rewarded. I see a child.'

Everyone's life.

'Boy or girl?' Melisanne asked eagerly.

'But the road you must travel is bumpy and steep. I see it strewn with obstacles, some large, some not so large. You must persevere to overcome them.'

'Will I die of old age?'

'The Fates spin the thread of life, child, not I, and only they know the length of that thread. As ever, a mortal's fate lies in the hands of the gods, though I, Hestia, sister of Zeus, tell you this. Apollo sends you health and Aphrodite wishes you well in ventures of love. Though I see Discord and Dishonesty skulking in the night, clouding the mind of your lover.'

'What about his wife?'

Air spat out of the tube. Shit. Iliona hadn't seen this one coming.

'Let me see, child.'

Usually she took her cues from the smallest of details. The way the subject stiffened or relaxed at her pronouncements. Changes in their breathing patterns, skin tone, in dilation or contraction of their pupils. From their reactions, she could determine whether she was on the right track, stressing those points where she had hit the target, moving on swiftly from those that elicited no response, whilst using these unwitting signals to predict what they wanted out of their future. This was different. Peace of mind might be the Oracle's stock in trade, and misdirection and distraction the tools that achieved it. But suddenly there was more than one person involved here. Possibly children, as well.

'You would give up everything to be with this man.'

'I would. I really would.'

'Because your lover is the kindest and most generous of men.' She crossed her fingers, hoping to heaven it was true. 'But I see a tree with a forked branch.'

What kind of monster would sleep with a trusting soul like Melisanne while still married to somebody else? If it was hot, dangerous, illicit sex he was after, it made him a bastard, who had no right to string her along and destroy any chance she might have for happiness with somebody else. He must know the lowlanders' view on virginity prior to marriage. On the other hand, if he'd genuinely fallen head over heels, then he should damn well stand up and be counted.

'A decision is looming,' she said. 'Maybe tonight . . . maybe tomorrow . . .'

She sprang the release on another contraption. Powder slid down her sleeve into the tripod, releasing clouds of white smoke, and at the same time as the goddess let out a loud sigh, Iliona slumped to the floor.

'What happened?' she asked woozily. 'Did Hestia speak?'

'She did.' Melisanne's eyes were shining.

'How did we do?' Iliona rubbed her eyes as she emerged, dazed, from her trance. 'Did you get all your answers?'

'Not all, my lady, but I am so *excited*. The things she said—! The goddess—! Everything was unbelievably accurate. It's amazing.' When she tried to stand up, she had difficulty finding her balance. Not the first time that Iliona had rendered a questioner quite literally giddy from the experience. 'I can't thank you enough, ma'am, I just can't.' She squeezed Iliona's hands with bone-crushing gratitude. 'I feel so *blessed*. I mean, to be touched by the gods—! I don't know what to say, really I don't, but I know, I just *know*, that everything will work out fine now!'

'I'm glad for you, Melisanne.'

Was she? She covered the tripod. No fire lives without air. Just as no life is worth living without fire.

Maybe tonight . . . maybe tomorrow . . .

With luck, this charade might just force the issue. Dammit, either stay with the wife or make a clean break! The current situation wasn't fair on either woman, and if there were children involved, the quicker he cut his ties to Melisanne the better. Little ones always came first.

Either way, though, someone was going to get hurt.

Maybe tonight . . . maybe tomorrow . . .

But hurt nevertheless.

In the windswept pass in the Macedonian hills, the sun slipped into the Lands of the Dead. Bats took to the wing. Fox, lynx, jackal and wolf moved from shadow to shadow.

Beside a soft, rushing stream, the gold train made camp. No lanterns were lit. No welcoming fire to cook by.

Six of the warriors stationed themselves for the first watch, accompanied by six auxiliary helots. They sat back to back with a stone between their shoulder blades, so if one fell asleep, the other would know. The rest of the squad turned in for sleep to take over in four hours' time.

Above their heads, the metallic fingernail of the new moon climbed above the horizon. Millions of stars twinkled and shone, so close you could almost reach up and touch them.

The new commander checked and counted the saddlebags, just as his predecessor would have done. Poor bugger, he thought. A broken leg was no joke for a soldier. He hoped for Gregos' sake that the break was a clean one.

Satisfied with the bag count, he took the first watch.

Nothing human moved in the hills.

If it did, the commander was ready.

By the light of lamps scented with lavender oil, Iliona slipped into a simple robe of pale pink linen with four narrow parallel lines round the hem embroidered with silver. She fastened it with gold clasps in the shape of grasshoppers, then belted it with a girdle from which nine small tassels dangled, one for each of the Muses. In the lamplight, her hair shone, silken and flaxen, as she brushed it, pinned it up then carefully fed the hoops of her earrings through her ear lobes. Pearl studs, subtle but elegant, with a choker and bracelets to match. Painting a thin line of kohl round her eyes, she tinted her cheeks with a cream made of wine lees, then dabbed perfume on her pulse points. Finally, she bound her sandals to her feet, clipped on the diadem her mother had given her and tossed a diaphanous veil over her head.

After thirty-five summers, Iliona of Sparta was still turning heads.

... *though you put on a public face of discipline and self-control, there are times when you are deeply, yes* deeply *troubled. In fact, there have been occasions when you have had serious doubts about whether you've made the right decision ...*

Words. Meaningless tosh, pure generalizations lacking in background and detail. And yet words which applied to everybody.

Not least the High Priestess of Sparta.

She stared at her reflection in the bronze-handled mirror. Maturity had rounded out her once coltish hips and given definition to her bosom, etching a few lines around her eyes in the process. Character lines, she decided. She ran her hands over a stomach that was as hard and flat as a discus. Maintaining the physical training that was indoctrinated into every citizen, regardless of age or sex, had kept her back straight and her shoulders square without marbling her long limbs with excess sinew, and yes, she thought contentedly, looking back was a confident woman. A woman of power. A leader, if only by example. The picture was exactly how it should be. Calm, authoritative and firmly in control. She peered closer to be sure, but no.

No indication of the pain that the return of a long-lost son would bring.

No indication of the agony of losing him for good—

'Damn.'

If that wound opened again because she'd just bumped into the table, Jocasta would kill her. The past was the past, there was no going back. Compose yourself. Decisions had been made which could never be changed, decisions made for the right reasons at the right time, so what was the point in stumbling around, feeling sorry for yourself? Blotting her tears with the hem of her veil, the high priestess lifted her chin, squared her shoulders and set off for the stables. Calm, authoritative and firmly in control.

For the next few hours, anyway.

FOURTEEN

L isyl was exhausted. More and more washing kept appearing through the course of the day, and the last thing she felt like was trekking up a mountain and then dancing. Much less having to go through the ordeal of meeting Morin's relatives for the very first time when her hair was all over the place, her hands were rough and wrinkled, and her eyeballs seemed to have slipped halfway down her cheeks. If Morin was still in the stables, waiting for her as she'd secretly been hoping, she would just tell him straight that she was too dog-tired to go.

Of course he wasn't. She checked in every stall, because you never know, do you? He might just have nodded off while he was waiting. Oh, well, never mind. Daft of her to expect him to hang around while she was finishing off that extra shift. It was his clan's festival, after all.

'Hello?' She thought she heard a noise up there in the hayloft. 'Morin, is that you?'

Nothing.

'Yvorna, if that's you buggering about up there, looking to jump down and scare the living daylights out of me like you did last week, I'm not in the bloody mood, all right?'

'It's not your sister.'

'Cadur?' She was surprised to see chiselled cheekbones peering down at her. 'What the devil are you doing up there at this time of night?'

The lower part of the stables was lit up well enough, but not the hayloft. I mean, you couldn't, could you? Oil lamps in dry grass? One slip and the place would go up like a . . . well, haystack!

'Nothing.'

'You must be doing something.' He looked too sheepish to be minding his own business. 'Here, have you got a girl up there?'

'No.' It came out too fast. 'No, I'm alone.'

'Come on, what is it?' she laughed. 'You're hiding something, I can tell.'

'Can you now.' His mouth tightened. 'Were you looking for Morin? If so, he left hours ago.'

'I wasn't,' she said airily. Hours, eh? 'I just wondered if he'd had time to grind up that bag of chestnuts I left him, that was all.'

'The sack's in the corner, by the trough.'

'Blimey!' It slipped out before she could help herself. Lisyl hadn't expected him to start, never mind finish, and her mood softened. 'All that peeling and rasping,' she said. 'He *must* love me.'

Cadur grunted, though whether from agreement, lack of interest or the effort of leaning upside down, she couldn't tell.

'It gets stains out, you know.'

'Huh?'

'Ground chestnuts. An old woman told me that, when she was passing through in the spring. She told me to steep them in water and keep stirring until it turns frothy. Once it's settled, she said, *strain the bits off and anything you soak in the liquid that's left will take all the mucky spots off your clothes.*' She pointed to his tunic. 'I'll get those grass stains out, no bother. If . . . you want me to, like.'

He looked at the marks, which hadn't washed out despite several scrubbings. 'I want.'

'Leave it by the sack, then. I'll do it tomorrow.'

'Don't you think you work hard enough?'

'I can't abide the idea of dirty laundry left lying about. What a pong, especially in this heat. And baked-in sweat stains something wicked.'

Eyes, darker than ebony, watched from under lowered brows. 'Does the station master know what you do?'

'I doubt very much whether he's interested in a laundress's stain-removal secrets,' she laughed.

'You should tell him,' Cadur said. 'He'll pay you extra, because then he can charge it as an additional service. He's canny on finance, is Hector, and anyway, he's interested in everybody's secrets.'

'That's what I said to Morin. About the extra money, not the secrets. But he told me not to be so daft, and it's not as if I'll be working here once we're married. Morin says a wife's place is at home, beside the hearth.'

'How do you feel about that?'

'He's right. I mean, it's not what I want. I love it here. But you never see an Eagle woman working, do you? It's not their culture. Only – well, it must get kind of boring. Still. I'll cross that bridge when I come to it.' She wagged a playful finger. 'Now, are you going to tell me what you're doing up in that hayloft or what?'

'I wasn't planning on it.'

'Then I'll just have to come up there and see for myself!' She belted her skirts and began to climb the ladder.

'Hey, hey, hey.' A strong hand grabbed her wrist. 'You be careful.'

Suddenly Lisyl found herself being whisked through the air, and for a second it felt like flying. And so what if Morin thought it inappropriate that his girl was in a hayloft with another man, her skirts kilted up to her knees, breathless with exhilaration? He never swung her through the air like that. Probably the only chance she'd ever get!

'Lisyl.' Cadur's voice sounded raspy. 'I've never asked anything of you before, but will you promise? Promise not to tell anybody that you've been up here or what you've seen?'

'Seen what? Either it's pitch black up here or I've gone blind.'

'Seriously.' He still had hold of her wrists, and he gave them a squeeze. 'You swear?'

Her heart was knocking louder than kettledrums. 'If it's that important, then yes. I give you my oath, Cadur. This will be our secret.'

'Then quietly.' Holding her arm, he guided her through the dark. She smelled sacking, which was odd, because she didn't realize they kept sacks up here. Odd place to store them, where no one could reach . . , Her thoughts were distracted by a series of squeaks, and as her eyes acclimatized she could see something squirming. Overlaid with a loud rattle of purring.

'Kittens!'

'Careful, their eyes have only just opened.' With one hand, he stroked the head of the proud tortoiseshell mother. The other fished into the sacking and came out with a minuscule lump of mewling fur.

'Oh, Cadur. He's perfect!'

'Don't you mean purrrr-fect?'

For half an hour she played with the kittens, one ginger, one tabby, two with black and white bibs, after which she didn't feel tired at all. In fact, a night of feasting and dancing with the man she loved no longer seemed remotely daunting, and so what if his family caught her with rough hands and her hair all over the place? She'd been working all day, what the devil did they expect!

The hut by the lakeside was so small you could almost touch the four walls with outstretched hands. It was timber-framed, with a low roof of thatched straw and a beaten-earth floor; the hinges on the door were ill-fitting and there was no chimney, either, so in the winter the room filled with smoke. For this, the landlord demanded a staggering five drachmas a month, though Dierdra would have paid double rather than share a dormitory with nine other women. Even the single rooms at the station were horrid. No windows, no peace, and just a curtain over the doorway for privacy. Nothing more than cubby holes, them.

She heard the knock, but didn't answer. The second time it was harder. Made with the side of the fist, rather than a rap of the knuckles.

'Dierdra?'

The door opened a crack. 'Cadur? Oh, thank Zeus. I thought it was that ruddy cloth merchant again. Talk about a bleedin' limpet!'

'You told me to come after I finished my shift.'

'I know, I know, I didn't realize the time, love. Come on in.' She glanced up the path. 'Anyone see you?' She squinted. 'Were you followed?'

'Who'd follow a stable boy?'

Dierdra shrugged. 'You never know. Funny things have been happening lately.' She stepped out into the path and yelled at the top of her voice. 'If you're watching, you pervert, we're just playing chess.'

Melisanne was no pervert, but she was watching. If her baby sister was involved with this creep, she wanted to know exactly what he was up to. Not every man was as decent and kind as her Hector, and if that was chess, she was a Phrygian. No one shoots the bolt on a simple board game. Or pulls the scrap of oiled skin over the only tiny window to shut out the night.

She listened to the slap-slap-slap of water on the shore. Heard something plop into the reed beds.

Dierdra called it a cottage. Hector called it a hovel. Melisanne called it a whorehouse.

Sure enough, the bolt shot again a few minutes later, and Dierdra emerged to draw water from the lake, wisps of badly

dyed hair hanging loose from their ringlets and her tunic practically off the shoulder, exposing half her breast.

All right, it was a good breast, she conceded grumpily. Round
and bouncy, not like her little poached eggs, and she shivered
with pleasure. Maybe Hector could slip away from the Eagles
and they could make love in the woods? Poached eggs or not,
he couldn't keep his hands off them, and she wondered what he
was doing right now.

Holy Muses, if Anthea made him wear that dreary rust-brown
tunic to the festival, she'd scream. *You look so handsome in
green*, she kept telling him, but he still wore the clothes Madam
ordered to be laid out. *Let her have her say on what I wear,
Mella. I have you. What does it matter?* Sometimes they'd make
love in the store rooms, sometimes in empty guest rooms, once
in Madam's own bed. *Catch!* That was the time he'd picked up
Anthea's favourite perfume jar. The little alabaster one. Then
threw it to Melisanne, who only just caught it, but the thrill of
that near miss was exquisite. After that, he would often toss a
fragile or precious object up in the air and catch it in the other
hand. Every time her heart fluttered that he'd drop it, but he
never did, and sometimes she wished he'd take the same sort of
risks when they met. *It would add even more spice*, she said. *I
don't want spice, I want security, Mella.* Then he'd kiss her, or
tickle her, or blow in her ear and suddenly she wouldn't want
spice any more, either.

Had he left for the Feast yet, or was he stuck in his office,
dictating lists, letters or endless reports to his scribe? Poor Hector.
If he wasn't sorting out piles of administration, he was stock-
taking in the cellars, checking the stables and dorms. *No peace
for the wicked*, he'd say.

*You can't keep getting up with the larks and going to bed with
owls*, she would chide, with a teasing pull on his beard. *It's
wearing you out.*

Not for much longer, he'd whisper back. *Not for much longer,
my love.*

Melisanne's heart leapt. Wait till she told him what the Oracle
said in her trance! This was just so exciting! She'd memorized
every word to pass on. *Love, warm and spreading, like the sun
in a hayfield. Hard work not always rewarded. Children.
Obstacles. Some large, some not so large*, but most importantly,
you must persevere to overcome them.

Persevere. The Oracle had been clear about that. *You must per-severe*, she'd said, but there was no doubt they would be overcome. *And children*. The gods had seen children as clearly as night follows day! Wasn't this just wonderful timing?

She listened to Dierdra singing while she drew the water.

Yvorna called Hector an old man, but he was mature, rather than old, and anyway, age counts for nothing when you're in love. When he lay in her arms and she smoothed out his frown lines with the back of her finger, it was the most wonderful feeling in the world.

I love you, he'd whisper over and over again. *It's as though a piece of me had been missing*. Melisanne brought him a sense of perspective, companionship and a warmth he'd never known. *For the first time in my life, I have a sense of belonging*.

Me, too, she would say, her eyes filling with tears, and for all Hector was married, being with him felt so natural. So right. Like they'd belonged together from the beginning of time. Two halves spinning through space that finally, amazingly, found one another. Two halves that made a whole which could not be parted. *Maybe tonight . . . Maybe tomorrow . . .*

Compromises would have to be made. Melisanne understood that. But it's not as though he and Anthea were happy. It had been a marriage of convenience for both parties. How many times had he told her the story? How Anthea's first husband divorced her to be with another woman, and how, at the humiliating age of thirty-eight, she'd returned to being the property of her father. Stifled by the restrictions and fed up with being an object of pity and shame, she knew marriage to Hector was her only chance to escape. He might have been born into the merchant classes, but he was competent, she was rich, and moreover her family had influence. Freedom came with a price for Anthea, though. Her father agreed to arrange that one last thing for her – Hector's appointment – then after that he disowned her. She hadn't cared, and Melisanne didn't blame her. Independence and happiness went hand in hand, and now the posting station was established and successful in its own right, Anthea was more than capable of running it on her own. All right, there would be red tape to cut through. The authorities would never countenance a female station master! But wherever there was a law, there was a loophole, Hector said. Melisanne saw the future as clearly as the Oracle had seen it.

Anthea taking over here. She and Hector running a small tavern wherever he wanted. Everyone would be happy and her heart filled with joy at the prospect of giving him all the things his wife never could—

'Ready to go a second time?' Dierdra called out with a chuckle. Hoisting the jug to her hip, she yanked her tunic back into place and tucked her hair back under its pins. 'Then we'll go off to the Eagles. That's if you've got enough energy left for the walk.'

Melisanne had seen, and heard, enough. Maybe tonight, maybe tomorrow indeed, but sooner or later she'd have to pluck up the courage and break the bad news to Yvorna. Apparently, Melisanne's wasn't the only road with a forked branch and bumps up ahead.

FIFTEEN

D rums echoed through the forest. Faint at first. A gentle pulse throbbing through the silence of the night. But with each beat of the stallion's hoof, the drums grew louder. Primal. Mysterious. Enticing. As Iliona drew closer to the summit, the torches lining the road opened into a cavern of light that was a clearing. Now she could hear pipes playing, too, along with triangles and hollowed-out rattles. There was the sense among the seething, laughing, drinking crowd that this was just the beginning.

A clansman wearing traditional dress of pantaloons and red leather headband took her reins. His eyes were already glassy from overindulging, and, like the rest of the men, a short, curved sword hung from his belt.

'It's called a "kopis",' Ballio said, noticing her staring. 'Very similar to the weapons worn by the Bulls, except the blade of these big mountain men has a forward curve.'

Held differently, used differently, Iliona realized. The kopis would be wound back over the shoulder to give a powerful downward swing. Definitely the sword of the hunter, who would also use it for cutting and sacrifice. Even though its principal design was for slaughter—

She thought of Gregos. The bloodbath that Lysander had described . . .

'I didn't think you were coming tonight.'

'I didn't say I wasn't coming, ma'am. I said men from Phaos weren't welcome.' The warrant officer patted the insignia gleaming on his sash. 'My responsibility extends further than merely checking the credentials of the couriers, you know.'

A likely story. He was just being nosey, and whatever secrets were held in this posting station, Ballio would have sniffed half of them out, while Hector would probably be aware of the rest. Very few would slip through the net, she thought. Those that did would be precious indeed.

On one side of the clearing, the biggest boar she'd ever clapped eyes on was roasting on a spit, the smell of cooking mingling with the apple wood over which the beast turned. The backs of the men who heaved on the handle glowed golden with sweat, and the fat from the meat hissed as it splashed into the flames. Nearby, beneath the trees, platters of figs and pomegranates almost obliterated the thick timber planks that acted as tables, alongside blood sausage, boiled eggs and wedges of yellow smoked cheese. Dried hams hung on ropes for people to cut their own slices, baskets of fresh bread were being constantly replenished, and clanswomen, also in traditional dress, dipped jugs into a huge krater of wine to replenish the drinking horns.

'Avoid that if you can,' Yvorna confided in her ear. 'Rough stuff, this mountain wine, you're better off sticking to beer.'

Iliona wasn't so sure about that. Her headache had only just gone. 'Another one I didn't expect to see here tonight,' she said. 'I thought lowlanders weren't welcome.'

The redhead laughed. 'I tell you, this lot couldn't have given me a wider berth if I'd been covered in spots. I told them I'm only here to support my sister, but between you and me, my lady, I really wanted to have a good look at the in-laws. See what Lisyl's marrying into.'

Iliona glanced across to where her pretty plump sister was being introduced to what she presumed was Morin's family. 'For a girl who's supposed to be looking forward to her wedding, she seems a little on edge.'

'Morin's been pressurizing her again, that's the trouble, and I think this time she's given in.'

'Your sister thinks Lisyl should stick to her principles. What do you think?'

'What I think is that Melisanne's in no position to be calling kettles black!' She tossed her thick auburn curls. 'Look at her and you'd think butter wouldn't melt in her mouth, and for the life of me I don't know why she wanted her fortune told.'

'Perhaps it's because her lover is married.'

Yvorna elbowed her playfully in the ribs. 'Aren't they the best ones?'

Iliona couldn't help smiling. 'What about you? Aren't you curious to know what's ahead?'

'Hell, no. I like a challenge – talking of which. You mind the bread, too. These highlanders let their flour and water ferment. Tastes heavenly, I tell you, but it don't half make you fart.'

She skipped off to chat to a bone-worker who had set up a stall under an oak tree, selling pins, beads and brooches in the shape of the new Hunter's Moon. With this amount of light burning, it was the closest any of them were likely to get to seeing the new Hunter's Moon tonight.

A battle horn announced a change in the tempo, the cue for a burly reciter to launch into his spiel, keeping time by waving a baton instead of accompanying himself on the lyre. Although the language was Greek, the accent was strong enough to cut with a knife, a tactic Iliona suspected was deliberate. Certainly the theme seemed to be *make war, not love*, and from the way the crowd made horns on their foreheads, you didn't have to look far to see who were the targets. Iliona bit into the bread, and to hell with the consequences. The aggression of these mountain tribes hadn't lessened with peace, prosperity or the passage of time, and however much they tried to pass off this festival as a case of one-upmanship, this was no light-hearted feud. The question was, was this show simply posturing and bravado, or was there a more serious motive behind it?

One that a large shipment of gold would go a long way towards financing?

'I don't know what you told my maid,' Anthea said, joining her, 'but it's certainly put a spring in her step.'

Hadn't it just. When Iliona saw Melisanne earlier – the sisters were obviously out in strength to support Lisyl! – she was eagerly telling Hector all about it. Iliona could tell, because Melisanne kept pointing at her, grinning like a cat with the cream, while Hector nodded with polite enthusiasm. Maybe it was easier to talk to a man, to the boss. Or maybe it was just not easy to talk to her sisters. For all their closeness, or perhaps because of it,

the girls found it difficult to confide about their love lives, and
it would take a brave woman to start confiding in Anthea. Madam
kept everything bottled in tightly. She would certainly expect no
less from her staff.

'Are you still planning on sacking Yvorna?' Iliona wondered.

Anthea glanced across to the wine krater, where Dierdra had
her arm round her friend's shoulders and was whispering in her
ear.

'That girl has the morals of a cat,' she snapped. 'Sees every
man as a trophy, whether he wears a wedding band on his finger
or not.'

Iliona stared at the space on the fourth finger of her left hand,
where her own wedding band ring used to be.

'Not for all of us does the vein of love run straight to the
heart,' she pointed out. 'Sometimes a vein is just a vessel carrying
blood, the same way that a ring isn't always an endless circle
that symbolizes the eternal nature of the marital bond, but simply
an adornment.'

In other words, when marriage is merely a contract, what the
hell do you expect?

'Yvorna has no idea of the damage she wreaks,' Anthea
continued bitterly. 'They might only be flings to her, but they
undermine the man's sense of stability. He starts to grow restless in his spirit.'

So that was it. She suspected the red-headed firebrand was
playing around with her husband.

Aren't they the best ones?

Iliona tucked into a slab of succulent boar meat and thought,
maybe so. Yvorna was quite blatant about enjoying a challenge,
but equally she was young and carefree. Love 'em and leave
'em was more in her line, and in any case Anthea couldn't be
blind. She must have seen her and Cadur, walking down by the
lake?

'If the affection is strong, nothing can break it,' she said gently.
'Take Nobilor. The way Yvorna flirted with him.'

'Yes, but who knows how he might have responded had his
bride and mother not been two miles behind.'

'Did he strike you as the flippant kind?'

Anthea's green eyes turned thoughtful. 'Actually, no,' she said
at last. 'He struck me as a very sincere and principled individual,
and he was besotted with Calypso, so maybe you're right.' When

she smiled, five years fell from her face. 'You know, it's strange. We have all manner of eminent personages passing through this station. Ambassadors, princes, lords and envoys, even the King of Arcadia once, though he didn't stay. He spent the night at the palace in Phaos.' She shook her pleats and adjusted her veil. 'But none of them, my lady, attracted half as much attention, or was anywhere near as popular, as Nobilor.'

'That's because ordinary people identified with him.'

Not simply because he was the best wrestler yet to don the victor's crown, or the fact that they couldn't believe their luck he'd come to this isolated outpost. More the fact that most youths from the ghettoes who set off with no money, just a burning ambition and a desire to win, don't usually find a rich sponsor to put them through Wrestling School, and often come home poorer than ever. That is, if they come home at all . . .

'His success was an inspiration to them,' she added.

And yet . . . *They'd spike his drinks, spread vicious rumours*, Calypso said. Spiteful, but petty, though, Iliona thought. Not in the league of sabotaging chariots. All the same, it was a point to bear in mind that the motive might not necessarily have been financial, at least not in a personal sense. Jealousy and resentment lie at the root of many murders, and if so, the killer wouldn't have hung around afterwards. What was the point? He'd done what he set out to achieve. Which means the bastard would have got away with it, too.

'Hector tells me you're interested in taking a tour of the stables,' Anthea was saying.

Carried away by bitterness, spite and extra-marital affairs, she'd almost forgotten the gold, and it was a pleasure to be able to discuss horses with someone who knew and appreciated them. For the next half-hour, Iliona immersed herself in the joys of cross-breeding native horses with Persian and Babylonian breeds, prized for their courage and stamina, and also Iberian mounts, famed for manoeuvrability and speed.

'When people think of Sparta, their first thought is of the massed phalanxes,' she said. 'What they forget is that all battles need scouts, and the advantages of an armed and mounted skirmishing and pursuit force cannot be stressed strongly enough.'

'The cavalry is elite, so why shouldn't their horses also be noble?' Anthea laughed. 'It's not just the riders that need to be fine-boned, swift, and smooth on the gait.'

Iliona confessed that her personal preference was for slender heads and thick crests, like her black stallion over there. 'They're so handsome.'

'Nobilor's pair were wonderful to watch, too,' Anthea agreed wistfully. 'I'd have expected a wrestler of his stature to have become hardened over the years, but Nobilor was as soft as dough with those mares. You could see it in the way he stroked them, watched where they were being pastured, made sure they were curried properly.'

'A dark bay and a gold palomino, weren't they?'

'Such a loss, two magnificent creatures like that. You should have seen them when they were in the harness. So graceful.'

How much of her old life did she miss, Iliona wondered. Watching chariots race was obviously one aspect, but if Anthea had been a victim of some hidebound divorce, maybe it balanced out. Not that her love of horses would fade. The nobility were quite literally born into them. In their world – Iliona's world – they were a crucial part of society, intertwined with the exploits of gods and heroes alike, and no expense was spared on their upkeep. When it came to appointing the master of this flagship station, she suspected that Anthea's background in horses would have counted almost as much as Hector's experience in running a tavern. A unique and powerful combination, but as Iliona knew only too well from experience, running stables was a costly exercise. Of course, the station would be awarded state funds to buy and equip its horses and maintain the stables, but, like the accommodation, Hector's facilities went far beyond the basics.

A labour of love that needed subsidizing, perhaps?

In which case, who better placed to swap and hide gold than the station master and his irreproachable wife?

'I hate to drag myself away from stimulating conversation, it's too rare a treat.' Anthea had to shout over the furious applause being given to the reciter as he finally wound up his incitement to war. 'But I promised to distribute honeycombs to the children, do excuse me.'

That would be another major adjustment, Iliona thought. From giving orders in her previous existence, to carrying them out herself in this.

While the crowd continued to whistle and stomp, she tried to picture how it must feel to be stripped of one's citizenship and disowned by the family. In the past, she'd imagined it as an emotional wilderness, in which the lovers clung to each other like barnacles in the hope that love would validate the sacrifices that had been made. What she hadn't stopped to consider were the day-to-day consequences that came in the form of inferior quality clothing, cheap footwear, loss of servants, not to mention the sheer bloody hard work. Anthea was making a good fist of it. Her robes were expensive, she'd retained much of her jewellery, and she used cosmetics with discernment and skill. All the same, a station master's salary, whilst comfortable, would not run to the luxuries Iliona had been seeing . . .

Flautists took over, but this time the tune was faster, picking up on the mood created by the reciter and whipping the crowd into a frenzy. The wine was flowing freely now, the conversation louder, and logic less balanced with each cup that was knocked back. Clearly the Eagles didn't believe in restraint, and even this early into the celebrations, the Festival of the Axe God was beginning to look exceedingly tame.

'So,' sneered a voice from behind her left shoulder. 'The charlatan has shown her true colours by telling fortunes.'

She turned round. 'Come on, Sandor, you can do better than that. Either I have the power to curse the posting station or I'm a fraud. I can't be both, so which is it?'

'Both presage danger.' Overcooked gooseberries pressed close to her face. She smelled thyme, hyssop and, oh dear. Lightly boiled cabbage. 'I can feel it in the air,' he intoned. 'Maybe tonight . . . maybe tomorrow . . .'

'Were you eavesdropping?'

'Zabrina of the Translucent Wave hears everything that goes on in her kingdom. I am only the instrument of the goddess.'

'Oh, I see. Melisanne told you.' It was a stab in the dark, but his narrowing eyes told her she'd just hit the bull's eye.

'You mock,' he said. 'You strut like a cockerel with your phoney pretend powers, but there is evil in the air, I can smell it.'

'Can you? The only thing I can smell are the home-made remedies of a man who is desperately trying to heal the bruising around his genitals and kidneys.'

'Go,' he snarled. 'Leave the kingdom of Zabrina and go back to Sparta, and take that black-haired witch with you.'

'Jocasta is a healer, not a witch, and if you dare so much as spread that for a rumour, I will personally rip out your liver and feed it to you, a mouthful at a time.'

She was hoping to anger him. Instead, he smiled smugly. 'Your malice is to be expected, madam. I do not take offence. Defeat, I am sure, cannot be easy to swallow.'

'I am not defeated, Eurotas is not defeated, and Sparta will never be defeated,' she retorted. 'I just don't take kindly to perverts who spy on women in quiet woodland glades.'

'She should not have been there,' he hissed. 'That is the pool of the maidens—'

'You like them young, eh?'

Now she'd got him. 'You deliberately make my words coil like a cobra, turning them back on themselves in distortion, but it is you who spits venom, not I.' He jabbed a bony finger into her shoulder. 'Tragedy is coming, trust me on this. "*Maybe tonight . . . maybe tomorrow . . .*",' he mimicked, 'but make no mistake, Iliona of Sparta. When it comes, it will be on your conscience. Not mine.'

He limped off, his white robes flapping in – what? anger? pique? contempt? Didn't matter. The crucial word there was limp, and Iliona made a mental note to pass the word on to Jocasta. Maybe that would put a smile on her po face.

'Take no notice of that old windbag,' a rough throaty voice said, stuffing a goblet of wine in her hand.

Dierdra's tunic was of loose, swirling linen that hung in elegant folds from the shoulder. Unfortunately, that was the only good thing about it. Iliona thanked her for the wine and thought, true, the flounces showed off her still-supple figure, but grey sucked the colour away from her face, while the heavy floral pattern emphasized the start of a wattle round her neck and exacerbated the severity of her yellow hair dye.

'He's been acting odd lately, must be his age,' Dierdra was saying, seemingly unaware that Sandor was a good five years younger than her. 'First he came on to me, and when that wouldn't wash – I mean, really, my lady! A priest! Do I look the pious type?' She tipped her head back and roared. 'Anyway, after I turned him down for the millionth time, he made a play for Yvorna, and you can imagine the effect that had on the poor girl. A priest, telling her it's her solemn duty to go to the shrine and . . . well, *purify Zabrina's altar with her love*, was how he put it.'

Dierdra looked round to make sure no one could hear.

'She was worried she might have to go along with it, but I

told her, he's just a dirty old man. You tell him, I said. You tell him you're more desired than Aphrodite herself, and that he can jolly well go hang himself.' She sniffed. 'Course, he didn't, more's the pity. Instead he's been wallowing around like a bear with a sore head, giving you earache, my lady.'

Sandor. A man who mistook misplaced youth for easy virtue, then mistook easy virtue for undiscerning. No wonder he was reduced to peeping through bushes.

'What did her boyfriend say, or didn't she tell him? Assuming she has one, that is.'

'Ah, well.' Dierdra's mouth twisted down on one side. 'Can't really talk about that, my lady. Wouldn't be right. Not with me being her confidante, and all. But I notice you're not wearing your amulet tonight.' She tutted. 'I tell you, you'll need all the protection you can get in this place. A right hotbed of gossip and malice, and I swear, if you look hard enough, you'll see imprints of ears against every wall.'

Iliona smiled. 'It's not that I didn't appreciate your gift, Dierdra.' Actually, with all that angst about her son and the stabbing, it completely slipped her mind. 'But I've multiplied its powers by leaving it on the altar in my room and asking Athene to infuse it with her strength and wisdom.' The smile broadened. 'I can feel it working already.'

'Then remind me to stand next to you, if a fight breaks out later. We'll be the only two left unscathed . . . Oops, must go. That's Yvorna, calling me over again.' She waggled her fingers across the heads of the revellers. 'Man trouble, I'll wager. Always is with us girls.'

With that, she sashayed off into the crowd, slapping a high-lander's face with a mighty backhander along the way for *trying to lose your eyeballs down my front, you dirty sod.* The clansman looked indignant, but his friends dismissed his protestations of innocence with loud bellows of with laughter, and who could blame them? The man was so drunk he could hardly stand up, and quite frankly Dierdra could count herself lucky that he'd stopped at just looking.

Oh, Dierdra, Dierdra, she thought. Instead of letting soft lines of loose hair flatter your face, you will torture it into ringlets, then dot them with ribbons and pins in an effort to look youthful. Worse, you douse the lot with enough perfume to mask even the heartiest tomcat's spraint.

'The Eagles are a hot-headed bunch,' Hector said, sidling up to Iliona as she snaked through the throng.

'They could always try using water to cool down,' she said, wrinkling her nose. 'There's little point in having a lake on your doorstep, if you don't bother to wash in it.'

Hector's beard creased into a smile. 'Baths are for rich folk and cissies,' he said, leading her to a less pungent part of the clearing. 'But then anything the Bulls do, the Eagles will do the opposite. Contrary isn't the word.'

Obstinacy wasn't a virtue, she thought. Just another expression of assertion and control, and this communal lack of hygiene business must be the worst case of cutting off noses to spite faces that she'd come across in a long time. Perhaps that's why Morin wanted to marry a laundress?

She watched the way the music continued to whip up the crowd, and thought, surely music was the mother of civilization. For without rhythm there would be no poetry, without poetry there'd be no song, and without song there would be no dance, therefore no traditions, no culture, no individual identity. Even if it didn't like washing. Most importantly, though, without music there would be no joy in the world. She tapped her foot to the beat and thought, from birth through to death, paeans and chants accompanied every step of the journey. Ensuring that whether it was setting the pace for reaping, sowing, threshing or fencing, warding off illness, or averting evil and witchcraft, the gods would be with you.

Ask and it shall be given.

'Ah.' Hector turned to the peacock advancing towards them, his long hair elaborately folded at the nape, apart from two precociously oiled curls that dangled, one over each ear. 'I don't believe you've met our latest guest.'

The guest wore a belt of Minoan blue, tied tight round the waist, and a kilt of expensive linen that fell to mid-thigh.

'A Cretan by birth,' Hector said, 'a banker by profession, his name is—'

'Lysander.' The banker placed his hand on his breast in an extravagant salute. 'Always a pleasure to meet a beautiful lady.'

She looked at the blue lily embroidered on the left hip of his kilt, the symbol of Knossos. Was it her imagination, or was the middle section the exact shape of the Spartan emblem, the lambda?

'Crete?' she repeated.

Grey eyes met hers without expression. 'Isolated, windy and deficient in harbours, but we invented chess, developed our own system of writing, use registered trademarks and employ our own methods for measuring weights, to ensure the highest possible levels of accuracy.'

'One would not wish to be double-crossed.'

'Indeed one would not.'

Hector's nod of acknowledgement across the clearing was faint, and in the crush Iliona couldn't see who it was directed at. Anthea, probably. 'Yes, well,' he said, rubbing his hands briskly. 'I shall leave you two to get acquainted, and don't forget, sir. If you need anything, anything at all, you'll find a triangle hanging in every corridor. No matter what the hour, a servant will answer the summons at once.'

Hector bowed. Lysander bowed. Iliona thought even his mother would be hard pushed to recognize him tonight.

'Cretan I can understand,' she said, as the drums throbbed. 'Cretans wear their hair long,' and it would take more than this mission for him to sacrifice his warrior's badge, 'but banker?'

'By definition, a banker is a man who takes care of his investments.' His cheek twitched. 'And I do have a great deal invested in you.'

He was in for low returns on this transaction, she thought. The gold train was due in tomorrow, yet she had no idea who the thief was and no idea where the rock dust was stashed, while the whole object of the exercise, to enhance Sparta's standing, had had completely the opposite effect.

But why go round telling the Krypteia he'd wasted his time bringing her here, when he'd work it out soon enough for himself?

'Thank the gods,' he growled, as the rhythm slowed, then faded to silence. 'I wondered how long it would take before they stopped this ridiculous bluster and finally got down to business.'

Silence settled over the crowd, and Iliona could sense the excitement among them. Drummers stepped into the clearing, nine in total. Three times three, the sacred number. Broad shoulder straps supported monstrous double-sided drum shells that balanced on their left hip, the underside of which was goat skin. Being thin, it was able to impart a light and sharp tone when swished with a thin willow switch, whereas the top face had much thicker wolf skin stretched over its frame, to impart a far deeper tone. What was unique was that the drummers used no accompaniment, such as the lyre or the flute. Music was made solely from the switch in the left hand, with accents made by a long wooden stick in the right. The result was hypnotic. Intoxicating. And like a vertigo sufferer drawn to the void, Iliona was sucked into the beat.

'I presume you're not the banker Hermione and Calypso are waiting for?'

'Sadly, the grieving beauties will have to wait a little longer for news of their inheritance, though I understand bets are being taken on which way the wind will blow.'

'Calypso being the hot favourite, I presume?'

'By a considerable margin, though my two drachmas are on Daphne inheriting the lot.'

'Tell me you didn't really bet on other people's misfortunes!'

'I am a flamboyant banker, remember? Who's lost count of the number of gold pieces he's lost, betting on Nobilor's opponent in the sure and certain knowledge that our celebrated wrestler was past it.'

'You'll lose your two drachmas, too,' she said. 'Daphne is a minor, and by law she can't inherit.'

'The estate can be placed in trust through an appointed guardian.'

'That'll be Hermione.'

'Nobilor was besotted with his gorgeous bride.'

'Not at the expense of his daughter.'

Take a burning house, with all three women trapped inside and only one who could be saved, and Daphne would be the one he'd rush to rescue.

Any father would.

She swayed to the hypnotic beat of the drums. *Boom, boom, boom-a-doom-a-dum-dum.*

Close to the spit roast, Cadur was leaning against an oak with his ankles crossed and his arms folded over his chest. He appeared to be watching the progress of some small beetle on the forest floor, and if she didn't know better Iliona would have thought he was deaf. As though aware of being watched, he slowly lifted his head. A hank of hair fell over one eye which he made no effort to push away. Iliona smiled. He looked at her for a count of maybe three before nodding. Then returned to watching the bug.

Herbs were thrown on to the fire, but all she could smell was the Krypteia's scent. Wood smoke with a hint of leather.

The drums drew her deeper into their spell. Now some of the drummers had muted the sound by wrapping gauze round their drumsticks, like clubs. *Boom, boom, boom-a-doom-a-dum-dum.* Mesmerized by the throb and deft twists of their wrists, she was aware of yet more herbs being thrown into the flames. Bay, hemp seeds, fir she recognized. Many others she did not. She could feel herself being sucked into their narcotic stupor, and made no effort to resist.

Boom, boom, boom-a-doom-a-dum-dum.

Surrendering to the hypnotic pulse, at first, she didn't realize. A dozen revellers wrapping their arms round each other's shoulders, moving in time to the beat. So what? Then others joined in, until slowly, imperceptibly, three hundred people had linked up, dancing as one round the fire.

'What bothers me,' Lysander rumbled, slipping a strong arm round her waist and sidelining her to the edge of the clearing, 'is how did Gregos' executioner find him?'

Iliona tried to concentrate, but her head had been stuffed with wool. 'It couldn't have been difficult to follow him to that abandoned shepherd's hut.'

'On the contrary. Even his own men didn't know where he hid out, and that was no mean feat, I can tell you. The boys are always trying to get an edge on each other. The word competitive doesn't begin to describe it.'

She thought of the annual cheese fight. A 'friendly' contest between recruits, where all Team A had to do was grab cheeses guarded by Team B and run off.

A contest where death wasn't uncommon.

'Suppose it was an accident?' she suggested, sipping the wine he had given her. 'Another warrior discovered the hut in your man's absence and decided to claim it as his own private bolt hole? Gregos returned. There was a fight. A spirited contest, if you prefer, in which things got out of hand.'

Grey eyes glittered. 'On the very day Gregos was supposed to meet me?'

'Contrary to what storytellers would have you believe, coincidences happen all the time,' she reminded him. 'Unless, of course, you're a high priestess, whose job it is to interpret the riddles. In which case, it's the will of the gods.'

For a moment there, he almost smiled. 'All things are indeed possible, but I'm sticking with the elimination-of-witnesses theory. I grant you, brawls can turn ugly, and it wouldn't be the first fatality in such matters. But hard as we breed our warriors, ma'am, none of them would choose to sleep on a blood-sodden pallet. The new tenant would have thrown that out straight away.' His mood darkened again. 'Gregos didn't trust anyone,' he growled.

Was it her, or was it hot? Sweat trickled down her collar bone. 'He trusted you.'

He shot her a sharp glance from the corner of his eye. 'I didn't kill him.'

Now she was finding it difficult to breathe. 'Let me put it another way, then. Who knows the whereabouts of your private hideaway?'

'No one.'

'Exactly. You trust no one.'

He leaned closer. His pupils were dark. 'Betrayal is everywhere, Iliona. Remember that.' Was it her imagination, or did a cloud cross those unfathomable eyes? 'And when you live and breathe treachery, you soon learn the only person you can trust is yourself.'

'Which is why you're head of the Krypteia and Gregos was only head of a mule train.'

'Donkeys.'

'Don't split hairs.'

'Why not? I can only make an ass of myself.' A strong hand grabbed hers. 'Come. We are guests here. We must join the ring.'

Before she could ask herself was that a joke, was frivolity part of the disguise, or was she just plain hallucinating, she'd been thrust into the circle, a bronzed arm round her shoulders, her hand somehow entwined round his waist.

Slowly, the new dancers picked up the steps. Simple, graceful, rhythmic and measured. Then a flute joined the drummers. A conical wind instrument, played with both hands. The sound was piercing and clear against the background of drums, setting the pace for the beat.

Little by little, the tempo increased. The whole crowd had now fused into one giant body, its very strength driving the dance. Faster and faster the flautist's fingers moved. Quicker and quicker the drumbeats. Iliona's skirts flared. Her veil soared behind her.

Her feet were barely touching the ground. Somewhere there was shouting.

Ay, ay, ay, ay.

It was the crowd. It was Lysander. It was her . . .

Ay, ay, ay, ay.

Faster. Faster. Faster and faster, until suddenly—

AY!

As one, three hundred dancers stopped dead on the spot. For a second, there was silence. Then cheers shook the mountain. The Hunter's Moon had been praised into a tumultuous crescendo. Now it was time for laughing and serious drinking.

At what point did he lead her into the woods?

When did he stand her against this horse-chestnut tree and press his rock-hard body against hers?

'I enjoy a breathless climax, don't you?' he murmured.

Was he laughing at her?

Somewhere along the way, she'd lost her veil. She must find it. No respectable woman would be seen outdoors without one, much less an exalted high priestess. But there was no strength in her legs to go and look for it. Would she fall, if he wasn't holding her up?

'What,' a gravelly voice rasped in her ear, 'was your point about Gregos trusting me?'

Oh, that. Yes, of course. Gregos. The gold. He'd brought her here, so they would not be overheard.

'What—' She cleared her throat. 'What was his marriage like?'

'I don't see—'

'Was it good?'

'N–not particularly.' He seemed puzzled by where this was leading. Though the branches, she saw stars in the sky. 'Like all warriors, he was away more than he was home,' he said, 'but you know yourself what it's like. Independence gives women strength and direction. Sometimes.' He brushed a wisp of hair from her mouth. 'Sometimes a man can feel out of place when he comes home.'

Someone had sucked the air from her lungs. 'They argued?'

'They argued, he'd get drunk, then they'd argue some more. But not enough for her to kill him, if that's what you're driving at.'

It wasn't. 'Was he faithful?'

A muscular shoulder shrugged against hers. 'He wouldn't be the first man to seek consolation elsewhere, if things weren't going too well at home.'

A picture of Anthea flashed through her mind. 'In other words,' she said huskily, 'you might not have been the only person Gregos allowed to get close.'

His little finger looped round a lock of long blonde hair that had fallen loose of her diadem and gently pulled it towards him. 'That's exactly why I need you, Iliona of Sparta. You read people.' Closer. 'You read situations.' Closer still. 'And you're smart.'

'If you're resorting to flattery, it must be bad.' Did he feel the shiver that ran down her body?

'Uh-uh.' His voice was more gravelly than ever and his breathing was rough. 'I would never even have considered the possibility, but you're right. The drag marks leading down to the river. A dead body is heavy.'

'Too heavy for a woman to pick up.'

'Exactly,' he whispered. 'Gregos' killer was also his mistress.'

The stars began to spin, but so what? Locked together under the canopy, she clenched her hands into fists.

'Were you faithful?' she asked.

She felt his breath in her hair. The breath smelled of mint. 'Were you?'

He was right, it was none of her business. Then his mouth closed over hers, and Gregos and gold became lost in desire. The stars turned somersaults. She didn't care.

In that high, windswept pass in the Macedonian hills, beside that rocky, rushing stream, the commander of the caravan prepared to be relieved. As expected, nothing had happened during his watch. His ears ached somewhat, from straining in the blackness, but all he'd heard was the occasional shuffle from one of the pack animals, a couple of snorts, and their strong, acid scent on the breeze.

In another few hours, they'd be at the posting station on the Lake of Light, with the riskiest part of the journey behind them. Bandits rarely attacked a major trade route. Especially one patrolled by Spartan hoplites.

Above him, the thin silver fingernail that was the new moon drifted across the star-studded sky. Pulling his cloak round him against the cold of the mountains, he noted Pegasus cantering towards the southern horizon. Hercules brandishing his club. The Dragon. The Pole Star. The Milky Way, of course. Once, he heard a faint slide of rocks from the other side of the outcrop, but this was followed by silence. He'd listened. Waited. An hour passed, maybe two, but who knows what creatures paced these dark, foreign hills?

Satisfied at a watch well kept, he saluted his replacement.

It was just unfortunate that when dawn broke, rosy and clear, over the mountains behind them, the replacement was lying face down in the dust. Shot through the neck with an arrow.

SIXTEEN

For the second morning running, Iliona woke up to find her vision blurry and a brain that matched. Squinting, she could just about make out the painted frescoes on the wall. The crumpled damask spread across the bed. The sunlight slanting through the open window across the oak floor. The only trouble was, these were not her frescoes. This was not her floor.

And this was most definitely not her bed.

'Good morning,' a voice beside her rumbled.

Shit. She lifted the covers.

'If you're wondering what happened last night, the answer's nothing,' Lysander said, cracking his knuckles. 'As you've just found out for yourself, you're fully dressed.'

'Then what—?' The last thing she remembered was spinning stars.

'I'm a hot-blooded Cretan banker, Iliona. Can I help it if the High Priestess of Eurotas finds me irresistible?'

She didn't understand, but then he did not expect her to. In fact, he was more than happy to explain.

'Hector introduced us. We got on well. So well, in fact, you drew me aside to whisper sweet nothings in my ear long before the dance, and then afterwards you led me into the woods.' He shrugged. 'At least, that's the way I remember it.'

'I'm sure you remembered it to many people, too.'

'Boys will be boys,' he said cheerfully. 'Of course, adding a certain something to your wine helped my cause.'

'And here's me thinking it was the narcotic-laden smoke.'

'That was just a mood enhancer. Not strong enough to knock your legs from under you.' He rolled off the bed, where he'd been lying fully clothed on the coverlet, and walked over to the window. 'Though to be frank, I've had worse missions in my time than propping you against a tree trunk in the dark.'

If that was a compliment, he could bloody whistle.

'You set me up.'

'I warned you. *Betrayal is everywhere.*' His eyes narrowed. 'You should know better than to trust me, Iliona.'

Lesson learned, and how else could her veil have worked loose? Tossed in plain sight, no doubt, so everyone would remark on the high priestess and the banker trotting off into the woods.

'Do you mind telling me why you found it so necessary to demolish my reputation?'

'Apart from giving us an excuse to be seen together?'

'Absolutely. I mean, since I couldn't keep my hands off you last night, why should today be any different? I meant the real reason.'

He scratched at the stubble that had formed on his jaw. 'Let's call it redressing the balance.'

That was one way to diffuse the power of this so-called curse, she supposed. Shameless hussies aren't taken quite so seriously as eminent priestesses.

'Remind me to thank you some time.'

'No rush. Any time you like.' Contrition was not in the Krypteia's handbook. 'Though during a romantic stroll by the lake might be an opportune moment.'

That's right. Make the affair as public as possible. 'I suppose the word no is out of the question?'

'It didn't seem to be the case last night, and, as all the servants will be able to testify, you were in no rush to leave this morning. Shall we say mid-morning, by the jetty?'

'I only hope I can contain myself that long.'

And to think she'd wanted him, too. Her cheeks flamed as she remembered his body hard against hers, and she quickly reached down for her sandals to cover the blush. Purely the drugs that he'd slipped her, where dizziness, breathlessness and trembling were part of the symptoms. She slipped on her shoes. That kiss, though . . . She jerked the knot tight. Except it wasn't a kiss, was it? Merely a collision when he caught her when she passed out. Engineered from the very beginning, and all, dammit, from a few bay leaves thrown on the fire and a guard she'd stupidly dropped—

Bay! Oil of bloody bay!

I don't trust him. Melisanne had been talking about Cadur. *He creeps down to Dierdra's cottage at night, I've seen him. Hard worker, but doesn't speak, doesn't mix. Even Hector has no idea where he's from – I meant the master, of course.'*

So that was Melisanne's lover! Iliona fluffed the creases out of her robe and thought, employed as his wife's personal maid, it wasn't hard to see how it started. Daily contact. Shared intimacies. An accidental brushing of hands.

She remembered the straw left at a precise angle in the stables. No word had been spoken, but a message was sent. A secret message repeated many times over, explaining the station master's frequent absences from duty and a scent robust enough to mask a perfume that Anthea would recognize straight away. Iliona also recalled the look of contentment, rather than sexual satisfaction, when Hector joined the women at the Axe God festivities.

'This is no casual affair between the station master and a servant,' she said aloud. 'Those two are genuinely in love.'

And love was a dangerous game.

Lisyl thought so, too. Last night, Melisanne lost no time in telling her what she'd seen when she followed Cadur after work, and Lisyl lost no time in reminding her that it was none of her damned business.

'Yvorna doesn't interfere with you and Hector—'

'Not so loud,' Melisanne had protested, even though no one could hear above the racket of those drums.

Singing as she pounded the linens against the rocks that lined this section of the lakeshore, Lisyl decided her sister had no right to go round spying on other people. Worse than bloody Ballio she was, in fact it was a wonder she hadn't bumped into him behind Dierdra's cottage. Nosey bugger was always prowling somewhere, saying it was work.

'You wouldn't like it, if someone crept up on you canoodling in the store rooms.'

'The difference is, we're not hurting anyone,' Melisanne shot back. 'But you know how Yvorna feels about Cadur, though only the gods know why. He gives me the creeps.'

'No,' she said, 'I don't know how she feels.' And just because a bloke keeps himself to himself doesn't make it sinister. 'But more to the point, neither do you.'

Wringing out Cadur's tunic – see? not a stain in sight – she'd been half-tempted to blurt out Dierdra's story there and then. How her husband had abandoned her with an eight-year-old son, propelling her once again as the property of her father, who promptly took over the child's upbringing and education, even sending him away to learn a trade. Poor Dierdra. Never saw her kid again, and no matter what connotations Melisanne put on locked doors and shuttered windows, Lisyl was convinced there was no hanky-panky going on. Dierdra looked upon Cadur as a substitute for her lost son, and this she knew, because he'd told her so, and she believed him. She stretched the tunic across the rocks to dry. Hand on heart, she couldn't say she liked the woman, and maybe that was because she didn't really know her. Quite frankly, she didn't want to, either, but if Dierdra wanted to keep her times with Cadur private, it was none of Melisanne's business. Which meant that if Lisyl were to tell Melisanne Dierdra's story, that would reduce her to the level of a fishwife herself.

'You can call it looking after her interests if you like,' she'd told her sister, 'but Yvorna will call it snooping, and she won't take kindly to it either way.' Melisanne's meddling would only drive a wedge between them, and open wounds don't heal. 'If there's anything to find out, let her find it out herself,' she'd said firmly, and that was that.

But was it?

Still singing softly to herself, she watched the heavy flight of a pelican heading for the islands. Every summer, a huge colony would nest out there, but once the chicks could fly, the whole lot took themselves off to the swampy end of the lake. Soon they'd be heading south for winter. Some might even have set off already.

Anchoring the edges so it wouldn't blow away, Lisyl turned her attention to the remainder of the linens in the pile. She'd hardly slept last night, tossing and turning, and it wasn't from excitement at meeting Morin's clan. In fact, most of them were blind drunk by the time she'd arrived, and she doubted they'd even remember her this morning. Instead, in between dreaming about kittens, she'd kept wondering, had Yvorna really fallen for those chiselled cheekbones and dangerous, dark eyes—?

'How's my favourite girl this morning?' Two big hands clamped round her waist and swung her round so fast she let go of the station master's tunic. 'Got a kiss for me, have you?'

'Morin! Shouldn't you be working?'

'Who's going to rat me out? Cadur? He's got his own secrets,' he chuckled.

Promise not to tell anybody that you've been up here or what you've seen?

'Anyway, I'm not stopping,' he said. 'Just wanted to tell you that I've found somewhere special, like you asked.'

'I've been thinking about that—'

'Don't go down that line again, sweetheart. You promised.'

I've never asked anything of you before.

'I didn't promise, Morin. I agreed.'

'Same thing.'

'No, it's not.' When you give your oath, that means something. 'But I've been having second thoughts, and honestly, I'd really like to wait until my wedding night – oh, no, Hector's tunic's bobbing off. Can you reach it for me, love?'

'Lisyl! I'd have to wade right in, and then I'd be soaked.'

'Oh, for gods' sake, Morin,' Yvorna called across. 'Fetch it for her. You won't bloody shrink.'

He glowered at the redhead, walking towards them. Cadur was beside her, looking at the ground. Or he could be watching through that stupid bloody fringe. You never knew with him.

'I've got a position to uphold,' he shouted back.

'Not if I tell Hector I saw you throw his favourite tunic in the lake.'

'You wouldn't bloody dare!'

'Oh, wouldn't I?'

'Shit. It was you who put glue on my stool, wasn't it?'

'You hardly ever leave it. I thought I'd save you the trouble of trying.'

'Yeah? Well, it's high time someone taught you a bloody lesson; you're getting right out of hand lately.'

'Here.'

While they'd been trading insults, Cadur had waded in and retrieved the station master's tunic, and Lisyl felt her cheeks burning in shame. For the life of her, she couldn't see how an incident this small had blown up out of all proportion, but that was Yvorna for you. Had to make her presence felt everywhere she went.

'Good heavens, look what the cat's dragged in,' Yvorna laughed, as Cadur squelched across the stones.

'Thanks,' Lisyl said.

'You're welcome.'

'Come on, you.' Yvorna grabbed his arm. 'Let's get you out of those wet clothes.'

Lisyl watched them run up the track, her sister laughing and tossing her red curls over her shoulder, Cadur bending down to whisper something in her ear. That's what it should be all about. Fun and games. So why did Lisyl feel uneasy? They made a handsome couple, Yvorna's blatant sex appeal, good humour and open, easy manner tempered by Cadur's brooding intensity and economy of speech—

'Any excuse to get a bloke out of his clothes,' Morin muttered.

The anxiety sharpened as she pictured them rolling naked in the hay. Was that his secret? she wondered. Was the hayloft the special place where he took Yvorna? Was that why he made her promise not to tell about the kittens, because he didn't want her sister to know she'd been up there, too?

It'll be the best thing that's ever happened, you wait.

She watched the way his tunic hung loose on his wiry frame. The lazy way he walked.

It'll open up a world of pleasure beyond your imagination.

Maybe Melisanne and Yvorna were right. Maybe sexual freedom was better than clinging to principles for no decent reason, and for goodness' sake, it wasn't like Morin was just passing through. In a few weeks, she'd be marrying him for better for worse until death did them part. What did it matter when you gave up your cherry?

You won't regret this.

Damn right. 'Where?' she asked. 'Where's this special place you found?'

'There.' He didn't even notice that she'd changed her mind again, but pointed to the circular wooden shrine perched high on the hilltop. 'Special place for my own special goddess,' he said gently. 'Tonight, Lis. Tonight, when the moon rises, we'll make love for the first time looking over the lake. There's no better spot to dedicate your virginity, trust me.'

Tonight? Bit soon, wasn't it? She'd have liked time to prepare for this moment . . . oh, what the hell. Yvorna and Melisanne didn't make such a fuss.

Just get the bloody thing over and done with.

*   *   *

This time, Iliona opted for the sweat-bath, a small, circular, window-less chamber into which rocks from the fire pit outside were carried on pitchforks and placed in a central tray. Water ladled over the hot rocks created steam, with branches of juniper, pine and laurel thrown on for their therapeutic properties. This followed a hot peppermint infusion to encourage sweating, and though an hour in the vapour room didn't quite live up to the attendant's exhortations that it would make her feel ten times better, it was just the tonic that Iliona needed. The slow release of resins cleared her mind as well as her nostrils. Either that, or the icy water of the plunge pool.

'What I like to do,' Dierdra said, 'is give my patients a good rub down before the massage with a rough, dry sponge. It opens up the pores and gets the circulation going, but I'll be gentle round that wound there, it looks nasty.' She scrubbed the rest of Iliona as if she was a stain. 'How did you get it?'

Gossip's the lifeblood of this posting station.

'I slipped and cut myself. Silly, really.'

'Accidents happen, and they change your life in an instant.' She settled her client on the massage table. 'Take one of the grooms. Lovely lad he was, just larking around one day last summer, when he fell out of the hayloft, cracked his skull like an egg. Such a shame.'

She moved across to the shelf, selected half a dozen oils and blended them.

'Still, if that was strange, it was nothing compared to that lady groom the station master hired in his place. I mean, honestly! A lone woman in the stables with all those men? No wonder she upped and left last week without giving Hector any warning. I'd have done the same thing in her place.'

'What happened?'

'Oh, I don't know the details . . . Now this blend's just the ticket after a heavy night, milady. Hyssop oil, with cypress, marjoram and a dash of sandalwood and I know you're not tense, but this'll make sure you stay that way. I'll just warm them up, then we'll let Dierdra's oils work their magic.'

It was obvious she hadn't a clue what provoked the woman groom into leaving suddenly. Just a tasty titbit to drop into the conversation, in the same way she'd been fishing to find out how Iliona acquired her wound. But in being passed on, every story changed a little in the telling. How many times did it need to be told before it changed out of all recognition? And in a small, isolated community such as this, what consequences would such a mutation have?

For the first time, Iliona felt a pang of pity for the masseuse. Lying on the black slate bench, surrendering to the slap-slap-slap of expert hands, she thought of the army of ageing admirers deceived by blonde hair tortured into girlish ringlets, their collective eyesight no doubt too short to see beyond the thick layer of kohl to the crows' feet beneath. Lonely men saw only what they wanted to see. The lamb and not the mutton. Yet Dierdra was isolated, too. Yvorna seemed to be her only friend, Cadur a stand-in for the son she'd been forced to give up because of unjust laws, work her only true companion.

'I like to start at the fingertips, firm strokes going upwards, a lighter one coming down.'

'Mmmm.'

'Harder or softer, depending on the state of the tissues. Always in the direction of the heart, though.'

It occurred to her that maybe Dierdra's appearance was a defence mechanism. To say her tunic was garish was an understatement, and it was no exaggeration that if the patterns round the hems were any louder, they'd have drowned out a set of kettledrums. Was that the idea, though? While you're busy gawping at the package, you don't see what's inside?

'Every muscle in your body gets a rub on Dierdra's table,' she was saying. 'Not just above and below, my lady. I apply the latest principles of making oblique and transverse circuits of the fibres. Feels lovely, doesn't it?'

Iliona looked at the gaping mouths of the bronze lion heads that served as showers. The rows of oils in little phials. And thought the gods' palace on Olympus couldn't feel this good.

'When the body is beautiful, the soul follows suit,' Dierdra pronounced with the final knead.

'There's an Egyptian proverb that says perfection can only come from harmony.'

'Is there really? Well, it's the autumn equinox tomorrow,' she said brightly. 'That should bring us enough harmony to see us through the winter.'

'Are you still thinking of leaving before then?'

'I have my plans, my lady. Everything's mapped out.' She winked. 'But don't you worry. I'll be around long enough to rub out all your knots and knobbles.'

Thank Hera for that, Iliona thought. She could get used to these modern techniques, and idly she wondered how much it would cost to add a sanctuary bath to the Temple of Eurotas. It would bring in pilgrims far beyond the boundaries of Sparta, increasing trade and promoting the temple's reputation. Oracles and healing baths were simply two sides of the same coin, since mental and physical health went together. *When the body is beautiful, the soul follows suit.* Well done, Dierdra.

The only thing now was to convince the king that the expense was justified.

Any news that she'd be opening the baths for the poor she could save for later.

'Have you seen Daphne this morning?' Hermione pounced on Iliona outside the bath-house door.

'Sorry.'

'Can't turn your back for five minutes and the wretched girl is off.' Her grandmother's face was pink and flustered. 'The banker will be along any second. I need her here.'

So then. The strain was telling.

'If I see her, I'll send her along,' Iliona promised.

The strain of waiting for the money, that is. Not grief. And whichever way Nobilor's will was likely to be cut, Daphne was still a loser—

Cutting across the yard towards the accommodation block, she ducked the crush of merchants, couriers, diplomats and students all being treated as if they were the most important visitor ever to have set foot in the station. Of course, hospitality veered on the sacred when it came to the nobility, where to deny even your enemies risked incurring the wrath of the gods. But the combination of Anthea's background and Hector's profession made this an inviting, comfortable, indeed memorable stop, and it would be a disaster if such an enterprise failed. Not simply for the proposals to link all major cities with key trade routes. It would be a personal disaster for the station master and his wife, not to mention the hundreds of people employed here. Worse, if word got out that Spartan gold had been stolen from the station, both the new communications system and Sparta would totter. Especially on top of a curse from the Oracle that had supposedly sounded Nobilor's death knell.

How long before the roof fell in on the bath house? Two years? Three? The stables would be torn down for firewood, winter storms would peel the frescoes off the walls and waist-high weeds would quickly lift the flagstones.

Thanking the janitor who opened the door for her, she thought there was not a more perfect springboard for a successful and efficient trans-Hellenic courier link than here, at the crossroads on the Lake of Light. Most communities, from the largest cities to the smallest hamlet, relied on fortification against enemy attack. The posting station had no such need. With mountains wrapped around it and a huge lake stretching out in front, the landscape provided an effective defence, and the very fact that the Eagles and the Bulls were locked in competition added to the bonus. Each would try to outdo each other to protect the station from attack, and if things got really bad, together they would make a creditable holding force until reinforcements could arrive. Also, where water supplies were often a weak link in a town's defence, there were no such risks here, where even the customary underground conduits had been dispensed with.

This could not – must not – fail.

'Haven't seen Melisanne, have you?' If Yvorna felt any contrition at being caught inside Iliona's room, it didn't show. '*Meet me in your break*, she says, *I need to talk to you, it's urgent*, and what happens? Someone tells me she's up here, but of course she's buggered off, and I bet I know where to, as well.' Green eyes rolled. 'What is she, half rabbit? I tell you, if I did it half as often as my sister, I'd be fit for nothing. Morning, by the way.'

And with that, the red fireball breezed off down the corridor, her skirts swishing with the swing of her hips.

For a second, Iliona was speechless, then she burst into laughter so loud it made the alabaster bowl rattle on the table. Sliding out of last night's robe, stained on the back by the bark of the horse chestnut, she wondered if the Krypteia would see the joke. Somehow she doubted it, but in any case she had no intention of sharing it with him.

Gossip might be the lifeblood of this posting station, but only among those who worked closely together. So many strangers came and went, they were of no interest. Maybe the source of a titbit to pass on, like how Iliona got her wound, for example. But when dozens of people passed through every day, like gnats, their antics only tickled the surface.

Belting a fresh gown of cream linen hemmed with green and gold thread, she wondered how many people had seen her this morning. Twenty? Probably closer to thirty, and that included Dierdra, Yvorna and Nobilor's mother. Yet none of them had remarked on her spending the night with the banker, or even alluded to it with a snigger or look. She could hardly thread her amethyst earrings through her ear lobes for laughing, never mind clip on her double gold pendant. All the trouble he'd gone to, and no one even noticed.

Betrayal is everywhere.

Wasn't it just! Let down by his own ego. Too clever for his own good. She rubbed wine lees on her lips to redden them and traced a narrow line of kohl around her eyes. Of course, it helped that most of the staff employed at the station were Bulls and few of the Eagles knew, or even cared, who she was.

Which meant a stranger could get away with just about anything without being noticed.

Unless Hector had picked up on it . . .

'Oh, for heaven's sake.'

The owl brooch that Dierdra had given her was no longer on the little altar. Must have got knocked off yesterday in her rush to leave, and now she was scrabbling around on her hands and knees in a clean robe, searching underneath the bed.

'Damn.'

Not there. She flicked the bed covers up and down. Not in there, either.

'Strange.'

An hour later, Iliona had covered every square inch of that room searching for that brooch.

So much for Athene's protection.

SEVENTEEN

F ive drops of oil of lemon balm in water, sipped slowly twice a day to relieve a nervous stomach. A poultice of eyebright to ease the wheelwright's stye. Wormwood, ground walnut husks and cloves mixed up to purge a mild case of worms. Jocasta's corner of the kitchen hall was proving popular, now that word had spread about her healing remedies, with clamps and retractors hanging where strainers and strings of onions used to hang, balances and flasks lined up on shelves in place of sacks and pickles.

At times, it was frustrating. The mincer appeared to be quite incapable of grinding pork for his rissoles without exchanging jokes with the fish cook on the far side of the room. No one could chop vegetables in unison, and whenever she needed to concentrate the hardest, the butcher always seemed to take a hacksaw to the thickest ox-bone he could find. The steam interfered with her preparations, too. Someone, somewhere was either poaching eels or stewing hares, putting black puddings on to simmer or boiling their pigs' trotters. But whatever they were stuffing marrows with smelled good, hot almond cakes made her mouth water every time they came out of the oven, and the sizzling of sausages on the gridiron made sweet music in her ears. Whenever the smell of turnips or smoked fish grew overwhelming, she slipped a few bay leaves on the fire to neutralize the odour. So on balance, she supposed, the system did work.

'Of course that coating on your tongue isn't a reaction to drinking too much wine last night. Your whole digestive system's out of order.'

She'd have thought he'd have noticed before, but at times we all see what we want to see. Her job was not to judge, but to prescribe sage tea for three weeks, with a chamomile mouthwash every morning, then move on to the miller's daughter's toothache.

In exchange for curing the kitchen steward's baby – a simple case of colic, as it happened – she had commandeered more space, more pots, more cooking implements, and felt very much at home juggling decoctions, tinctures and infusions.

'Chew five of these after lunch,' she told the head baker, handing him a pot of what were nothing more than dried cherries. 'Then lie down in a dark room for half an hour.'

He had been embarrassed at consulting her, but, newly married and with a wife half his age, he was having problems sustaining an erection. She wasn't remotely surprised. A combination of middle age, fatigue and a constant need to prove his virility was taking a psychological toll. Rest was the best antidote to anyone's flagging energies, but of course the baker would not see beyond the miracle cure.

'I am surprised you take no payment for this sorcery,' a voice intoned.

The priest shooed the line away and pressed his face close to Jocasta's.

'A herald will make the announcement tomorrow,' he said quietly. 'Those who wish to consult your services will be free to do so at their leisure and convenience, but they will no longer be welcome at Zabrina's shrine.'

She slammed the pestle on the oak table so hard that several pills bounced on the floor. 'You aren't seriously making them choose between the goddess's protection and their health?'

'Categorically not!' His thin nose lifted in indignation. 'The very notion is offensive, madam, an insult to both to me and the goddess whom I serve. But charms and potions wreak more harm than good. I will not allow this absurd practice to continue.'

'In what way is easing a wracking cough absurd, Sandor? Or helping that blonde maidservant overcome her morning sickness? And is it equally preposterous, do you think, to suggest massaging thyme oil on swollen testicles, or adding a comfrey tincture to a bathtub every day?'

'You are not a physician, madam. You are not trained—'

'Precisely why I don't examine the patients, or treat acute underlying conditions.' She replaced the lid on her box of poppy ointment. 'Already, I have suggested two of them consult a physician over in Phaos. They won't, of course.' His fees were far in excess of their humble means. 'But I can at least mitigate their pain, while helping scores of others manage their minor ailments.'

Would he rise to the bait? she wondered idly. Would he reject her recommendations for treatment, or would temptation get the better of him? Her money was on him smelling of thyme oil and comfrey next time she saw him.

Hypocrite.

'And what's the alternative to my remedies, Sandor? Will you be telling the women to bathe naked in – what was it you told my friend it was called, the Pool of the Virgins? In the name of your sacred duty, where you will personally oversee their recovery?'

'Friend.' His lip curled. 'You? A helot? Perhaps you amuse her, like a puppy amuses a child, until it grows into a lumbering dog. Then again, perhaps your countertop remedies suit her own policies for the moment, but mark my words, your so-called friend will tire of you. You will be cast out like filth on the middens.'

'Overworked similes are tedious at the best of times, Sandor, and quite frankly, neither your insults nor your threats will change my mind about healing, much less my opinion about my employer.'

'She keeps secrets from you.'

Jocasta shook a jar containing a garlic and dandelion infusion. No one said convalescence would taste good. 'Does she really.'

The priest smiled. 'Did you know she lifted her skirts in the woods for some wayfaring stranger, then spent the night in wanton abandon in his bed?'

Liar. 'Good for her.'

Iliona did take lovers from time to time. They both did. Casual affairs, because everybody needs release. But, by definition, the High Priestess of the Temple of Eurotas had to be discreet.

'You don't believe me.' Sandor hopped round the table, pushing salves and tongue depressors aside. 'Suppose I told you it was the Cretan banker.'

Now she knew he was lying. Even overlooking the fact that Lysander was calculating, detached and a natural-born killer, Iliona might still have succumbed to physical desire. He was an attractive bastard, Jocasta gave him that, but to behave in such a shameless manner in public with the head of the Krypteia?

'Holly leaf tea,' she pronounced. 'Works wonders for delusions, and now if you don't bugger off and let me round my patients up, I'm going to scream and say you grabbed my breast, the choice is yours.'

'Go,' he warned. 'Leave Phaos to the balance and harmony of the autumn equinox. Take your brews back to Sparta, but remember. The sun is setting on the likes of you, madam. Female physicians are an abomination of nature, and Athens has already put one on trial. The impostor will hang, mark my words.'

He stomped off, leaving Jocasta reflecting on how a wounded lion is the most dangerous creature of all . . .

'He wasn't pushing you to anoint Zabrina's altar with your virtue, was he?' Dierdra asked.

'No.'

'Because if he does, you tell him where to go, the dirty sod.' The masseuse smiled. 'Haven't got anything for a burn, have you? Oh, bless you, darling, you're an angel.'

Jocasta wasn't so sure about that. Mixing a salve using mucilage from a lily for the burn on Dierdra's elbow, she decided there were two reasons for that. One, only Jews and Babylonians believed in them. And two, even if such creatures existed, angels wouldn't plot the overthrow of governments, bringing about a war in which innocent women and children would surely die.

EIGHTEEN

Small puffs of clouds dotted the northern horizon, white wisps chafed the sky over the mountains, but above the lake the sky was cloudless and blue, turning Zabrina's kingdom into a sheet of shimmering sapphire. Out on the water, fishermen applied different strategies for different catches. Some used spears with trident heads, a skill that required patience and strong arms in equal measures. Others cast nets weighted by perforated stone rings, though the majority relied on the old-fashioned but reliable hook and line technique. If the boats were large enough to warrant a sail, and on a lake that size many were, the canvas was white. This was in stark contrast to any other vessels that Iliona had come across. But then those had been seagoing ships, where the sails needed tanning to prevent the salty air from rotting the canvas. Only sweet, fresh water from streams and underground springs fed the Lake of Light. Only the sweetest, freshest fish were caught for the table. For this reason, the nets of the lake fishermen were also bleached white hemp.

'My apologies for keeping you waiting.'

'Not at all,' she told her ardent lover. His hair had been neatly refolded at the nape in Cretan style, and freshly oiled curls swung around his ears. She wondered why the effect was not effeminate. 'I've been perfectly happy watching the birds and biting my nails. Anticipation, I'm told, is good for the soul.'

'Hm.' Measureless eyes looked up to the mountains. 'If you expect me to apologize again, you'll have a long wait. I need to find this gold—'

'And I'm bloody helping you.'

His lips tightened. 'Despite what you might think, I am not unappreciative. However, my country comes above everything, Iliona, and time is running out.'

'Please don't insult my intelligence with that *desperate times need desperate measures* crap. You set up that seduction to put me in my place. I only hope you told everyone how good I was in bed and how you could hardly stay the course.'

'Would you have preferred I told the truth, and said you spent the whole night snoring like a goat?'

Who said romance was dead?

'I suppose the theft couldn't be political?' she said, *and would it have hurt him to have said kitten?*

'No.'

Foal, or puppy even?

'A single heist would have been enough to leave us with egg on our faces, and it wouldn't need to have been sophisticated, either. With politics, it's the principle, rather than the amount, and the seas close soon,' he said. 'Athens would want to spread Sparta's embarrassment far and wide, inflicting the most damage possible. They certainly wouldn't want to risk any chance of us catching the perpetrators.'

And another thing, Lysander reminded her. If Athens knew they were trading gold from Macedonia, they'd have broadcast the fact in advance. This would have the benefit of publicizing Sparta's economic discomfort, as well as sending an open invitation to every bandit in Greece to attack the caravan.

'Public humiliation is an effective weapon, which,' he rumbled, 'rather brings us back to the Oracle foreseeing a rosy future for this flagship enterprise.' He shrugged. 'Better the gold than a triumph of self-promotion, I suppose.'

'At this rate, you might not get either,' she said sweetly. 'So far the only thing we've managed to establish is what you already knew. The gold wasn't destined for Sparta, and the accomplice could be anyone.'

Anyone at all.

'Hm.' He scratched his cheek. 'Let's take a walk,' he said.

They followed the path in silence, the islands shimmering in the equinox heat, peninsulas melting into the waters. As her hem brushed the creamy clusters of meadowsweet it released waves of almond fragrance. She heard the cry of a peregrine falcon.

Would he ever find out that his plan to blacken her reputation had fallen at the first hurdle? Too many times for comfort this morning she had found herself back against that tree, reliving the pressure of his lips against hers. If she closed her eyes, she could taste the salt on his skin. Smell the mint on his tongue.

'Not anyone,' he said eventually. He stopped. Skimmed a stone over the water. Skip-skip-skip, eight times. 'Gregos picked up a horse from this station and rode like the wind to meet me. Which meant someone from this station followed him. Someone who's good with horses and whose absence would not be remarked on, and yet . . .'

This was ridiculous. No one in their right mind would choose a man who didn't laugh.

Then again, how many men whose wives and children had been murdered find much to laugh about?

'It doesn't add up,' he was saying. 'Gregos could not have been killed by a woman.'

'A female groom worked here until recently.' Iliona ticked the points off on her finger. 'Good rider. Familiar with horses. Left without warning, and strong. If it wasn't uncommon for Gregos to find consolation outside the marital bed, she could easily have seduced him.'

Hot sex in the hay. Passions kindle. She rides after him, tells him she loves him, can't live without him, maybe she even rides with him.

'The point is, he'd trust her,' she said. At least, he wouldn't mistrust her, there's a difference. 'He takes her to his hut in the woods, and he's not worried, because he's not meeting you until dawn. Plenty of time to relax after a long ride.'

'Sex is a powerful weapon,' Lysander agreed. 'It's broken stronger men than Gregos.'

And women, she reflected.

'It suggests your man in Lynx Squad has more than one accomplice.'

'Not more than two, though.' He skimmed another couple of pebbles. 'If the gang was any bigger, their best bet would be to make a lightning strike in one of the wide, open passes. On horseback, they'd have had a fifty-fifty chance of making off with an entire delivery of gold. Twenty-five thousand drachmas.'

'Whereas these thieves only stole what they could carry.'

Iliona watched clouds of butterflies dance over the meadows and thought, when a robbery relies on this amount of planning, the gang members need to stay tight.

'Their strategy,' he said, 'is to steal as much gold as possible without jeopardizing the escape.'

She focused on the cloud banks on the horizon, fluffing up

into balls, then dissipating. Once this last caravan reached Sparta, all twelve members of Lynx Squad would be placed under close surveillance, shadowed day and night in a bid to unmask the traitor. Unfortunately for Lysander, it seemed the thieves had the advantage.

'With the Lake of Light straddling two major trade routes,' she said, 'escape is easy for them, but it makes pursuit a nightmare for you.'

No doubt he'd have men stationed along each of the four highways, the same as he'd know exactly which ships were waiting at the coast, and where they were headed. But exactly who were they looking for, that was the question. He'd only assumed the accomplice was employed at the station. Suppose it was a messenger, a muleteer, a philosopher, a poet, who timed his visits to coincide with the caravan? Factor in a second accomplice, and the problems multiplied tenfold.

'Like you said, the seas close in less than three weeks. If they make it,' she pointed out, 'that gold buys an awful lot of alibis, puts a lot of distance between them and Sparta, and, more importantly, it will buy them anonymity.'

'Oh, I have my work cut out with this one.' A scorpion crunched under the heel of a fancy Cretan slipper. 'But if there's one thing the Krypteia is famous for, it is patience.' Grey eyes bored into hers, as measureless as a winter sky. 'Patience and stealth, to be precise, and the arm of the secret police is long. Decades might pass, but a Spartan warrior never, ever yields. One day, Iliona. One day that gold, and the thieves, will be traced. You have my word of honour on that.'

Word, yes. But honour . . . ?

'I notice you used the past tense,' he said. 'You said this woman *used to* work here.'

A snake slithered under a stone. 'What of it?'

'To me, it makes more sense to return to the station and get on with the job as before. Head down raises no suspicions. Business as usual until the last gold train passes through.'

'Maybe the last one already has. At least from the thieves' point of view.'

Moorhens dabbled in and out of the reed beds. Storks wheeled over the water. Glossy ibis croaked and grunted up in the trees. In fact, Iliona passed quite a lot of time getting acquainted with nature before the Krypteia finally answered.

'It's a possibility,' he acknowledged. 'Ten per cent of three gold trains, rather than four, is still rich pickings. It would buy time by throwing us off the scent, but I'm sticking with good old-fashioned mathematics.'

She watched a pair of swans flap lazily over the water, their reflections pearly in the heat haze. 'Mathematics?'

'Ten thousand drachmas divided by three is a tidy little sum,' he murmured. 'Divide it by two, though, and it becomes even tidier.'

'Holy Hera. You think she's been eliminated, too?'

'It's what I would do.'

Yes, but not everybody is a cold-blooded killer.

Though at least she knew why Lysander had taken so long to answer. He'd been thinking it through, the way the gold thief thought it through. Trying to cover every angle.

'If she's dead, we're back to square one,' Iliona said dully.

She'd never met this groom, and probably wouldn't have even liked her. Women who kill for money don't usually have sunny personalities and empathetic dispositions. From some angles, she deserved exactly what she got. And yet . . .

The thread of human life had nevertheless been cut before its natural span, cheated of everything life had to offer her. The love of a good man. The tug of a babe at her breast. Even the simple joys of a glorious sunrise. But Iliona's sorrow didn't centre on the death of a killer. This had been a woman who'd forged a career in a man's world. Who'd have had to scratch and claw every step of the way. And who, had she lived, would have set a precedent. Making it easier for other women to follow—

'Not quite square one.' Lysander skipped another stone over the water. 'The dead still talk. If I find this woman's body, it might give me clues to how she died, and therefore who killed her.'

Iliona understood. A stab in the back would indicate a surprise attack. An up-and-under thrust to the heart meant a professional killer, as well as someone she trusted enough to get close, while poison was a woman's weapon. Of course, the body might yield no clues at all, though Iliona didn't see this as his biggest challenge.

'The lake is clear to ten fathoms, but its depth is far greater,' she said. 'Your arms would drop off from rowing before you found her.'

Skip-skip-skip. Another seven ripples.

'He didn't throw her in the lake.'

She couldn't help it. She laughed. 'Are you serious? Why, when he has a hundred and seventy square miles where only the fish would find her, would he risk the body being found?'

More pebbles. More ripples.

'Because every fishing boat is accounted for,' the Cretan banker said. 'At night, they're brought up on the beach, stern first, which means anyone taking one out would be noticed. The killer wouldn't want to risk it.'

'Yes, but you said yourself a corpse is heavy to lug around, and in any case, what makes you so certain she came back?'

'The same reason she left in the first place.' He patted his heart. 'Love.'

Oh, god, yes. What else explained it? Working at the posting station, among so many men, love sparks. She pictured them sneaking away, perhaps running hand in hand to their special place in the woods. He'd serenade her on the lyre, they'd play chess, drink wine, make love until the cock crowed, while planning their, quite literally, golden future together. Until Gregos put a spoke in the wheel. He had to be stopped, and she imagined the groom's lover convincing her there was only one way. The lure that had distracted the Spartan soldier at the posting station in the first place, while the gold was being switched, would also be the lure to his silence. And because she loved her man, even though he'd pimped her like a common prostitute, she had followed, and then killed, the one person who threatened their happiness.

Only to discover that once she'd outlived her usefulness, the heart of greed was black, and cold, and empty . . .

'My guess,' Lysander said, 'is that he met her at a prearranged spot and killed her there.'

When she arrived at the meeting place, breathless from terror and guilt but most of all love, little did the poor bitch know that her grave had already been dug.

'Not too close to the station, where they risked being interrupted,' he said. 'But not so far away that their absence would be remarked on, either.'

Well, that's all right, then, Iliona thought. Instead of a hundred and seventy square miles to search, he's narrowed it down to a thousand.

That should keep him out of her hair.

NINETEEN

Mountains that were misty blue in daytime had turned violet in the dying light. The islands in the lake fused with the shadows. The setting sun had turned the autumn leaves to molten gold. An old man leading a donkey down the twisting, narrow path nodded to the young laundress marching up. But if he wondered why she was out alone at sunset, curiosity didn't show in his leathery, gnarled face. He and the donkey plodded mournfully on. The young woman strode purposefully up.

Pausing for breath, Lisyl heard a horse whinny in the stable yard, watched as a column of smoke from the spit-roast searched out a breeze to carry it off. There was just enough light left in the sky to make out the usual scrum of visitors, now the size of ants down below. Scribes and administrators, in need of a decent night's sleep. Dispatch runners, grateful for a plate of good food and a bath. Messengers, wanting a change of horse and some rest.

They'd be lucky, she thought wryly. No one works overtime on the eve of the equinox, and that was the trouble when you employ citizens, instead of keeping slaves.

'You should use more slave labour,' she'd told Hector, as she'd stripped the sheets off his couch the other morning. 'Everybody else does.'

'You think that makes it right?' He'd smiled gently. 'With this new alliance growing richer by the year, don't you feel the wealth is better spread among ordinary people?'

Lisyl most certainly did not! Excuse her, but what slave ever had to work more than an eight-hour shift? *They* never had to worry where their next meal came from, did they? Lodgings were free, their owners clothed them, physicked them; slaves didn't pay taxes, plus they got pocket money on top. She'd rolled the linen into a ball and pointed out that several slaves owned businesses over in the town of Phaos. Barbers, dressmakers, one ran a bakery, another had a forge, and every last one owned slaves of their own.

'They're far richer than me and Morin,' she'd protested, stuffing her chin on the bundle to keep it in place.

'Only financially,' Hector murmured, opening the door for her. 'Don't forget, you're free to live where you wish, wed whom you choose, and live in the safe and certain knowledge that you will never be separated from your loved ones unless it's by the Herald of Death.'

The station master was right, she supposed, but only up to a point. The difference was, he was married to rich, aristocratic Anthea while Lisyl was plump and, well, let's face it, poor. Oh, and the other thing he'd forgotten was that she was indeed free to marry anyone she pleased . . . provided he wasn't an Enkani.

'Oh, Morin.' High above, the Evening Star twinkled in the sky. 'Why couldn't you have been born in bloody Phaos?'

Personally, Lisyl blamed the Persians. If they hadn't invaded, Greece would never have had to go to war, and if they hadn't gone to war, no one would ever have thought of this posting-station lark. Stirred everything up again, it did, Eagles and Bulls always trying to get one up on each other, and what was the point of it, anyway? Absolutely stupid. Like Hector said, freedom was a rare and precious commodity, and it wasn't as if both sides didn't know how lucky they were to have it.

The Eagles believed freedom was their right, which it was.

The Bulls believed they'd earned the privilege. Which was also true.

Holy Hermes, would they *ever* rub along?

She sighed, imagining herself and Morin becoming the bridge between the clans. That was how they'd pictured themselves when they first got together. Star-crossed lovers that kick-started a new and blissfully harmonious relationship between lowlanders and the mountain men . . .

Only Morin didn't see it that way any more. He saw her as becoming an Enkani woman through marriage, giving up her work and raising babies the Eagle way, in which boys effectively reported to their fathers from the age of eight.

'Every other nation in the Greek alliance does it, what's your bloody problem?' he had snapped.

'Not every nation, Morin. The Spartans don't, and it's the same down here in Phaos—'

'Yes, but you won't be in Phaos, will you, Lis? You'll be one of us now, and I'm proud to have you as my wife.' He'd kissed her. 'We'll make lovely babies, Lis.'

Was that all he thought about? she wondered. Hopefully, he

wouldn't be so grouchy once she'd surrendered her virginity, and she tried to remember what it was like at the beginning, when love was fresh. He wasn't bigoted back then. None of this foot-stamping, I'm-a-man-and-I'm-the-boss in those days. He'd always insisted that celibacy wasn't natural for a man, and perhaps that's what changed him, but with luck, after tonight, it would put the fun and games back into fooling around.

I mean, honestly. When was the last time anyone heard Morin laugh?

Glancing back down the stony track, she could just about make out a rider hurtling into the yard. Bit late to be riding at that speed, she thought. The poor horse could fall and break a leg – and the rider wouldn't fare too well out of the arrangement, either! She wondered what the hurry was, as he jumped down and sought out the Cretan banker. Not difficult to pick out in that fancy gear. The blue stood out even from here! Now there was an odd cove, she reflected, pressing on. Most bankers who passed through kept themselves to themselves, but this one played dice with the grooms like he was one of the boys, and the funny thing was, they opened up to him, too. Though quite why a banker should be interested in a woman working in the stables, Lisyl couldn't say. Curiosity, most like, and she must admit, she was shocked herself at first. But like everything, she supposed, you soon get used to it.

Mind, wasn't it shortly after she arrived that Morin started getting uppity? Funny how men felt threatened by a woman doing what they thought was their job! Still, she squared her shoulders. All those bad moods would be history after tonight, which reminded her. What was going on between Yvorna and Cadur when Lisyl was putting the washing away earlier? She'd been taking the short cut, round the back of the stables, when she noticed her sister shaking Cadur's shoulders. Lisyl couldn't remember the last time she'd seen such an angry look on Yvorna's face.

'Tonight, Cadur! Don't you understand? You have to act *tonight*.'

Whatever his answer might have been, Lisyl would never know. He saw her, loaded up with linens, from the corner of his eye. Locked gazes with her for a beat of three, and then walked off. The last thing Lisyl saw or heard was her sister shouting at him, and Lisyl didn't know why it should make her eyes sting, but there you go. She mustn't let a lovers' tiff weaken her resolve. She'd promised and it was too late to go back on it now. Besides, she'd gone to all the trouble to dig out her embroidered turquoise tunic, the one she kept for best, and though ideally she'd have picked a floaty, feminine wrap to go with it, the evenings did tend to get a little chilly up here in the mountains. Special moment or not, she'd brought a woollen cloak. Morin wouldn't notice, anyway.

At the fork in the path, she made the sign of three. Silly really, because what's to fear from the Blue Goddess? Also, no wolves prowled round here this time of year, bears rarely ventured so close to the cliff, and dragons hadn't flown over the mountains for as far back as anyone could remember. Even so. Lisyl tweaked a strand of hair behind her ears and found the rasp of cicadas oddly comforting, the twitter of bats round the temple entrance strangely welcome.

Zabrina's shrine wasn't anywhere near as glamorous as the temple of Aphrodite in Phaos, for example, which was new and built of stone. Or even those of Zeus, Apollo and Poseidon, which were brick, faced off with stucco and then painted. No terracotta tiles. No marble columns or ornate pediments up here. A simple timber structure with a roof that had been newly thatched last year, whose door was opened twice a year, no more, for religious rites.

Unlike most deities, the goddess did not reside inside her shrine. Her palace was in the deepest part of the lake, where her throne was guarded by dragons that laid eggs of pure gold. But on her festival days, the doors opened to reveal her statue, and she was as beautiful as Calypso, Lisyl decided. Dressed in blue robes and carrying an eight-pointed star that represented all the points of the wind, her face was pale, since she rarely came to the surface. But when she did, every seventh year at the spring equinox, she would dance over the lake at midnight, when everyone was asleep, because her waters had been formed from the tears of the River God, and this is the only way she was ever able to touch her beloved, who cried so when they parted.

Her heart twisted at her own beloved being so romantic as to choose this shrine. She honestly hadn't thought he'd had it in him!

'Morin?' She squinted among the wooden columns, where poppies sprouted in the fissures in the rock, their soft grey heads unfurling alongside rosemary, thyme and hyssop. 'Morin, is that you, love?'

Probably Nobilor's accident making her see shadows, and in all honesty, who could blame her? Made you stop and think, it really did. Strapping chap like that, here one minute and gone the next. What thoughts flashed through his mind as he plunged over the edge, poor sod? And how far it must have seemed, that drop to the bottom of the ravine . . .

As the tiny crescent moon rose higher in the sky, Lisyl chafed the goose pimples on her arms.

Tough as it was on the wrestler's bride and mother, it was the girl she felt sorry for. Only eight years younger than Calypso, but what a difference, eh? And she might be thick as two short planks, that widow, but what Lisyl wouldn't give to have legs like hers! Went up to the clouds, they did, whereas poor Daphne's were like tree trunks, her neck was short, her waist almost non-existent, and her skin was ever so spotty, poor love. Still. Lisyl shrugged. Now that Nobilor was dead, that was something she could take pride in, don't you think? Being the spitting image of her dad?

'Morin? Morin, dammit, if that's you larking about . . .!'

It wasn't. Just votive ribbons that had been tied in the trees. Dancing, Lisyl liked to think, for Zabrina of the Translucent Wave, whose statue stood sentinel over her watery kingdom. In any case, it was daft, imagining Morin would have got here before her. He'd had to work the stable shift after Cadur, and that was the trouble with this blooming posting station. Even at the best of times, there was too much work for too few workers, and Phaos wasn't exactly on the beaten track for itinerant labourers. God knows how Cadur found this place, but that wasn't the point. Hector really *ought* to take on more slave labour—

'Hello?'

Again, Lisyl thought she'd seen something moving in the darkness. A quick flash from left to right. But only the rustle of mice in the undergrowth answered her call, and the distant bark of a fox. Stretching upwards, she flicked one of the pottery doves suspended above the temple's portal. The pebbles inside jangled a soft tune in reply. Besides, she thought, flicking it again, Morin wasn't the type to play practical jokes, not when the occasion was so special.

'Sandor?' Hardly. Apart from Zabrina's festival, the priest was only in attendance in the mornings. That's why Morin said this shrine would be so perfect, and it was, it was! The lake was a sheet of purple velvet. The lights of Phaos twinkled in the distance like fireflies and fairies.

'Look, if that's you messing about, Yvorna, you can bloody stop it now. Anthea's all for sacking you as it is.'

Madam made no bones about not being happy with the way she carried on with the customers, flirting and teasing, and slapping them down, albeit with a laugh and a wiggle. Yvorna insisted the punters loved it, and probably they did. But the punters didn't run this blooming station! Melisanne said it was only because of his tenderness for her that Hector hadn't caved in and dismissed her, though Lisyl wasn't sure. Hector did love Melisanne, she was certain of that. But he didn't seem the sort to bow under pressure. Still. If that's how Melisanne wanted to see it, that was up to her, and anyway the threat of being fired might just be the shock Yvorna needed.

Take the Axe God festival the other night. She was quite unrepentant about spilling beer down Hermione's frock, but for heaven's sake, you can't go round leaving bereaved mothers reeking of booze and not expect a bollocking afterwards. All right, she didn't like Morin, so she put glue on his stool, and you had to admit that was funny. Him jumping about with three legs stuck to his bum, but she needed to tone it down a bit, did Yvorna. Lisyl watched a barn owl float through the air on silent, white wings. The trouble was, if she said anything to her sister, she was nagging. If she tried to rein her in, she was being spiteful.

You're just jealous because I can have any man I want, whereas the only man who wants you is a self-centred, lazy Eagle, who'll go to fat the minute you get married.

Lisyl had learned not to bite back. *There's a rumour going round that your latest beau is married*, she said instead. *You just be careful, Yvorna.*

Folk are only jealous because I'm young and having fun.

Fun? You've gone through that many men, it's a wonder there are any left.

Lisyl tried to make allowances. Yvorna only went off the rails after their parents died, and she was pretty sure rebelling was her way of burying the pain. The trouble was, Yvorna wasn't the only person who was devastated, and the other two weren't earning a reputation for themselves in the process!

She'll settle down once she finds the right man, Cadur told her once.

Exactly Lisyl's point. The way Yvorna was carrying on, no decent chap would ever offer his ring—

The snap of a twig made her jump.

'That's it, my girl, I've had it to here with your damnfool silly pranks.' She marched down the portico because, seventeen or not, Yvorna was not above a bloody good spanking. 'I know you're trying to give me the jitters, but this fish isn't biting, so cut it out.'

She stopped. Looked. Nothing!

'For heaven's sake, Yvorna, why don't you just grow the hell up?'

At first, Lisyl didn't see it. Then the thin sliver of moon shifted behind the pines, and its thin light caught something swinging in the shadows. A life-size puppet dressed in her sister's tunic, with her sister's frizz of curls.

'That –' she gulped – 'that's not even funny.'

All the same, her heart seemed to be all over the place as she waited for Yvorna to jump down with that old familiar *Got you!* giggle. Instead, the only sound to cut through the blackness was the creak of rope against rafter—

'Dammit, Yvorna!' She tried to keep the panic out of her voice, but from somewhere had a feeling she was losing. 'You win, all right? Now get the hell down, you're scaring the shit out of me!'

Lisyl was still screaming when Morin cut her sister down ten minutes later.

TWENTY

S tanding at the bend from which Nobilor's chariot plunged into Hades, a figure stared into the blackness. So this was how it felt to be a killer. A murderer. A taker of life not just once, but twice over. A double executioner.

I should be feeling happy. I ought to feel relief. Instead, I have nothing but sorrow. Sorrow, and unimagined fear—

Far across the lake, the lights of the town rippled out in sensuous, golden arcs.

Everybody makes mistakes.

A weary hand rubbed weary eyes and knew that this was true. Error was the lynchpin of human nature, for without it lessons could not be learned, progress could not be made, for what was life, if not a journey in itself?

But not everybody cocks up on such a colossal scale.

As little as a week ago – no, even yesterday – the plan was on schedule. The future looked good. Bright. But then tonight . . . Tonight . . .

The pain inside was deep and crushing. *It should not feel like this. It should not.* But it did, it did, oh yes it did, and here was yet another lesson that had been learned.

Death is so very final.

TWENTY-ONE

'Hector.' Anthea's voice cut into the stillness like a knife blade, now that the keening and wailing in the yard had stopped. 'Hector, are you absolutely certain about my having a heart-to-heart with Nobilor's bereaved?'

The station master looked up from this latest dispatch from the Council for Interstate Communications and ran a weary hand over his face. His wife was growing older by the day, he noticed. The grey in her hair might be dyed with discretion and that gown might flatter her sixty-two years. But her jaw line was sagging, liver spots dotted her cheeks and, as her skin dried with age, so the lines round her eyes and mouth deepened.

'It's not a question of reopening old wounds, Anthea.' He laid down the scroll. 'Both women might give the *appearance* of having taken his death on the chin, but I'm pretty sure this is because neither wants to let the other see how vulnerable she is. This tragedy coming so soon after their own will cut deep scars inside.'

The impact of sudden death dangled in the morning air like dust motes in the office.

You can never tell, can you? the staff would be saying.

You never really know what goes on inside someone else's head.

From bread being kneaded to stables mucked out, the shock

that Yvorna, of all people, was so troubled that she hanged herself would be disguised by gossip and chit-chat. Inside, though, it would be a different story. Some would find blessings to count that they hadn't previously considered worth the counting, while others would be discovering a shallowness among family and friends that they hadn't been aware of until now. But for everyone who worked here, from supervisor to flunkey, official to traveller, troubles would be put into perspective. This morning everyone at this station would have seen their own mortality in the mirror—

'I understand that,' Anthea said, 'but why me? You're this station's master. Wouldn't it be more appropriate for you to comfort an Olympic champion's widow and his grieving mother?'

'Probably.'

Hector lined his quills in a row. Mella collapsed when her sister's corpse was brought into the yard, and all he could do was call for help.

'But what can I possibly say to two women who hate each other's guts and where the only thing they have in common is the charred remains of a corpse that's lying at the foot of a ravine that I, personally, insisted on rolling a barrel of burning tar down the mountain to block the stench of rotting flesh because it was putting visitors off?'

'You can't blame yourself there. It was Hermione's idea to cremate him, not yours.'

Rather than meet his wife's eye, he let his gaze wander over the array of wax tablets and bronze styluses on his desk, scanned the piles of coins waiting to be counted into the official money box, found solace in the familiar mix of parchment, ink and vellum.

'Her son had just died, Anthea. No one thinks straight under those conditions.'

For gods' sake, he should be holding Melisanne now. Rocking her, while the tears flowed . . .

'I callously took advantage of a grieving mother to suit my own ends,' he said levelly. 'I don't feel I'd have the right words today.'

'And I do?'

'You're a woman. Women talk to other women.' He produced a crooked smile. 'Or so I'm told.'

'Very well.'

Anthea let out a sigh of good-natured resignation, and he thought she seemed more contented in herself this morning. Less melancholic than she had been for some time, as though a weight had been lifted from her. Or was that just his imagination? Seeing smiles, where Mella was distraught?

'I suppose if nothing else I can sit between them to prevent further bloodshed, but you did the right thing, Hector. Nobilor may have behaved foolishly, driving his chariot on these roads at full tilt, but even so, it wasn't fitting for an Olympic hero to be left as fodder for vultures and wild beasts.' She twirled her wedding ring round and round her finger. 'I suppose you want me to call in on the daughter as well?'

'That would be kind.'

'Do you know how she's bearing up?'

'Strangely quiet, by all accounts. No tantrums, not even tears.'

Which surprised everyone, because until her father's accident, Daphne had divided her time between showing off to Daddy, playing up to her grandmother and being perfectly vile to Calypso.

'Shock plays strange tricks,' Anthea said. 'Nobilor never disciplined the girl. In fact, he indulged her every whim . . .'

'Except when it came to his new bride.'

The atmosphere in the room changed abruptly.

'That's just sex, Hector.' His wife's voice was tight. 'When it's new, it's exciting, but after a while, the passion wears off and in any case, sex like that isn't deep or spiritual—' She broke off. 'I think what I'm trying to say is that thrill . . . thrill is no substitute for—'

'Sorry to disturb you, sir.' One of the scribes poked his head round the door.

'Not at all.' Hector vowed to sacrifice a white lamb to Hera in gratitude for her divine intervention. 'What's the problem?'

'There's a messenger outside on urgent business for the King of Illyria, and the warrant officer needs your seal on the authorization for a fresh ride as quickly as possible.'

'Tell Ballio I'll be along in a minute.' Hector waited until the door closed before turning back to his papers. Suddenly, he felt as old as his wife. 'While we're on the subject of tragedy,' he said, straightening his inkwells, 'I know we're short-staffed, with the equinox coming straight on top of two festivals, but I've given Lisyl and Mella three days off.'

'That's ridiculous! One morning is quite sufficient, Hector.

What they need is hard work to take their mind off it, and I know I sound harsh, but quite honestly, there's no better antidote. You should countermand the order.' Anthea tutted with an affectionate smile. 'Really, Hector. You can be such a softie at times.'

Torn between wanting to leave Mella to mourn in peace with her remaining sister and having her around so he could comfort her, he said nothing.

'How on earth you manage to run a posting station so efficiently when you indulge the staff, I've no idea,' she was saying. 'But at least the problem of Yvorna has been solved—'

'Anthea!'

'Oh, don't sound so shocked. Business is business, and of course I'm sorry she hanged herself, but life goes on, Hector.' She indicated the open scroll with a nod of her immaculately coiffed head. 'What did the Council have to say?'

The station master leaned back in his chair and at last lifted his gaze to his wife.

'They are of exactly the same opinion as you, it seems, regarding the disposal of Nobilor's remains. They remind me, in their usual pompous terms, that this posting station is sited at a critical crossroads for trade and is a showcase for the new alliance of city states. Therefore, leaving a champion's corpse to rot would not have reflected at all well on Greece. In fact, they commend my decision to cremate our unfortunate hero in poetically fulsome terms.'

'And why not?' Anthea said softly. 'You run a tight ship, but a fair one, Hector. You don't fiddle the expense account, the rooms are clean, aired and welcoming, and there's never any trouble.'

'That's because there's a bloody great garrison on the other side of the lake.'

'Yes, but by the time it takes them to march round, brigands could have stolen the horses, raped all the women and burned this place to a cinder.'

'You exaggerate,' he said smiling, 'but I appreciate the sentiment.' He covered her hand with his. 'I am grateful to you, Anthea, you do realize that? I . . . I always have been.'

The hand beneath his slid away.

'I'd better go and see Hermione and that dreadful widow creature.' Halfway across the room, Anthea turned. 'Oh, and Hector. My maid's sister has just hanged herself,' she reminded him gently. 'Please don't call her by the wrong name if you speak to her, she'll think you don't care. It's Melisanne, not Mella.'

Shit. He'd just called her by his pet name in front of his wife—'Melisanne. Thank you, I'll try to remember,' he said, but the door had already closed.

For several minutes, he remained at his desk with his head in his hands, staring deep into space. Then the station master stood up, flexed his shoulders and marched off to keep his appointment with the warrant officer.

No one who saw him would have imagined there was anything wrong with his marriage. Or that tragedy had struck his posting station twice in six days.

The lifeblood of the station was certainly spilling freely by the time Iliona disrobed in the bath house, and now there was no question of the place not being cursed.

'The gods have taken against us,' the hair-plucker wailed. 'I can feel it in my vitals.'

'Poor Yvorna,' sniffed the sponge girl. 'I miss her so much.'

'You hardly passed two words with her,' the coal-carrier retorted. 'Not a girl's girl, that one, but you know, I think you're right about the gods. Someone's upset them, and now we all have to pay.'

In the antechamber, where the attendant was busy damping down Iliona's skin and scrubbing it, Iliona was surprised, but not displeased, that the staff no longer blamed her for the curse. Thanks to Melisanne, they'd decided the high priestess was merely an instrument of the gods, because Melisanne had seen her fall into a trance, and Melisanne did not exaggerate or lie. She had heard for herself the unearthly voice in which Hestia had spoken . . . which was all very fine and dandy, but the end result was, they still accepted Sandor's word about the curse.

And maybe he was right, she thought, as the attendant smothered her from head to foot with olive oil and ash, then scraped it off with gentle strokes of the strigil. Maybe the gods had cursed this enterprise. First the gold, then Gregos, the female groom who'd killed him and who herself might well have been silenced, not forgetting Nobilor, and now Yvorna.

She lay in the hot bath, thinking of the lush red curls and unforced laughter. A bright beacon of light that had deserved happiness in return, and who Iliona had seen as some lucky chap's ticket to a life that was one long round of joy . . .

'Dierdra.' She hadn't expected her to be working this morning. 'I'm so sorry about Yvorna. I know how you felt about her.'

For itinerant workers, friends would be more important than family, and Iliona could only begin to imagine the poor woman's grief, masked behind a professional smile.

'Thanks.' The masseuse looked drawn, her eyes hollow underneath the plaster of her make-up. 'But life goes on, my lady. Terrible as it seems, it really does.'

Iliona was spared any further awkwardness by Calypso, who tossed her towel on the floor of the massage chamber, swung her long legs on to the spare bench, then fussed to settle her little lapdog next to her.

'Isn't it simply awful about Yvorna?' She combed Pookie's fur with her fingers. 'You just wouldn't have imagined her as the type to go hanging herself.' Big blue eyes turned to Iliona. 'All sorts of rumours have been flying around. Like, she'd been robbing guests blind and was about to be unmasked, that's why she committed suicide.'

'Yvorna was no thief,' Dierdra rasped.

'I must say, she didn't strike me as the type, either.' Calypso pushed her hair away from her face with both hands. 'But over breakfast I heard someone say she'd been promised marriage by some wealthy visitor who rode off and left her . . . Oh, for heaven's sake,' she squealed. 'What now?'

'What now is that you should have been taking Daphne out on the lake an hour ago.' Six tons of flab wobbled inside an overstretched linen towel. 'And I'm going to have a word with the management, too. Quite unsanitary, allowing animals into a bath house.' Hermione sniffed. 'Not to mention vulgar.'

'Vulgar?' Calypso's outrage came out in the form of a squeak. 'When you wear red with orange, and pick your teeth at the dinner table! But as I was *saying*, Iliona, whatever drove her to it, it's a real shame about Yvorna.'

Hermione plumped down on a stool. 'From what my maid was telling me, she was a wanton strumpet with a wasp of a tongue and a malicious idea of what's funny. By all accounts it's good riddance to bad rubbish and with all due respect, Dierdra, no one else here's going to miss her apart from her sisters.'

'That's a beastly thing to say.' Calypso snorted in indignation. 'According to the girl who does my hair – who has this *amazing* technique, by the way. She twists it round this way, like so, and then back on itself like this, and see? Now it looks twice as thick—'

'If only you'd been this vague with your wedding vows,' Hermione muttered, 'my Billi would have died of old age before the service was finished and then we'd all have been spared.'

Calypso poked her tongue out. 'What I'm driving at is that apparently Yvorna was mending her ways. Now who was it told me she was in love . . .? Doesn't matter. The point is, people *will* miss Yvorna, won't they, Dierdra?'

'I think your her mother-in-law's probably closer to the truth of it, ma'am. She wasn't the most popular girl on the station.'

'Sounds more like a cry for attention that went wrong,' Hermione said.

'Well, Cadur will notice the draught, that's for sure,' Calypso declared.

'Perhaps,' Dierdra said, as she continued to pummel Iliona's flesh. 'But I don't like to talk about my friends, dear. It wouldn't be right. Now I think you'll find this blend's just the job, milady. Jasmine, with cypress, honeysuckle, basil and rose. It'll pep you up all day long, as well as keeping your skin soft and supple right through to the morning.'

Not so much a mix of essential healing oils, more a case of blending chalk and cheese, Iliona mused. Nobilor and Calypso. Hector and Anthea. Yvorna and Cadur.

'So are you going or not?' Hermione chided.

'Suppose so.' Calypso shrugged herself off the table. 'Come on, Pookie. Mummy's turn to babysit, though lord knows what the rush is. Daphne wasn't waiting in the garden like she was supposed to, and if she can't be bothered, I don't see why I should.'

Hermione shot Iliona a tight smile. 'It's a habit of hers lately. Wandering off.'

'What do you expect?' Calypso trilled. 'Poor girl's lost her daddy, she's on the cusp of womanhood and a million miles from home. Now, Pookie, say bye-bye.'

She waggled his tiny paw up and down, then trip-trip-tripped across the tiles, warbling a paean to Apollo.

'Hector's arranged for them to go out on a boat,' Hermione said. 'Asked me if I wanted to go. I said not bloody likely. Told him, I don't care how long I'd live happy-ever-after in the Blue Goddess's palace. I'll settle for my three score and ten up here, thanks all the same.'

'You're not worried about Daphne out on the water?'

'Heavens, no. She's fifteen, and they have no fear at that age, do they? Anyway, it'll do her good to get out for a bit, even if it does mean being stuck with you-know-who.' She leaned forward on the stool. 'Besides.' She winked. 'The banker's due any day. Won't do any harm if I'm the only one around to greet him, will it?' She stood up. 'I'll skip my rub today, Dierdra. Better go and chivvy up Daphne, otherwise that poor fisherman will have wasted a whole morning waiting for Her Ladyship to put in an appearance, and it'll be me who has to apologize for the lazy little cow.'

'Do you believe Yvorna committed suicide because a rich lover deserted her?' Iliona asked once they were alone. Because despite what Dierdra said, everyone who's grieving needs to talk.

'Yvorna wasn't in love.' Dierdra rolled Iliona on to her front and massaged her lower back with the flat of her hand. 'If there was someone special, she'd have told me. We didn't keep secrets from one another, us two, but what folk round here don't understand is that if men sow wild oats, why can't women?'

'I know. When it's a man it's called freedom, when it's a woman, it's brazen.'

'And you tell me that's fair, milady.'

As it happened, Iliona could not recall a single moment from the time she was born when life had been fair. 'Why *do* you think she hanged herself?'

The pause was long. 'I don't believe she did,' Dierdra said at last. 'I know she was my friend, and I loved Yvorna deeply, but between you and me, there was a mean streak in that girl.' She moved on to using her fingertips, going up and down, sideways, then crosswise. 'If you want my honest opinion, I think she went up there to frighten Lisyl and the prank misfired.' She sighed. 'Not suicide, milady. Just misjudgement, but then that's the trouble with these things. One just never knows.'

Strangling slowly on a noose, suffocating slowly and painfully, could certainly be termed lack of judgement, Iliona thought, as Dierdra kneaded between her shoulder blades. But was it really coincidence that Nobilor misjudged a bend and Yvorna miscalculated on a practical joke? Within a few days of one another?

'Oh, that's it, I've had enough!' Calypso dropped both dog and tunic on the bench. 'If Daphne can't be bothered to make the effort, I'm damned well going to have my massage.'

She released her long strawberry-blonde hair from its clips. 'I tell you, I've deserved it—'

'Calypso!' Hermione was red in the face and wheezing, as though she'd been running. 'Look at this.'

She stuffed a scrap of parchment under her daughter-in-law's nose.

'Shit.' Calypso sprang off the couch like a gazelle, grabbing Pookie and her clothes in one fluid movement to dash off after Hermione.

'Well, now.' Dierdra wiped the excess oils off her hands. 'Wonder what that was about.'

Iliona had no idea, either.

But for the very first time, the women looked worried.

Outside the bath house, a chisel-cheeked groom leaned against one of its pillars, his profile silhouetted against the morning sun. His feet were crossed loosely at the ankles and in one hand he held a piece of wood, in the other a whittling knife. The piece he was carving was a cat, its head turned as though waiting for a stroke, and for the first time Iliona noticed that he held the knife in his left hand. His lowered head turned slowly in her direction, and for a second eyes as dark as Hades locked with hers. This man's best friend has just died, she told herself. But saw no sign of grief in his expression.

Blowing the shavings into the wind, Cadur turned away and sauntered back into the stables. A full minute passed before it occurred to Iliona that he'd been standing directly outside the massage-chamber window. Listening to every word that had been said.

TWENTY-TWO

'Lady Iliona!'

As he changed tack and strode across to meet her, she decided Hector also looked like he'd been through hell and back. A result, no doubt, of longing to comfort Melisanne in this, her darkest hour, but not being able to.

Maybe tonight . . . maybe tomorrow . . .

Prophetic words indeed.

'My favourite station master,' Iliona replied with a smile. 'What can I do for you?'

'Rather the other way round, I believe.' He pointed towards the jetty. 'I had arranged for a boat ride for Calypso and the girl, but it seems they are unable to make it. Since the boatman has already been paid, my wife wondered if you'd care to take the trip instead.'

Why? So the oarsman could take the priestess out beyond the islands, then throw her in without anyone seeing?

'I'd love to.'

'And tonight, of course, in place of the customary equinox bonfire, we shall be lighting Yvorna's funeral pyre. You are welcome to attend, if you wish.' He didn't wait for an answer. Probably took it as read. 'So vibrant and full of passion,' he said sadly. 'What a waste of a young life, and how sad that she didn't feel that she could talk to either Anthea or me. If she had, maybe she'd still be alive.'

Not Anthea, Iliona thought.

'It's a long way to trek to commit suicide,' she said. 'What on earth took Lisyl up there?'

'She was due to meet Morin.' He shrugged. 'They thought no one knew, but—'

'You know everything that goes on in your station.'

'I try to, which is not the same thing.' He shot her a deprecating grin. 'Information is a contributory factor to the station's smooth operation, knowing what issues to act on, which to leave alone. I can only make these assessments by understanding the people who work for me.'

The same principle Iliona worked to herself at Eurotas.

She turned her eyes to the little round temple perched on top of the cliff. 'In your opinion, was Yvorna too hasty in committing suicide?'

'In my opinion, everyone who commits suicide is too hasty, but Yvorna?' He blew out his cheeks. 'I hate to admit failure, but that was one member of staff whose behaviour I found impossible to predict. She could be extremely wilful, when she put her mind to it.'

Either you have a word with Yvorna or I will, Anthea said.

'Yet you didn't sack her?'

There was a longer pause this time. 'No,' and when he continued, his voice was stiff. 'Yvorna was very popular with the customers.'

She plays practical jokes on them, and all sorts.

'But not the staff?'

His glance turned to Anthea, her arms loaded with linens which were presumably Lisyl's responsibility, though it didn't look like the first time the master's wife had rolled up her sleeves and got stuck in herself.

'Not all of them, no,' he said slowly.

Let's not bicker over a servant girl, Anthea.

Iliona pictured Melisanne, her silver hair contrasting sharply with Lisyl's black mane and Yvorna's springy red curls, her boyish frame completely at odds with Lisyl's curves and Yvorna's buxom wiggle. There would be more than bickering if that affair came to light—

'Yvorna's death will have hit the girls hard. First their parents, now their sister.' She smoothed her pleats and asked casually, 'Remind me again how the parents died?'

'Winter fever.' Hector shook his head from side to side. 'Takes a heavy toll every year, and this was no exception. But the poor always bear the heaviest burden, don't they?'

Vulnerability. That was what drew Hector to Melisanne, she decided, watching him greet the latest merchant with unforced bonhomie. The girl was trustworthy, competent, honest and reliable, witness her rapid rise to the post of Anthea's personal maid. But she remained a simple soul at heart, gentle and artless. Almost childlike in her inexperience of the world beyond the Lake of Light, she was just the antidote Hector needed in a job where the pressure was relentless and breaks non-existent.

Demands that equally applied to his marriage.

And with handsome, eloquent, irreproachable Anthea grinding away on the domestic front, a model of style and elegance in a place where appearances mattered, the refreshingly ingenuous Melisanne offered the perfect refuge.

His wife didn't know him well, Iliona thought, if she imagined Hector would tumble a capricious creature like Yvorna. True, Yvorna would never kiss and tell, but Hector wouldn't risk his career, his marriage, his whole reputation on a casual roll in the hay. Though clandestine, his relationship with Melisanne was no cheap, sordid affair. With her, he had found spiritual love, something he'd probably never experienced – and probably never expected to.

The question was, now that Iliona had unwittingly forced the issue, what was he going to do?

'Well, well, well, a banker of many talents,' Iliona said, as a bronzed hand guided her into the boat. 'Now tell me. I need guidance on this. Do I ravish you here, or am I allowed to control myself until we get out on the water?'

A muscle twitched in the fisherman's cheek. 'Both, if you like. I won't stop you. Though I'm hurt you treat my Cretan affections so lightly, lusting after a humble boatman so soon after leaving my bed.'

'So I'm not promiscuous, then. What a treat.'

Part of her said, don't do it. Don't antagonize the head of the secret police, there will only be repercussions. The other part said, why the hell not?

Trust no one.

Unsure what motivation lay behind this magnanimous offer, she'd cobbled together a selection of items that might come in handy on this trip. A potion. A powder. A couple of conjuring props. The usual paraphernalia one might be required to call upon, when the oarsman was under fish-feeding instructions. Plan A, of course, would be to bluff her way out of it, by calling upon the gods and getting an immediate response. Plan B was the long, narrow blade up her sleeve.

Betrayal is everywhere, Iliona.

Who knows, she'd thought, strapping another to her calf. Maybe the boat trip really was Anthea's idea, in which case her travelling kit was redundant. On the other hand, if this was someone else's suggestion – someone who'd become suspicious of her questioning – the precautions would be more than worthwhile.

When you live and breathe treachery, you soon learn the only person you can trust is yourself.

Sound advice from a master betrayer, but the tactics she'd had to work out for herself. Then again, the Oracle didn't interpret riddles for nothing. Straight out of the smoke-and-mirrors department came the high priestess's stock-in-trade. Diversion. Humour, irritation, anger, contempt, they all served the same purpose. While the subject was distracted, the magician turned tricks. The quickness of the hand deceives the eye.

Betrayal is everywhere.

Wasn't it, though?

The apprentice, she thought sadly, was learning.

'I thought you'd ruled out searching the lake for the groom's body.'

'I have.' He unhooked the painter as though he'd been doing it all his life. 'But there have been developments,' he said. 'I need to take precautions.'

Developments, as in a hanging, which well and truly sealed the curse on the station? Precautions, as in eliminating the person responsible for shredding Sparta's reputation?

The only person you can trust is yourself.

'What kind of developments?'

The powder would blind him, and while he thrashed at the burn, the knife would be deep in his heart. Because what Lysander didn't know was that Iliona, too, knew how to kill. A skill she had learned from her father, the arch kingmaker and executioner, who disguised death with charisma and friendship.

And this was not her first time.

'One of the guards in Lynx Squad is dead,' he rumbled through a mouth full of gravel. 'Shot through the neck with an arrow, which is a pity, because I really, really wanted a chat with that soldier. Man to man, and all that.' He clucked his tongue. 'Once again, though, it boils down to mathematics. Because if ten thousand divided by two is a nice round number, divided by none, it becomes even nicer.'

Iliona stared across the shimmering blue lake, all one hundred and seventy square miles of it. The realm of Zabrina of the Translucent Wave, where those who plunged into her depths didn't drown, but were carried to her palace on the backs of sea eagles, where they lived happily for one thousand years. A kingdom of tranquillity and beauty, and justifiably named.

Then she lifted her gaze to the mountains. Mysterious, unforgiving and dark.

And yet were they? Perspective can be an illusion, just as perspective can change in an instant.

When a storm whips up, the lake is the danger zone, and the mountains become the refuge. Everything goes in reverse. Just as blackberries can be brambles, depending on viewpoint. And the soldier in Lynx Squad, who she'd thought was the mastermind, turned out to be merely a puppet on the end of a string.

A string which was also cut when he was longer needed . . .

'The gold will be arriving tomorrow,' Lysander said, 'where I will personally be counting it in.'

'Be careful.'

'Haven't you realized yet?' The smile from the side of his mouth was wolf-like as he loosed the little white sail. 'I am invincible.'

'That's what Gregos thought, too,' she reminded him sweetly. 'And look where it got him.'

Something hardened in those fathomless eyes. 'I am not Gregos,' he said. 'Gregos made a mistake. A very, very big mistake.'

Yes. He was foolish enough to let his guard down, whereas, with Lysander, no one would ever discover the location of his personal refuge.

'We all make them,' she said.

'Not on my watch,' he growled back.

Out in the marshes, hunters with throwing sticks and nets were snaring widgeon and duck. Was that all life meant to the Krypteia? One long round of stalking and death?

Iliona dabbled her hand in the crystal-clear waters of the deepest lake known to man, watching the sandy beaches and stony shores slowly recede, while the islands loomed larger and larger. Black Isle. Snake Island. Devil's Isle. Nothing to offer a fisherman comfort out here, should a storm spring out of nowhere. That's why they painted eyes on the prows of their boats. To watch for evil, and keep them safe on the water.

Geese sailed between the islands like a fleet of triremes, their orange bills held high, facing into the breeze. Once migration started, they would be among the last to leave. Perhaps that's why they sailed with such poise and conceit. Kings and queens of the lake.

But what of the creatures who lived in the mountains, forced to endure snow, ice and gales for months without end? There were risks in migration, but greater hazards in surviving the cold. In a matter of just weeks, the wooded hillsides, now a patchwork of rich autumn colours, would be a leafless desert. Howling Mountain was the name given to one. Wolf Canyon. While the hills of dry scrub were no less forgiving. Dry Spur. Mount Hopeless. Vulture Peak.

Both the Eagles and the Bulls, it appeared, treated their territories with caution and respect, knowing exactly what the seasons

and the gods were capable of. Quite right, too. Without fear there
is no sense of danger, she thought. Presumption is a deadly indulgence.

'Here.'

Once they were clear of the islands, Lysander drew a small
red clay flask from under his seat, unstoppered it and offered it
across.

'A liqueur made from the root of those huge yellow gentians
that grow so abundantly in this particular region. Stimulates the
appetite and improves the digestion, I am told.'

The little parcel of elecampane powder slipped into her hand.
'Thank you, but my appetite's fine and my digestion robust.'

'Try it. The taste will surprise you.'

'I don't doubt that.'

'Hm.'

His lips pursed for two or three seconds, then he took a swig
from the bottle himself. The stiletto slid down her arm as she
studied the muscular, bronzed thighs that bore the scars of more
than one battle. The bulging biceps that dealt death with sword,
rope, dagger and more.

'You really are too quick to condemn a man, my lady.'

In an instant, the powder and knife had been twisted out of
her hand and were sinking into the water. She hoped he did not
see her flinch.

'And you are too slow to trust.'

Who knows what manner of commander they would appoint
in his place, if push came to shove and she was forced to use
the bevelled blade strapped to her calf. But surely no successor
could be as cold, calculating or callous.

'These gentians,' he said, through a mouthful of gravel. 'Did
you know that each tiny flower lasts only one day? But during
that one day, it is visited by scores of insects, and so many flowers
make up each whorl that the display continues to flower for weeks.'
He took another swig. 'The word, I believe, is symbiotic.'

The word, Iliona believed, was bullshit. She looked at him,
completely at home in his rough fisherman's tunic, and thought,
hell, it might even be true, that he needed her here. But when
those services were no longer required, she would be cast away
like dust in the wind—

'Yvorna was murdered,' she said.

Measureless eyes stared into hers for what seemed like hours, but was, in reality, no more than ten seconds. 'I know.' He leaned back in the boat. 'On the pretext of helping to carry her home, I examined the body. I found several large wounds on the back of the girl's head, suggesting a sustained and vicious attack.'

'But everyone thinks she hanged herself.'

'That's because people always believe what they see, and since the blood had been carefully washed out of her hair, what would make them look beyond the obvious?'

The art of illusion doesn't rely so much on accuracy, as the conviction with which it's carried off.

'What made you look beyond the obvious?' she asked.

'Same reason as you.' A muscle twitched at the side of his mouth. 'Gregos, the gold, a missing groom, a dead wrestler. Even before my soldier was killed, that was a lot of activity, even for a busy posting station like this.'

This time when he offered the clay flask, she accepted.

'Surprising, isn't it?' he rumbled. 'For a bitter root, you'd expect a bitter liqueur, but when it's been mashed, fermented, boiled and matured in oak barrels with honey, it's not bad.'

Like mead, the liquor trickled down her throat and curled up like a cat in her stomach.

'Not bad at all,' he said levelly.

She watched dragonflies zip back and forth across the beds of placid yellow water lilies. Listened to the screen of reeds rustling softly in the breeze, while eels seethed in the clear blue lake many cubits down. At the bottom, it was said tall, waving palm trees grew out of the sand. But then legend also had it that fairies colonized these islands and dragons lived in caves deep inside the mountains. That's why the Eagles built altars under the stalactites and left fresh meat as a sacrifice.

But whether you believed in such stories or not, Yvorna would never again watch white puffs of clouds drift low over these hills. She would not run in the snow or skate on the ice, feast on the freshwater crabs that made their homes in this lake, or hear the cry of the ravens.

Aren't you curious to know what's ahead?

Hell, no. I like a challenge.

What challenges are you facing right now, Yvorna? Are you happy at being reunited with your parents? Sad, that you never told your sisters you loved them? Angry at whoever did this?

According to some, she'd hanged herself out of desperation, while others felt it was a cry for attention that went horribly wrong. From the outset, Iliona had no doubts it was murder.

'Are you saying Yvorna was dead before she was strung up?'

'The probability is extremely high. There was no blood in the hair after it had been washed, because dead bodies don't bleed.' Lysander steered the boat round Devil's Isle towards the middle of the lake. 'Neither do those on the cusp, though. But if you're asking did she suffer, then I can reassure you on that. I suspect the first blow came from behind, taking her by surprise, given there were no defensive wounds on her hands and arms. If that didn't stun her into unconsciousness, it would certainly have sent her flying, where other blows would have rained down very quickly. Murderers aim to kill,' he added quietly. 'Not engage in a fight.'

The fact that his gaze was fixed on the circular shrine, reflecting in the tranquil waters, didn't make this easier. Iliona thought of the tumultuous emotions boiling and churning within the confines of the station, becoming more concentrated with each day that passed.

I'm not sure I can stick another season of noses poking where they don't belong, Dierdra said.

Who could blame her. From the outset, Iliona knew that keeping secrets was nigh on impossible.

Those who kept them would need to guard them with their life . . .

Scenes played in her head. Yvorna flirting with the men, as she filled their goblets with beer. Her dramatic winks, her controversial remarks, her couldn't-care-less toss of the head. In her mind she saw her skipping off to chat to the bone worker at the Feast in the mountains. Yet there was another side to Yvorna. There was the girl who'd been shaking Cadur's shoulders down by the lake. The same girl who'd emerged, wiping tears from her eyes, from the store room.

Bold-eyed and inviting one minute, solemn and earnest the next, what did that tell her? That Yvorna was the sort of girl with whom you never knew where you were? Or simply well-balanced and rounded?

'Her murder may not be connected to the gold,' she said, as much to herself as Lysander. 'It could have been a spurned suitor—'

'Who wouldn't have gone to such extreme lengths.'

He was right. This was personal.

Her mind drifted back to the Axe God festivities.

Drink up, girls. Yvorna's voice echoed over the lake, as did the rap of her knuckles on Calypso's and Hermione's goblets. *Otherwise your throats'll be too dry to cheer the little squirrels when the Axe God lifts them up to hang their dolls in the branches.*

Iliona's throat contracted. *Adorable*, she'd said of the little fur tots.

Not so adorable once you know the history. In the old days, those dolls were alive and kicking.

The remark had spurred Iliona to take a keener interest in the white, woollen offerings. *You mean hanged?*

I do mean hanged.

Coincidence?

'There's something else,' the Krypteia said. 'Do you recognize this?'

In the flat of his hand lay a small silver owl, its unblinking eyes made of coral.

'Where did you find it?'

'Pinned to Yvorna's breast.' He'd noticed it in Iliona's bedroom, sitting in the little altar niche, the morning he slipped in through the window. 'I'm assuming you didn't give it to her, because she wasn't wearing it at the Feast of the Eagles.'

Haven't seen Melisanne, have you?

Oh, come on! Surely, if Yvorna had stolen the brooch, she would have looked – at the very least – uncomfortable at being caught in the act?

What is she, half rabbit? she'd tutted instead. *I tell you, if I did it half as often as my sister, I'd be fit for nothing. Morning, by the way.*

Was any neck made of such brass?

All sorts of rumours have been flying around, Calypso said earlier. *Like, she'd been robbing guests blind and was about to be unmasked, that's why she committed suicide.*

Yvorna was no thief. Dierdra was adamant about that.

Iliona tended to agree.

She probably found the brooch, *Finder's keepers*, she could hear her trill. Or was that just wishful thinking?

The world looked different when you were drifting in the

middle of the lake. From here, Zabrina's kingdom seemed to stretch out for ever, a perception that was further distorted by the unusual clarity of the water. The Lake of Light. Named for its brightness and radiance, but also, perhaps, light as in weight-lessness, too. Out here, with nothing below, there was a feeling of flying. Disconcerting and exhilarating at the same time. A space where time lost all meaning . . .

'There were other things, too,' Lysander said.

From a small pouch, he tipped out a selection of rings, cloak pins, earrings and brooches.

'During the commotion of the girl's body being brought home, I searched her quarters. This pouch was under her pillow.'

Damn.

'If you're interested,' he murmured, 'the pouch is made out of crane skin.'

Cranes could fly. Iliona wished she could fly with them. High, high in the sky . . .

'I'm worried about Daphne,' she said slowly.

Lysander adjusted the sail, then the tiller, to turn the boat back towards home. 'In what way?'

'To be honest, I'm not sure. She's lonely and confused, some-times chewing her lip till it bleeds. But . . . Well, you only have to look at Lisyl and Melisanne. Their grief breaks your heart.'

She's fifteen, Hermione said. *They bottle everything up at that age.*

'Her reaction's not natural,' she said. 'Hermione and Calypso saw Nobilor as their meal ticket, so I assumed it was one of them who loosened a wheel pin on his chariot, or sawed part-way through the axle.' Or at least paid someone to do it. 'But all that resentment, Lysander.'

From her mother abandoning her, to her lack of good looks, from being raised by servants to Calypso's arrival.

'Suppose it vented itself on her father? The one man who really cared?'

He brailed the sail as they approached the shore. 'Can you prove it?'

'No.'

'Then talk to her. Not as a friend, but as Dike, demanding justice. As Nemesis, wanting retribution. Burn some herbs, blow some smoke, be her father, wanting to know why.'

'Then what?'

The wolf smiled. 'One step at a time, Iliona of Sparta. First, you prove your case against Daphne.'

The implication, of course, being that the Krypteia would take care of the rest.

Iliona let her arm trail in the water. Warm on the surface, cooler the further her hand went down. Cold, so cold, at the bottom. The legend was comforting, that Zabrina rescued the drowned and gave them happiness for one thousand years. But the truth was, there was no comfort in death. None at all.

And the centre point of death was the stables.

TWENTY-THREE

B elow the path where Jocasta was standing, the silver sheet that was Zabrina's kingdom sparkled under Helios's rays. A heat haze melted the distant horizons, and the air was heavy with the wild thyme and oregano that grew by the waysides. If anyone asked, she was collecting lilies to take home to the new temple garden. The ones with curled-back, yellow petals and bright orange stamens. According to the porter, the best ones were up in the hills.

'They grow best in the cracks in the stones.'

Cracks that, when she was a child, Jocasta used to call the rock's smile. There was nothing to smile about today.

Help! She'd been packing up her physick table for the night when she heard the cry. *Somebody help!*

At first, Jocasta was confused. She'd heard the unmistakable wailing and keening that accompanies death, even though, at that stage, she'd had no idea who had died. None of her business, and the kitchens had emptied like bats out of a cave, so there was no one to talk to about it, anyway. So when someone called for help, she immediately assumed the diagnosis was wrong and that the 'corpse' was actually alive. Instead:

It's Melisanne—

—she's collapsed—

—had a seizure—

—she's dead!

With everybody talking and screaming at once, it was like

walking into a beehive. *Quiet*, she ordered. *Move back and give me room to work and this poor girl some air.*

Melisanne wasn't dead, of course, nor had she suffered a seizure. She'd simply fainted, which was not surprising in her condition. Jocasta had been mixing her infusions of peppermint, chamomile and lemon balm to calm the morning sickness, and had also prescribed drinking more fluids and taking more exercise. Sitting around, she explained, was exacerbating the nausea.

As is hanging around the kitchens, she'd added wryly.

Melisanne did not see the joke. *Please don't tell anyone.*

Fine, Jocasta had promised, though the secret would be out soon enough. Sickness didn't start until the second month of the term, and the girl told her she'd been fighting it for a while. *But you can only bind a bump for so long, Melisanne. After that, you're risking your own life, as well as the baby's.*

Maybe shame was holding her back, who knows. Certainly, no man stepped forward to help when she fainted. Perhaps the father was a traveller who had long since moved on? Like she said, it was none of her business.

However, with Melisanne too weak to lay her sister out, Jocasta stepped in to close Yvorna's eyes and slot the two obols between her teeth for the Ferryman's fee. It was only when she was tying the chin strap, to prevent the jaw dropping open, that she noticed Yvorna's hair was still damp. And when you plot rebellion, war and destruction on a regular basis, you quickly become attuned to the nuances of suspicious death.

I ought to be doing this, a rough, throaty voice rasped. *I'm her friend. It's my job.*

You have enough on your plate, Jocasta said gently, easing a teary, trembling Dierdra out the door. *I didn't know the deceased, so it's better this way.*

She fastened the shutters, shot the bar on the door and turned up the oil lamps. Expert fingers quickly discovered head wounds beneath that wild tumble of curls. She lifted an eyelid. No sign of the tiny red spots that were characteristic of ligature strangulation. No discolouration of the whites of the eyes that would indicate a desperate fight for survival. None of the unusually pale skin that might be caused by the sudden pressure on the neck from a high hanging. No facial congestion and purple, protruding tongue if the victim had asphyxiated.

Washing and preparing the corpse for its funeral rites,

anointing it with fragrant myrtle and mint oils, Jocasta continued her examination, though by that stage she was already certain she was looking at a murder victim. Yvorna's skull had been smashed and her body strung up, to make it look like suicide.

So on the pretext of gathering lilies, she was now making her way to what she considered the scene of the crime, rather than a place of sanctuary, beauty and worship. But the path was steep, and the late summer air warm. Wiping the sweat from her forehead, she paused to marvel at the sculptured cliff faces that plunged into the lake, said to be carved by the Titans, back in the mists of antiquity, before even the Olympians were born. In one or two places, close to the shore, tall pillars of grey rock stuck out of the lake. All that was left of a race of people who displeased the gods and were consequently turned into stone. Maybe it was true, she thought. Probably not. The gulls nesting on them couldn't care less.

As she continued up the twisting path, she noticed a field hand crouched on his haunches, counting the fish, or perhaps the swirls of the current. Then she remembered that field labourers wore broad-rimmed hats to shade them from the sun as they ploughed, planted beans or dug carrots. When he shifted to a cross-legged sitting position, she saw that his tunic hung loose on his wiry frame and that his face was as finely sculpted as the rocks that he sat on.

Jocasta watched Cadur for another couple of minutes, but he didn't turn or move. Just remained staring out over the water. She continued her climb to the shrine of the Blue Goddess, pausing at the lustral basin to purify herself before entering the precinct. According to the men who worked at the station, the wood of this shrine stayed warm to the touch through even the coldest days of the winter. An illusion, no doubt, the oak being warmer than their freezing cold hands, but a comforting legend nevertheless. She filled her lungs with the air that was redolent with the scent of the rosemary, hyssop and thyme that made their homes in fissures in the rocks and were used to purify the goddess's altar. The oak columns had been garlanded with flowers. Mainly cornflowers, asters and a few late roses, while pottery doves dangled from the gateway, the pebbles inside them chiming soft tunes in memory of the dead, whose souls they represented.

In the name of plant collecting, Jocasta began a thorough search of the area. Unfortunately, the precinct and portico had

already been swept. Another purification ritual in a shrine tainted
by death. Also, if Yvorna's killer had gone to the trouble of
washing the blood from her hair, they would certainly have
cleaned the spot where the life was bashed out of her body. Then
again, she thought. The killer confidently expected the hanging
to be taken at face value. In which case, a cursory sluice-down
would be enough to avert suspicion. Also, Yvorna was most
likely killed close to where she was strung up, if not directly
underneath – and hey presto, what do you know. A dark, damp
stain, which no one would have noticed in the dark. According
to the various accounts, there was a stool here that had been
kicked away, when Yvorna jumped. Was it the same stool her
killer had sat on, waiting patiently for her to arrive?

Jocasta sat on a rock, listening to the bees drone round the
herbs. The murder weapon would be impossible to find, no doubt
thrown as far as was humanly possible. But now she had all the
proof that she needed. Nothing concrete, it was true. Enough,
though, to set her mind at rest that they were dealing with a
cold-blooded killer.

The question was, what was she going to do with this knowledge?

She remained at the shrine, watching the sun sink slowly
towards the Isles of the Blessed, while crickets rasped in the
trees and the breeze carried the scent of ripe blackberries, apples
and change. The sky turned first to pink, then to fire, casting a
lavender shimmer over the landscape, transforming the harsh
valleys into enchanting, mellow, mysterious places and turning
the water to silk.

She couldn't say when she first became aware of the flute.
Perhaps it had been playing when she arrived. Part of the natural
mood of the shrine. But it seemed to have been here from the
beginning of time, with notes that were poetic, haunting.
Breathtaking, almost. Captivated by the curiously soft, ethereal
sound, she let her thoughts drift, while votive ribbons fluttered
in the branches. Colourful, happy and free.

Flute . . .?

Jocasta jumped up, dagger in hand. Stupid bitch. How could
she have let her guard down? She, who was so in tune with the
nuances of nature and suspicious death! Stupid, stupid bitch!
Stealthily, she followed the melody. As she approached the altar,
it suddenly stopped.

'My apologies if my music disturbed your contemplations,' a low voice intoned.

Major religious sites, in fact even smaller sites such as the Temple of Eurotas, generated spiritual tourism on a scale that required a massive contingent of clerical and manual staff. Not so Zabrina's. The spring carnival that was held in her honour took place at the lakeside, and at midsummer young girls collected dew beneath a full moon to sprinkle on her waters like tears. Other than that, the role of her priest was a part-time profession, with equally part-time acolytes to call on, when needed.

'On the contrary, Sandor. I found it relaxing, and to be honest, you play exceedingly well.'

Pale bulging eyes looked at the knife in her hand. 'Just as well it meets with your approval, then,' he murmured.

She was more concerned with the pipe. Long and conical, it boasted seven finger holes down the front and the same number of vent holes on the cone, explaining the soft, breathy sound it produced. 'I've never seen an instrument like that.'

With a wide sweeping gesture, he indicated for her to take a seat on the stone, then launched into another poignant lament, his cheeks bulging as he blew in a strange, almost circular pattern. Hypnotized by the music, Jocasta felt herself being lifted out of her body, drifting across a landscape lush with mint and bulrushes, over soft, marshy swamps and white, rocky beaches. It was, she felt, as though he had conjured the Blue Goddess herself, and shivers ran down Jocasta's arms.

'That was lovely,' she said, once he had finished. 'Genuinely lovely.'

'A gentle tune for the gentle goddess who fills men's barns, as well as their nets.'

'Tell me, Sandor.'

She picked a poppy and began making a doll, by bending the petals down to form the skirt and pushing a stick through the stem for the arms.

'Why is it that, when gods are served by priests, goddesses by priestesses, and virgin goddesses by virgins, you tend the shrine of Zabrina?' She paused. 'Is it your sense of inferiority – a man doing a woman's job – that makes you so bitter and twisted?'

'How dare you! How dare you come to this sanctuary and

spill poison and spite in front of my lady?' The knuckles clutching the flute were as white as his robe. 'I tend my goddess, madam, for the same reason your mistress tends the shrine of the river god, Eurotas.'

'Ah. So you were also appointed by a king, who broke with convention in the mistaken belief that he thought he could control you?'

That shook him, but his recovery was commendably quick. 'I'll have you know I was elected by the twin Councils of Elders,' he said. 'Both Eagles and Bulls, it was a fair and democratic decision, and I was appointed to this post for seven years.'

Jocasta smoothed a strand of her jet-black hair. 'Which, I am guessing, ends at the midwinter solstice?' All appointments ran solstice to solstice. But given his attitude towards the future of the posting station, and the changes he had seen since it opened, it seemed reasonable to assume that his term was expiring. 'And you're seeking re-election. Obviously.'

'Who else is qualified?'

'Who else would put up with trekking up here every morning for no pay, and not even their food and lodging thrown in.'

Although, to be fair, he would get a front seat at the Odeon . . .

'What does it matter. Why can't you just go! If you're the physician you claim to be, madam, send the high priestess home for the good of her health. Surely that can't be beyond your abilities!'

Jocasta twirled the poppy doll between her fingers, making it dance, as fields and pastures merged with the hills in the fiery glow of the sunset. Groves that had provided shade for count-less generations of cattle slowly slipped into shadows themselves. In the distance, the cowgirl was calling her herd home. 'Was that the same silver tongue that invited Yvorna to sacrifice her honour on this very altar? For the life of me, I can't imagine why she didn't jump at the chance.'

Sandor's face turned as red as the sunset. 'I . . . did no such thing.'

'Yes, you did. After pestering Dierdra for sexual favours.'

'I – I—' He stood up, his eyes burning with hatred. 'This is scandalous, madam. You bring your wickedness to Zabrina, through your lies and your curses, while a girl waits for her funeral pyre. It's outrageous.'

'My apologies, if my truth disturbs your contemplations, Sandor.'

'I – don't know what the world's coming to,' he stuttered.

'People lie, they fornicate, they even die, yet nobody cares.'

'I care.' She stood up and looked him squarely in the eye. 'I care about Yvorna.'

'Oh? What about Nobilor, then? An Olympic hero dies, who gives a toss about him? Not his wife, not his mother, not even his daughter.'

Typical of the con-man response. Change the subject.

'When people don't like each other,' she said pointedly, 'they tend not to want to expose themselves to the enemy.'

'Really? Then how come the girl has gone missing and they haven't called in the army,' he stormed. 'Doesn't that sound an alarm horn to you?'

Missing? Daphne? Holy bloody Hera.

Jocasta tossed the poppy doll over her shoulder and flew back down the path to the station.

Cadur was nowhere in sight.

TWENTY-FOUR

As the daylight faded, the atmosphere in the station changed with it. While it was light – while they were busy – the fragility of life could be pushed to the side of their minds. But when darkness settled its cloak over the landscape, there was no escape. To the west lay the Realm of the Dead, where Yvorna would be taking her first tentative steps. But the Realm of the Dead lay in darkness, for once Helios had finished driving his fiery chariot across the sky, he would disembark, to sail back to his palace in the east in a boat made of gold. Taking his warmth and light with him . . .

'Regrettably, the posting station is not in a position to allow employees the luxury of the customary three days' lying in state,' the warrant officer said. 'If –' he cleared his throat – 'luxury is the right word.'

Iliona watched the pyre being piled with firewood down by the lakeside and thought, given a choice, few people would opt

for oblivion. They'd much rather be with their loved ones, running
through wheat fields, splashing in puddles, feeling the rain on
their face.

'There is little indulgence in Hades, Ballio.'

'There is little indulgence in trade, either, ma'am. Given the
volume of traffic that passes through here, a corpse lying about
would be quite inappropriate.' He smiled smugly. 'I shall be sure
to put in my report that the Master followed the rules to the letter.'

'Yes, you mentioned at the Feast of the Eagles that your responsibility extended further than merely checking the credentials of
the couriers. But when I asked around, I discovered that is exactly
what your role is, Ballio. In fact, you can't even sanction a fresh
mount without the station master's approval.'

He sniffed. 'Not yet, ma'am, not yet. But there will be changes,
you'll see.'

'And when these changes come, the information contained in
your reports will prove you are qualified for much more than
merely inspecting warrants?'

'Exactly. My reports are meticulous in every detail.' He tapped
his thin nose. 'Very little escapes Ballio's notice.'

*I'm not sure I can stick another season of noses poking where
they don't belong.*

'I can well believe it,' she said.

And yet secrets were kept here . . .

One only had to look at the stables, where the tired donkeys
and mules of the gold train were being brushed, fed and watered,
and the warriors of Lynx Squad stropped their blades on the
sharpening stones, children staring bug-eyed at their faceless,
bronze helmets and marvelling at greaves etched with Hibernian
cobalt.

The Cretan banker, of course, was nowhere to be seen, but
the wolf was still on the prowl.

'Callous as it may seem,' Anthea said, joining her on the path
to the lake, 'I believe the Council for Interstate Communications
is right in ruling on immediate burial for those who do not have
the funds to pay for a funeral in Phaos.'

Her black mourning robe fell in elegant folds, pinned at the
shoulders with brooches of gold and girdled with a belt hung
with tassels. Through her diaphanous black veil, amethyst
earrings glinted in the night, and a pearl choker matched the
bracelets that hugged her wrists.

'I would agree with you, Anthea, that a corpse lying in state is less than desirable, had I not seen the accommodation on offer.'

Lanterns lit the way. Tiny glow-worms of light, flickering in the dark on both sides of the track.

There were no lights on the River Styx.

'I don't follow you,' Anthea said.

'Let me put it this way. Fevers, heart failures, respiratory diseases obviously take their toll, but how many of the staff actually die at this station? Five a year?'

'At the most.'

'Yet the station doesn't consider subsidizing the cost of transporting bodies across the lake worthwhile.'

'Hector's budget has little room for manoeuvre.'

'I'm sure,' Iliona said evenly. 'Yet the accommodation is luxurious and the fittings quite opulent. I half expect to see a ceremonial barge on the lake offering pleasure tours any minute.' She paused. 'How much of your money is left?'

For a moment, she thought Anthea would tell her to mind her own business. Instead, 'Not one obol,' she said. 'When Hector was given this appointment, I sank every last drachma into making this the best posting station in Greece. The standard to which all the others would want to aspire.'

With its bath house and vapour room, vast kitchens and attention to detail, she had certainly achieved her aim.

'But it still hasn't made you happy.' It was a statement, not a question.

Anthea stopped on the path. Around them, tree crickets pulsed their repetitive mantras and bats flew low on the wing. The air smelled of roast goat and manure, incense and honey cakes. 'It is not a pleasant experience for a woman of independent thought to be rejected by her husband, then returned to being the property of a father who treats her with nothing but contempt for shaming the family name.'

'Marriage to Hector was your escape route, but then you found yourself in a worse trap than ever before,' Iliona said gently. 'You made the mistake of falling in love with your husband.'

'He was young.' Anthea swallowed. 'Very young. But even then Hector was ambitious. After the Persian Wars united the city states and the first designs for a communications network were being thrashed out, my father managed to secure him this

job as station master.' She laced her hands in an elegant gesture.
'And all the time this place was being built, while my husband
attended meetings with the various commissions and – well,
organized everything from the ground up, I prayed, oh how I
prayed, for a child.'

Because maybe then, his love would grow.

She smiled. 'Of course, no baby came—'

No love either, Iliona thought.

'—and it wasn't long before I grew too old to bear him a
child.' Anthea's sigh was deep and came straight from the heart.
'He tells me, can you believe, that he is "grateful" to me.' She
shook her head slowly from side to side. 'After all these years,
that word still drives nails into my heart.'

That was the key, Iliona thought. *All these years.* She was
thirty-eight when her husband rejected her, nearly forty when
she married Hector, who was just twenty-two. For more than
two decades, they had lived with this uneasy alliance. Inevitably
the distance would either close – or increase.

'Still. The relationship limps along without incident,' Iliona
said, 'until, one day, his routine starts to change. He tells you
he's working in his office when you know he is not. He disappears at odd times of the day. Takes to wearing oil of bay.'

'I am not a fool,' Anthea said bitterly. 'As soon as he hired
the sisters after their parents died, I knew what that little bitch
was up to. So if you think for one second I'm going to splash
out one copper chalkoi so she can be buried in Phaos, you have
another think coming.'

Oh dear.

'Yvorna wasn't sleeping with Hector.'

'The hell she wasn't. The bitch even bragged about it at the
Feast of the Eagles, I heard her. You were telling her about
someone's fortune you'd read, whose lover also happened to be
married, and I remember her response very clearly. She elbowed
you in the ribs in a quite common manner. *Aren't they the best
ones?* she said.'

'A typical Yvorna quip, and quite frankly, if you'd taken the
trouble to get to know your staff, any of your staff, Anthea, you
would have realized that.'

She should stop. High priestesses don't swan around insulting
their hosts. She should apologize. Admit that she had stepped
out of line, forgive and forget and all that. Should . . . But

wouldn't. Yvorna's death had hit her hard. Someone had to fight for justice.

'The trouble is, you're still trying to hang on to a life that has gone. When you married Hector, you relinquished your status in society, and at the time you were happy to do so and, to be blunt, that was the person he married.'

She'd changed. Not him.

The colour drained from her face, throwing lines and age spots into sharp relief. 'Are you saying I drove him away?'

'I'm saying your hurt did.'

The more grateful he was, the more barriers she erected, disguised as efficiency, rigidity, but most of all snobbery. More and more Iliona could see how Hector was drawn to Melisanne's uncomplicated, unconditional love.

'Is it too late? You're the Oracle, you speak to the gods. You'll know if it's too late to save my marriage, because I know, I *know*, he has a mistress.' Tears flowed unchecked down her cheeks. 'Is it love? Is it a servant? Iliona, I beg you. Read my future. Read his—'

'I'm sorry.' She'd done enough damage reading Melisanne's fortune. One mistake was plenty, thank you. 'You will need to petition the gods yourself for this.'

She left Anthea facing the consequences of her own actions, and hurried down to the lakeside. Yvorna lay on her bier, red hair streaming over her shoulders and clutching a laurel branch in hands that had been folded over her chest. Like Lisyl at the shrine of the Blue Goddess, she expected her to jump up any second, laughing at her latest wheeze.

Except this was no wheeze. Rigor had set in: she was as stiff as a statue, and colder than Hades itself.

At the side of the stretcher, Melisanne was slumped on her knees, weeping uncontrollably, while a hollow-eyed Lisyl sat beside her, hugging her shoulders, her mourning garland cockeyed and wilted. Iliona wondered whether to go up to them, but what could she say that could bring comfort in the wake of this tragedy? Instead, she hung back while big, burly Morin stood over his girlfriend, patting her head with his hand as though she was a dog, looking uncomfortably out of his depth.

Well away from the pyre, Cadur leaned against the trunk of a willow, his thumbs looped in the belt of his tunic and his head half turned away. The only part of his body that touched the bark appeared to be a thin band of bone on one shoulder blade.

'The green tunic was my idea.' Calypso came over to join Iliona, the dog stuffed underneath her arm. 'I told Lisyl, Yvorna was too lively a creature to be wrapped in a boring white shroud, and she agreed. After all.' She shifted Pookie to the other arm. 'If you break with tradition about burial times, you can break it with other things, too.'

Yvorna would agree wholeheartedly with that. Close your eyes, Iliona thought, and you can picture her rolling around on the floor, tickling three-headed Cerberus, who guarded the entrance to Hades. Tossing her hair, as she teased the shades on the Isles of the Blessed.

The trouble with being dead is you feel so stiff the next day.
Joking with the Ferryman as he rowed her over the Styx.
Who are you?
I'm death.
Then I'll shout up a bit, so you can hear me.

Iliona swallowed. Took a deep breath. Turned her eyes away from the pyre. 'Where's Daphne?'

'Oh – lying down, I suspect,' Calypso trilled. Her beautiful hair was tied up in a fillet, her pink robe fell in elegant folds. But her cheeks were too red, her face was too pale, and if she shifted that dog of hers just one more time, the poor thing would spin on its own. 'Bit upsetting, this funeral lark.'

'There's a rumour going around that she's run off. In which case, you should call out the army.'

'No need for that, dear.' Hermione practically slapped Iliona on the back. 'I know my granddaughter. She'll be back soon enough.'

So it was true, then. 'The kitchen staff say she's taken a sack load of food.'

'She paid for it,' Calypso said quickly.

'She's fifteen years old, her father's just died and she's been cosseted her whole life. Surely you must be worried?'

The two women swapped glances.

'She's only trying to annoy us,' Hermione said. 'Thinks it's funny, I suppose. They do at that age.'

'I reckon it's that Sandor,' Calypso said. 'Scare the life out of anyone, with that nonsense about curses and stuff. Honestly, the number of times he's told me to –' she pulled a face – '*leave this realm and never come back.*'

'Oh, did he?' Hermione frowned. 'Well, he never told me to bugger off, because if he did, I'd have soon put him straight.'

'Really? I'd have thought you'd be the first person he'd want gone.'

The bickering was halted by the uneasy hush that settled over the lakeside. Draped with a ceremonial fishing net over his robes and holding the horn of consecration, Sandor addressed the mourners. From the corner of her eye, Iliona noticed Dierdra sidle up to Cadur, wiping away tears with the back of her hand.

'In the absence of male relatives,' the priest intoned, 'I call upon a volunteer to head the procession.'

The crowd, of course, expected the station master to step forward, but Iliona didn't share their optimism and faith. Given his feelings for Melisanne, he would want to keep the lowest of profiles. Wisely, Hector had absented himself altogether.

'I will,' Morin said.

Lisyl rose unsteadily to her feet. 'That's a very kind offer, love.' She pushed the hair out of her eyes and squared her shoulders. 'But Cadur was Yvorna's best friend. I think he should lead it.'

Morin leaned down and whispered something in her ear, but Lisyl looked straight past him.

'Will you?' she asked.

Cadur's lips pursed white. 'Of course.' He prised himself away from the tree. 'It would be an honour.'

Morin muttered something else that Iliona didn't catch, but Lisyl simply indicated that he should station himself at the bier. On a count of three, the pall-bearers hefted the stretcher on to their shoulders and, to the sound of Sandor's soft breathy pipe, the mourners formed a thin file, the sisters clutching each other's arms for support.

With the priest at the front and Cadur behind, Yvorna set off on her very last journey.

Iliona stepped back into the shadows. This was a private occasion, where grief should not be intruded on. Dierdra was beating her breast and scattering ash in her hair. Wailing women drove off evil spirits. Holy water purified the procession's path. Once the bier had been laid on the pyre, Sandor offered prayers to Hermes, Guider of Souls, laying sweet oregano over the body, then covering it with a cloth, which he tucked in tight.

O Cerberus, guarding the gates of the Underworld,
O Charon, ferrying souls over the Styx.

The singing drowned the first crackle of flames being lit.

Guide this shade
To the Elysian Plain,
Land of ambrosia, nectar and figs.

'Pity I missed the start,' Hector said, joining Iliona in the shadows.

The lines on his face were deeper, or so it seemed in this light, his skin was an unhealthy grey, and his beard was just that tiny bit less well trimmed.

'Unfortunately, greeting an amber merchant took longer than expected, what with showing him around, pouring libations to Apollo, to whom amber is sacred, and then, of course, he would insist on telling me about the family business. How the men scour the Baltic shores after the storms, sorting out nuggets that become trapped in the seaweed and scooping any floating pieces in nets from boats.' His smile was tight. 'Interesting enough stuff, but rather long-winded in the telling, I'm afraid.'

She was only surprised he didn't ask for chapter and verse about working the amber into beads.

'Anthea thought you were sleeping with Yvorna.'

'What?'

'Well, you didn't want long-winded again, did you?'

'Yvorna, though?' He pressed a clenched fist to his forehead. 'What on earth made her think I would bed a girl like that? Please don't get me wrong. She was a breath of fresh air, just what this station needed, and we're going to jolly well miss her spark, that's for sure. But she was a hot cinder, that girl. Not my type at all.'

'Whereas Melisanne is.'

There was a pause, while the station master tried to figure out how much she knew. Iliona saved him the bother.

'Did you know she's carrying your child?'

Hector's sharp intake of breath was audible above the dirges and wails. 'I – I don't know what to say.'

'The big question, Hector, is not what you're going to say, but what you are going to do.'

Dripping holy oils from the horn of consecration, the skeletal figure of the priest circled the pyre. He sang of the River of Forgetfulness from which Yvorna would drink to erase the pain of departing. He sang about the apple orchards to the west, beyond the White Rock, where the skies never clouded and the fields were lush with asphodel. But he did not sing of the tiny heart that beat inside Melisanne . . .

The equinox, Iliona reflected. The true balance of nature and life. That as one dies, so another is born.

'Mine is a marriage of convenience, nothing more,' Hector said flatly. 'Anthea and I both hoped, I believe, that something warmer would grow, and for my part, I deeply regret it did not.'

'But you won't leave her.'

Haunted eyes looked into hers. 'I forgot you see through the eyes of the blind and hear through the voice of the deaf.' He shook his head. 'I would never have achieved such an exalted position without Anthea's influence, and the station would not be half the success it is without Anthea's money. But that aside, I would not shame my wife by seeing her divorced for a second time. I owe her that, if nothing else.'

'Then you have no choice. You must give up Melisanne.'

His mouth pursed as he watched his darling Mella, howling and rocking with grief at the foot of the pyre. 'Never.'

'Would you twist the knife further into her heart, by letting your wife find out for herself?'

Two decades of unrequited love had congealed into bitterness, and for Anthea, barren and lonely, Melisanne's pregnancy would be the last straw.

'She would see it as the ultimate betrayal of her personal maid. She'd throw her out without pay, sacking Lisyl, Morin, and anyone else here that Melisanne might also be friends with. She would destroy you, Melisanne and herself. And what of the baby? What would become of your child then?'

Anthea would not tolerate the humiliation of having her husband's bastard anywhere that he might have contact with it.

'The sooner you break the bad news, the better.'

They were tough girls, the sisters. They'd find a way through.

The dirge for Yvorna played on.

Further along the lakeshore, where the soft, marshy ground deadened the fall of footsteps and not even the moon was bright enough to cast shadows, the commander of the gold train met

with his boss. He could not explain it. If they were bandits, why
did they not attack the caravan? Why pick on only one soldier?
The only theory he could come up with was that it was an accident. A plainsman hunting night game had either mistaken the
guard for his quarry or else blundered with his aim. No wonder
he disappeared silently into the night!

Lysander did not disabuse him. The Spartan phalanx was
trained to fight, not think, and warriors with acumen soon
stood out. Gregos was a thinker, that's why Lysander chose
him to supervise the gold train. If anything went wrong, Gregos
would know exactly how to deal with it, and the Krypteia's
faith was justified when Gregos fathomed out how, and where,
the switch was made. The new commander needed no such
brains.

'Do you have a good marriage?'

'Sir?'

'Yes or no.'

The commander blinked before answering. The closest to
subordination he would ever come. 'No, sir. Not particularly.'

No. He wouldn't. It went with the territory that strong men
who were absent a lot of the time would clash with strong women,
who managed farms and ran the house in their absence.

'How do you propose to rectify that?'

'I – er – obviously I shall review the arrangements when I
retire. But that's not for another nine years, by which time the
boys will be grown up and serving in the army themselves. Sir.'

'In other words, you have no intention of changing the current
situation?'

'No, sir.'

'Suppose you're on the battlefield. The phalanx is locked,
shoulder to shoulder, but you can feel the enemy pushing you
back. The ground is flat. There are no hills. It is sunny. What
do you do?'

'Order the men to press harder, sir. Remind them they are
fighting for their country and defeat would bring humiliation on
Sparta.'

'You would use encouragement to drive the enemy back?'

'Yes, sir.'

Yes, sir. Always *yes, sir*. Lysander would give the order to
unlock and retreat, thus unbalancing and confusing the enemy.
He would then order his men to face the sun, blinding their

opponents with the glare of bronze armour and shields. Then re-form and slaughter the bastards.

Just as Gregos would have done.

But then the commander, who never looked beyond the rigid lines he'd been taught, would never be sidetracked either . . .

The head of the Krypteia did not enjoy making mistakes, any more than he liked having his judgement called into question.

Especially when it was he, himself, doing the calling—

'About the dead guard, sir. We buried the body and marked the spot with a cairn. Once the caravan arrives in Sparta, we will return and cremate him, and I will personally bring his bones home on his shield.'

'Good.'

Except traitors don't return home on their shields. Their bodies are left to rot in the wind, so their souls never rest and they may never find peace.

Even that was too good for the bastards.

'Tell me his exact words again,' Iliona said.

Jocasta moved downwind of the flames and repeated the conversation she'd had with Sandor verbatim.

'So he thinks Daphne might have come to some harm, yet Hermione and Calypso aren't worried,' Iliona murmured.

'I spoke to Dierdra when I got back.'

Jocasta didn't like funerals. The pyres brought back the stories of plagues, wars and earthquakes that her grandfather used to tell her when she was a child. She couldn't sleep afterwards for fear of Poseidon striking open the ground with his trident, or flaming arrows landing on the thatch.

'She blamed Anthea for the girl running off.'

Put the fear of the gods into the poor girl, I reckon.

How so? Jocasta had asked.

Stupid woman has this idea in her head that those three needed some kind of counselling. I heard Hermione tell her, 'Forget it, love, we're just fine,' but does she leave it alone? Oh, no, not Madam. I'm at the window. I see Daphne skulking off into the stables. I see Anthea follow, and I hear her call out, 'I'd like to talk to you later, young lady, if you don't mind' – and that was it. Ten minutes later the silly cow's gone.

'I don't like this at all,' Iliona said.

'Me, neither.'

After what Sandor had told her, Jocasta flew back to the station faster than Pegasus. She made enquiries, and eventually came to the conclusion that the priest was the only one who was worried about Daphne wandering off. If that wasn't odd, then what was?

'He was wriggling on a hook at the time,' Iliona reminded her. 'Could that have been a cheap ploy to get you out of his hair?'

'I think it's safe to say he doesn't like me in particular and women in general. Unless it's for ogling purposes.'

Yvorna's ashes were being quenched with water and wine. Sandor was using cypress, juniper and laurel to waft away the smoke, and the women sang laments for her soul.

'Yet you said he played beautifully on his pipe for Yvorna.'

'I said he played beautifully, but only to negate the damage her death had caused to his shrine.' Most peeping toms feel emasculated by women, why should Sandor be an exception? 'I'm betting that, to him, Yvorna's death was just one more nuisance. Another reason why the station should close.'

'Either way, I find it amazing that such a hypocrite and pervert can produce such sweet music,' Iliona said, watching him work in his ceremonial fishing net. The catcher of souls for his Blue Goddess. 'It's like he's almost two people.'

They stood in silence while he sprinkled poppy petals over the ashes in the promise of resurrection.

'You know,' she said slowly, 'it's as though everyone at this station is two people. It's the only way they can survive.'

'Balls.' It wasn't often Jocasta disagreed with the high priestess on matters of human nature, but for once Iliona was wrong. 'Look at all the foreign trade passing through these crossroads. Nearly everything that comes through is either new or fresh or stimulating, and the very nature of the traffic, not to mention the sheer bloody volume, is going to breed a far freer and open society than anywhere else in the Greek alliance.'

'That's what I thought, at first.' Iliona hadn't packed black for this trip, but her midnight-blue gown was close enough for the occasion. She adjusted the matching diaphanous veil, tucking it under her diadem, and shook the folds of her sleeve. 'Actually, it works in reverse.'

Too many people, too much stimulation, and none of it relevant to them. Consequently, the station had closed in on itself, creating a community within a community almost.

'Right at the beginning I was told that gossip was the lifeblood of this station, and it's true. But if rumour sustains it, then secrets are the glue that holds it together.'

They walked along to the shore, to where the fishing boats had been dragged on to the beach, their painted eyes watching over the water. The mountains seemed to creep closer at night, the snowy caps glowing like ghosts.

'Maybe Hector's principles about not employing slave labour are noble,' Iliona continued 'More likely it's a cheap way of exploiting itinerant workers. Low pay, without any responsibility for them.'

And you could bet your boots he had a financial investment in this enterprise, she added. Anthea might have sunk her money in it for love, but Hector's family had been running taverns for generations. Shrewdness was his middle name.

'For some of the workers, it would be a case of having a past they'd want to hide.' Iliona sighed. 'Others have different secrets they'd want to protect.'

Jocasta looked out across the kingdom of the Blue Goddess and thought, don't we all. 'You mean Melisanne's pregnancy?'

Iliona sat on the stones and crossed her legs. Jocasta remained standing, arms folded across her chest.

While she'd been changing Iliona's dressing earlier, it came as quite a shock to discover that they'd reached the same conclusion regarding Yvorna's death. This at least took the heat off the physician, who'd had no idea what to do about it. Go to the station master with her suspicions? What would he care? A serving girl killed at the shrine was nothing to do with him. Ballio would quite rightly argue that, although technically neutral, the shrine was not actually within the boundaries of Phaos, and was therefore a problem for the Eagles, not the Bulls. Sandor would only accuse her of malicious accusations. Worse, with no tangible evidence, no body to examine, not even a decent suspect for the murder, who'd take her allegations seriously? A woman physician was on trial for her life in Athens, relegating the likes of Jocasta to the status of healer/witch/wise-woman, take your pick. Throw in the fact that she was a helot, despised by every class in every city state, and the case was doomed.

'When you stop and really look under the surface,' Iliona said, 'you start to see how secrets shape the personality in a small, tight-knit world like this. Not the other way round as it would for, say, you or me.'

Speak for yourself, Jocasta thought.

'Even the sisters. Very different in looks, outlook and character, of course, but the overall impression is that all three are exactly what they appear to be. What you see is what you get, yes?'

Jocasta shrugged. 'I suppose so. I really haven't given it much thought.'

'Bubbles of protection also build bubbles of illusion, though.' Iliona rose to her feet and brushed off the dust from her robe. 'The danger comes when you start to believe your own script.' She squeezed Jocasta's arm. 'Throw petals on the pyre for me, will you?'

'Why? Where are you going?'

'I need to talk with a banker about his investments.'

'At this hour? You do know it's past midnight?'

'Don't worry. Wolves on the prowl never sleep.'

Jocasta threw up her hands in exasperation. 'What on earth's that supposed to mean?'

'It means,' Iliona said levelly, 'I think I know where the female groom has been buried.' She paused. 'It's a long story. I'll tell you later.'

Damn right, Jocasta thought, watching her go. She tossed the poppy petals into the water and watched them bob away on the night. No way was she going back to that bloody pyre, but one thing was clear. There was more to this trip than Iliona first told her. All that crap about Sparta's reputation!

Now it appeared there were at least two murders to deal with. Jocasta was wise not to trust Iliona.

TWENTY-FIVE

By mid-morning, the station yard was the usual ant's nest of porters running back and forth with sacks, packs and baggage. Exhausted runners passed their scrolls to a fresh pair of legs over a meal of warm bread, cold ham and goats' cheese. Couriers poured libations to the gods at the various shrines while the inspector scrutinized their warrants. Scribes took dictation from visiting merchants, water-bearers topped up the horse troughs, and the balances of the money-changers clanked a merry tune under the awnings.

Pushing through the crush, the air a curious amalgam of incense, ink, horse sweat and metalworking from the forge, Iliona was surprised to see a froth of dyed ringlets going the other way.

'Not working this morning, Dierdra?'

'No, milady, not today.'

The ribbons in her hair were brighter and more numerous, the jewellery on overload, and her tunic was covered with so many flowers you felt you were walking through spring Alpine pastures. But it seemed to Iliona that the make-up had been more artfully applied this morning, with none of last night's tear-streaked rouge on her cheeks or smudges of kohl round her eyes.

'My boy's feeling very low today.' The ribbons nodded towards the stables, where an expressionless Cadur was unbridling a stocky grey pony. 'Thought I might take his mind of it by cooking him a nice hot meal later. Really push the boat out, with good wine this time. None of the rough stuff, you know.'

Having hooked up the bridle, Cadur began kneading the horse's tired muscles, starting at the fetlocks and working upwards. 'I showed him how to do that,' Dierdra said proudly. 'Works a treat, that technique. In an hour, I guarantee that pony will be galloping round the paddocks like a yearling.'

Either side of the great, wide stable doors, two guards from Lynx Squad stood stiller than statues, the red crests of their helmets ruffling in the breeze.

'You do have the most astonishing hands, Dierdra.'

'That's what all the boys say!' She laughed. 'Must fly. Want to pick out a couple of crabs from the nets, before someone else snaffles the best ones. See you later, eh?'

The groom had moved up to massage the horse's stifle, the equivalent to the human knee, on its hindquarters.

Tonight, Cadur! Don't you understand?

On the pretext of trying to find a lost treasured bracelet, Iliona had been prodding the manure piles with a pitchfork when she'd heard Yvorna shouting at him. Hidden rock chips were quickly forgotten as she ducked behind one of the stalls to listen.

You have to act tonight.

The redhead's eyes had been blazing with unaccustomed anger, but whatever the cause, it stopped abruptly when Lisyl turned the corner with her arms full of clean linen and Cadur stared at her, then walked off.

Five hours later, Yvorna was dead . . .

'You were right,' a gravel voice murmured in her ear. Iliona jumped. 'The grave was exactly where you said it would be.'

The eyes of the Cretan banker locked into hers. *Trust no one*, they said.

'The heat and ants had taken their toll,' he said, his voice low so only she could hear. 'But it appears our female groom was killed with a single stab to the heart.'

None of the overkill in the abandoned shepherd's hut, then. This was cold-blooded murder.

'You were also right about her sleeping with Gregos. I asked around, and by all accounts he was quite smitten with her.'

He watched the amber merchant setting up his stall outside the porter's lodge, spreading out beads and bangles for everyone to see. Heard the horses snickering, as the grooms rubbed them down. Watched an itinerant acrobat turn somersaults in exchange for a meal.

'You probably noticed that the gold train arrived last night. I counted the sacks when it came in. There was no shortfall. And I can personally vouch that the saddlebags haven't been touched since.'

'Could you be wrong about the switch being made here?'

A feral sound came from the back of his throat. 'All things are possible,' he acknowledged. 'Except, of course, that.'

A cinnamon-trader rode in on an ass, his hair shaved in a circle above his temples, large golden bands in his ears. The dry sticks that smelled and tasted so good poked out from a basket on the donkey behind. An Argolian silver-worker rode out, accompanied by a Corinthian vase-painter, both having decided there was safety in numbers. They exchanged pleasantries at the gate with a portly Babylonian, complete with red leather slippers and brightly bejewelled turban, and a somewhat effeminate fringe to his tunic.

'How can you be sure?'

'Where's the best place to hide a pebble, Iliona?'

'You must know I set this riddle regularly at the temple. On the beach, is the answer.'

'Exactly. The bolder the act, the less people notice. Even your helot set up her treatment table knowing the kitchen staff would accept her authority without question. Even the head steward didn't query it.'

'And your point?'

He smoothed the knot at the nape of his neck and patted the Cretan iris emblazoned on his chest. 'It means that among such a gaudy cosmopolitan crowd, I have become invisible, even to my own men.'

Not having taken them into his confidence, she had been wondering what Lynx Squad's reaction would be, upon seeing the head of the Krypteia at the posting station. Through oracles, divination, omens and riddles, Iliona employed every trick in the book to ensure the eye saw only what it was expected to see. She hadn't imagined the wolf would also be able to blend into sheep's clothing and still fool the rest of the flock.

'What are you going to do?'

'What I do best,' he said, with a twitch of the lip. 'Set a trap. You?'

'I, Lysander, am also going to do what I do best.'

See through the eyes of the blind, then talk through the mouth of the dead.

'You bastard, Morin!'

Every head in the yard swung round in unison. They were just in time to see a plump girl with dark hair slap the face of a big, burly groom. Despite the purple hollows round her eyes and pale skin that was stippled with grief, the girl was still pretty. Everyone stopped what they were doing to watch.

'I can't believe you said such a wicked thing!'

'Lisyl.' Hector stepped between them, before the girl could land a second blow. 'Lisyl, please.'

The crowd seemed to multiply out of nowhere. Neither Hector, Morin or the girl seemed to notice.

'Why don't you tell me what happened, and let me take it from there.'

'It's nothing, sir. My future wife is naturally upset after the death of her sister—'

'Upset?' For a moment, her eyes didn't focus beyond her fury, then she pursed her lips. 'I know you two hated each other, but to say, *What do you expect of a bloody lowlander, taking the coward's way out* is inexcusable, Morin.'

'Is this true?' Hector asked the young groom.

He rubbed the flaming red mark on his cheek. 'In my view, sir, suicide is for cowards. I've always said that, and I don't believe in changing my opinion now.'

'Nor should you, though I have to say your timing isn't exactly diplomatic. Yvorna's ashes are barely cool.'

The groom shrugged an apology. Hector nodded its acceptance.

'But that part about the lowlanders,' he said. 'Was that true?'

'I'm an Enkani, sir. We don't hang ourselves when the going gets rough. We face things, no matter how unpleasant they are.'

'Good,' Hector said. 'I'm pleased to hear it, because you're obviously well equipped to start a new job somewhere else. Collect your belongings, please, and be gone in an hour.'

'But – but – you can't do that, it's not fair. This was just a lover's tiff. I spoke out of line, I admit it, but my comments weren't intended for Lisyl's ears. Lis, I swear. I never meant you to hear that.'

Hector sucked his breath between his teeth. 'You don't understand, do you, Morin? Lisyl didn't just find Yvorna's body. She then had to break the news to her other sister.' His eyes alighted on the ashen creature hovering at the edge of the crowd. 'Now I dare say, if Lisyl had been a man, she'd have punched you on the nose, everybody would have cheered and we'd all have carried on exactly as before.'

He drew a deep breath.

'Morin, I'm not sacking you for what you said about Yvorna committing suicide,' he said, 'or even the insensitivity of the remark. But I am the station master, and my job isn't merely to recognize the problems that arise when tribal differences become inflamed. It's to prevent them from getting out of hand.'

He turned to address the gathering.

'As far as I'm concerned, everyone at this station is Greek, nothing more, nothing less, since the city states are now all united under a single banner. If any of you hold a different opinion, that's fine by me. Everyone is entitled to his or her own viewpoint. I wouldn't have it any other way. But I've made it clear on several occasions that I will not have prejudices voiced within my domain.'

'He started it,' Morin said, pointing.

Cadur stopped massaging the horse's withers to hold his hands up, palms out. 'I told you I didn't want any trouble.'

'Calling me a loudmouth is your idea of not wanting trouble?'

'Did you?' Hector asked. 'Did you call this young man a loud-mouth?'

'No.' Cadur glanced at Morin, then at Lisyl. 'I called him a pathetic, gutless, work-shy loudmouth, and Yvorna would have hated it that he, of all people, should find her hanging and vulnerable.'

'That is an extremely inflammatory statement,' Hector said. 'Especially when Morin had to cut down the victim, and the bereaved are distraught.'

'You're not really going to fire them?' Lisyl wailed. 'If it was anyone's fault, it was mine. I'm the one who lashed out.'

'You reacted under extreme provocation, you're a woman, you're also in mourning. I don't hold you to account, but most importantly, this is not your fault, Lisyl.' Hector looked Cadur straight in the eye. 'I do not tolerate disorder at my posting station. Do you understand?'

'I do.' There was a beat of three before Cadur turned to Lisyl. 'Sorry, Lisyl, but if I'm going to be sacked, I may as well enjoy it.'

Swinging his fist, he laid Morin out flat.

There was still no change in the hot weather, and the serenity of this impossibly blue, impossibly clear lake was even more pronounced at the top of the cliff. Up here, the air was sweet with the smell of overripe apples, loud with the drone of wasps made woozy from the intoxicating juice. Iliona drowned the sound by flicking one of the painted pottery doves that hung from the portal, and making it rattle.

Wooden dolls hanging in the trees. Substitutes for sacrificed virgins.

Doves hanging over the entrance, chiming for the souls of the dead.

Yvorna hanging from the rafters—

The scent of herbs permeated the softness. Rosemary, hyssop and thyme.

Why here? she wondered. Why lug a rope all the way up here, when it was so much easier to hurl the poor girl off a cliff? Of course, if Yvorna had gone over the side, the body might not have been found. Gentle as it looked, the continual pressure of underground springs, combined with the thrust of the rivers that fed into the lake, caused a constant momentum. Three days might pass before she bobbed up again, if at all. Was timing a factor, or simply that the killer needed the body to be found? Why was it important that her death was made to look like a suicide? Few of the motives put forward held water. That Yvorna had been harbouring a secret crush on Morin and was unable to live with the realization that he was serious about marriage with Lisyl was risible. Was she just jealous of her sister's committed relationship, and wanted to spoil Lisyl's big moment? No one could take such theories seriously. Yvorna truly despised Morin, and there were easier ways to sabotage Lisyl's transition to womanhood than the taking of her own life! The rich, married lover who rode off and abandoned her might have held true, had Yvorna not been so resilient.

A prank gone wrong, Dierdra suggested. Possible. She was known for her practical jokes, though surely that would be taking things to extremes? Which, really, narrowed the field down to just one motive. That Yvorna took the honourable way out, rather than being publicly exposed as a thief.

There was no denying the small silver owl Lysander had found pinned to her breast. Or the selection of rings, cloak pins, earrings and brooches under her pillow. *If you're interested, the pouch is made out of crane skin . . .*

'The Blue Goddess welcomes you to her lofty abode.' Sandor bowed. 'She presumes you come to say prayers for the deceased?'

You mean hanged?

I do mean hanged.

Iliona looked at his shadow, long and thin like himself, before eventually lifting her eyes. 'Actually, Sandor, I came here to see you.'

Like her own, his duties varied from presiding over rituals and sacrifices to preparing and participating in festivals. The difference was, the Shrine of Eurotas was busy night and day, every day.

He's been acting odd lately, Dierdra had said. *First he came on to me, and when that wouldn't wash, he made a play for Yvorna. Telling her it was her duty to go to the shrine. Purify the altar with her love . . .*

'But now you mention it, I wouldn't have any objection to offering a prayer for Yvorna, or pouring a libation in memory of her irrepressible spirit.'

'Then let us make sacrifice to Nemesis the Inescapable,' he intoned, brushing the altar with herbs. 'For Nemesis avenges wrong, punishes arrogance and redresses the balance of excess.' He lifted the phial of sacred water high with both hands. 'Even happiness, madam. For nothing must upset the balance of life.'

Yes, god forbid one was ever too happy.

While he consecrated the altar with apples and figs, laying his ornate bronze crown of roses, almond flowers and holly on top as a mark of devotion, Iliona let her mind wander.

What made Morin choose this particular site? Yes, it was romantic, and at night there would be no one about. There were no treasuries to maintain here. No records to keep, no eternal fires to watch over, no sacred cats to take care of, or burning of incense that demanded constant attention. Just this tiny round shrine built out of wood, with its little thatched roof and tiny stone altar, requiring the ministrations of a part-time priest, nothing more.

Zabrina of the Translucent Wave. A beautiful name for a beautiful place. But benign or not, Zabrina was an underworld goddess.

Even the moon had a dark side.

'And now for the libation,' he said.

'We found the girl's grave.'

The phial fell from his hands, holy water splashing over his robes as it bounced off the altar and on to the floor. 'G–grave? What girl?'

Iliona picked up the phial and refilled it from the lustral basin. Three times she passed it over the stone, tipped it out and refilled it, before drenching the apples and figs.

'You know damn well what girl. The female groom. Now let's not play any more games.'

White-faced and shaking, he slumped to the ground. 'How did you find out?'

'The gods see everything, Sandor, and in my trances they talk to me. Tell me exactly what happened.'

'But if you already know—'

'Alathea, virgin goddess of truth and daughter of Zeus, stood in white beside the Gate of Dreams and commanded it. Will you insult the Olympians by refusing her request?'

He buried his face in his skeletal hands. 'Zabrina is a virgin goddess. It is only fitting that I collect holy water from the Spring of the Virgins. I make the trek every day.'

'You were hardly collecting holy water when Jocasta found you.'

'No.' He swallowed. 'But that day – the day of which you speak – I went down with my krater, and as I approached, I saw the woman from the stables standing beside the pond. It was obvious she was waiting to meet someone. A tryst, no doubt. She had a reputation for fornication, just like this one.' A bony finger pointed to the rafters above their heads. 'She must have heard me, because she called out, *Is that you?* For obvious reasons, I did not wish to intrude on their privacy. It is enough that these people defile the sanctity of the site with their vile lust and their—'

'Let's just stick to the story, Sandor. What happened next?'

'I returned a couple of hours later, but this time I took a different route, that I might be able to look down over the pool. If they were still sporting, I would try later, but no. The spring was deserted. Only the birds in the trees.'

'Except it was not deserted, was it?'

'Yes, yes, of course it was.' He seemed irritated by the question, swatting it away with his hand like a fly. 'You already know that. But as I approach from this different direction, I see a long mound of freshly turned earth.' He made the sign of the horns to avert the evil eye. 'I know a grave when I see one,' he whispered hoarsely. 'But what should I do? My hand shakes as I uncover the soil, and suddenly, to my horror, the eyes of this poor girl are staring up at me.' He shuddered. 'I close her eyes, I open her mouth that her soul may escape, then I place a coin on her tongue for the Ferryman.'

'For gods' sake, you're a pest! How could you leave her there, knowing her soul would never rest?'

'What options were open to me?' he asked miserably. 'She'd been stabbed through the heart. Murdered. If I reported the crime, it would look like I was guilty. Who else could have done it? On the other hand, if I ignored it, I would have to live with the consequences of a soul damned to hell. I opted for self-preservation.'

'Is that why you warned me off? Why you tried to make Jocasta leave, too? And Calypso.'

'Too often you hear tales of men who kill for sexual pleasure. My Zabrina is a gentle goddess. I will not have her tainted by such baseness.'

Thanks very much, though at least it explained why he hadn't tried to discourage Hermione. He obviously didn't deem her capable of firing sexual passions, no matter how perverted the killer.

'So now you hang around the Pool of the Virgins, to protect other girls from coming to the same sticky end?'

'No, madam.' Sandor stood up and drew a deep, juddering breath. 'I go there to make sure she is never alone.'

TWENTY-SIX

D iversionary tactics. Brilliant. Just what the gold thief was after.

Once the altercation in the yard broke up, it was back to work with much catching up to be done. Heads down, the workers returned to their duties, the grooms currying horses and strapping mules at double their normal speed, and even the merchants and couriers, distracted by the impromptu entertainment, needed to compensate for the time wasted gawping. As a consequence, the flurry in the courtyard was even more chaotic than usual. It made a gold thief's heart swell.

Only the soldiers of Lynx Squad, standing guard at the stables, remained rigid and watchful at their posts. Battle-scarred hands rested over their short-swords. The eyes behind the faceless helmets glittered in vigilance.

'Fire! Fire in the stables!'

No one was able to say how it started. Milling about, trying to catch up, they'd been either concentrating on the backlog of work, or thinking about what had just happened. Drama on that scale doesn't come round every day. That would be something to talk about long after the autumn rains had set in, that was sure. So the first wisp of smoke passed unnoticed. As did another, and another. Only when straw began to crackle and flames were licking the beams did any one realize what was happening.

'FIRE!'

The alarm horn blew then, long, low and piercing, sending the horses into a frenzy of rearing and whinnying, as dogs barked, mcn shoutcd and women screamed. In a flash, thick plumes of smoke had smothered the courtyard, spreading panic, fear and confusion.

'Fetch buckets,' the soldiers from Lynx Squad ordered. 'Form a chain to the lake, each of you an arm's span apart. The rest of you, use water from the troughs. Towels from the bath house. Anything you can find to douse it and smother the flames.'

But the hay was dry. Within minutes, the stables had become an inferno.

'Faster,' the guards urged, as the flames crackled and spat. 'If we don't contain it, the whole station will go up!'

'Cadur!' Lisyl cried, as he dipped a cloth in the trough and covered his mouth. 'For gods' sake, what are you doing? Don't be stupid!'

'I'll be fine,' he said, tying it round the back of his head. 'I'll be fine.'

One of the terracotta roof tiles cracked and shattered at her feet. Lisyl screamed. 'This is madness, Cadur!' The smoke was stinging her eyes. 'Don't go in there.'

'Get back, ma'am.' One of the soldiers pushed her roughly aside, as his colleague formed the head of the chain. When she looked round again, Cadur had gone.

Inside, Lysander, too, had covered his mouth with a cloth. The wolf waited.

He did not have to wait long.

'The gold's not there,' he said, when a hand pushed through the smoke to grab at the saddlebags.

'What?'

Torn between turning round to see who was speaking and checking the saddlebags, the gold thief failed to notice the rake handle coming towards him. Then a thousand stars exploded inside his head, and nothing mattered any more.

Iliona noticed the smoke from the top of the cliff. As she hurtled down the path towards the station, she saw a human chain swinging leather buckets up and down to the lake. Not particularly well organized, a lot of water was slopping, but panic makes for enthusiasm. The chain was nothing if not fervent. In the yard, the smoke had driven people and animals into the fields. It was pure pandemonium, with roof tiles raining down, people coughing and yelling, money-changers scrabbling to gather up coins, scribes trying to save their vellums and parchments, grooms trying desperately to calm panicking horses.

'Cadur,' Lisyl screamed. She pointed. 'He's inside and no one will go in to help.'

Iliona thought of Lysander setting his trap. Did he sacrifice the stables to catch the man who tried to cheat Sparta? Or was this the mastermind's idea, setting a fire so he could switch the gold while the guards were distracted?

'Get away from there, Lisyl.' She tried to pull her away from the door. 'There's nothing you can do,' she shouted.

Smoke and flames licked up the sides of the building. There was an ominous crack of timber deep in the stables.

Then a figure emerged from the inferno. His chiselled cheekbones were black, his tunic scorched down one side, his forearms were blistered and raw.

'I couldn't leave them.'

In his hands sat four tiny kittens.

Lisyl looked at them. Blinked. Then did the only thing she could sensibly think of. She fainted.

Praise be to Apollo, the building survived. Of course, twelve professional soldiers plus twelve helot auxiliaries soon made short work of the job, and its very size also helped to save it. The central supports made from giant oak trees just smoked a bit, charred a bit, looked like a crocodile afterwards, but were thankfully too thick to catch fire. Only a dozen stall partitions were lost. Those, the hayloft, a few carts, some tools, and a whole load of straw. Everything else just needed elbow grease, along with a hammer, some chisels and nails.

But with crisis comes change.

Sudden death had already adjusted their values once. Now people were forced to assess them again.

For Iliona, this moment of clarity had come earlier, up at the Shrine of the Blue Goddess, when she realized, silly bitch, she had been reading everything here back to front.

Those theatrical warnings of Sandor's should have alerted her. With so few duties to perform, what he did have, he took seriously. Any sacrifices and prayers were undertaken with finely honed dramatics, which had gradually been absorbed into his priestly persona.

You would do well not to compare yourself to the Olympians, madam. Arrogance does not become you.

Such pomposity!

First you swagger, then you lie, until finally the Oracle shows her true colours.

He'd accused her of 'making magic' to curse the posting station, causing Nobilor's death, and it was well known that he'd be happy to see the place closed. Could he, she'd wondered, have messed with the wrestler's chariot to serve his own ends? Stealing the gold to finance a string of covert sabotage operations that would guarantee the trials were not working?

If he'd asked Yvorna to sacrifice her virtue on the 'altar of love' (or whatever Dierdra had called it), wasn't it also possible he'd either sweet-talked, brainwashed or blackmailed the female groom into working with him? Even to the extent of killing Gregos?

But she had misread the signals, and once she looked at the thing from the proper perspective, Iliona found herself looking at a man who hid beside pools, not to spy on naked physicians, but to protect other girls from suffering the same fate as the groom, as well as keeping vigil over her grave.

Make no mistake, priestess. You will rue the day you came to Phaos.

For all the bluster and bluff, Sandor wasn't a bad man. Hell, he wasn't even a weak one. Just a lonely one, out of his depth, and frightened that if the enterprise became successful, the shrine would be enlarged and embellished, Zabrina's cult would grow stronger – throwing him out of a job. For a man for whom that shrine was his life, there would be nothing left if he lost that.

Afterwards, of course, everything else fell into place.

Like the Lake of Light, you think you're looking at the placid, bountiful kingdom of a beautiful, gentle goddess. But the clarity, colour and light are deceptive. The lake can be a very dangerous place, and Zabrina is a goddess who feasts with the dead.

Treating the fear, as much as the various cuts, burns, blisters and scratches that queued at her treatment table in the kitchens, Jocasta was coming to terms with Iliona's bombshell about Sandor.

'So who killed the female groom?' she asked Iliona.

By necessity, the conversation was as brief as it was hushed. Lisyl had fainted, Cadur was burned, and Iliona's arms were full of squirming, terrified kittens. On top of that, their mother, whose survival instincts had forced her to abandon them, was now suffering a clear case of conscience, and was howling and trying to climb Iliona's robe to reclaim what was rightfully hers. There was little Jocasta could do about that, but she sat Lisyl up, stuffed her head between her knees and ordered the groom to stand with his arms in a bucket of cold water until she told him to move.

Iliona picked the ginger kitten off her shoulder. 'My guess is that she must have been killed by some traveller on his way through.'

Lisyl was still too stunned to take in what they were saying, and was it surprising? She'd been through the wringer, with her parents last winter, the shock of Yvorna, the terror of seeing a friend walk into the flames, and, the last straw, her fiancé thrown out of a job.

'These –' cat claws don't make for smooth conversation – 'opportunists can strike anywhere,' Iliona told Jocasta. 'Wrong place at the wrong time, poor girl.'

Something about that didn't quite add up, but Jocasta wasn't sure what. After all, if he was an opportunist killer, why bury his victim? Why go to all the trouble of taking a shovel along? And how did he know about the spring in the first place?

'This is lavender oil,' she told Cadur, applying it carefully to his arms. 'It will soothe the burn, relieve the pain and reduce the inflammation. Give it an hour or two in the air, then come back and I'll put on a light, porous dressing with calendula cream to prevent any infection.'

'This'll be fine.' He looked at her through his fringe. 'Thank you.'

'Do I look the type who starts jobs, then leaves them half-finished? You'll bloody well come back in an hour, is that clear?'

'Yes, ma'am.'

She turned to the next patient. A small girl, with not so much as a blister, but her soot-blackened face was streaked with tears and her hands were shaking with terror. Jocasta washed off the dirt with elderflower water, tied a bandage round a finger that hadn't seen so much as a scratch, then gave her a honey cake from the griddle.

'That's not a burn, it's a boil,' she snapped to the next in the queue. 'Go and put a baked onion on it and stop wasting my time.'

The stables catch fire, the station's in crisis, and what do they do? Whinge about a bloody pimple.

Applying ointments and salves to the various injuries, she regretted kicking Sandor so hard in the balls, and punching him twice in the kidneys. *Get in first*, was her father's maxim. *Guilty until proven innocent in emergency situations. Remember that, and you won't go far wrong.* Well, now the priest had been proven innocent, so maybe she should mix a special painkilling cream for him to rub in? Even though it would deplete her precious stocks of balm of Gilead, it seemed the least she could do—

The hell, no. However righteous he might be when it came to standing watch over graves, she hadn't forgotten the lies he spread about Iliona bedding the Cretan.

The bruises could bloody well take care of themselves.

Hermione and Calypso were fanning the smoke out of Nobilor's window when Iliona burst into the bedroom. The wrestler's quarters were twice the size of her own, and sumptuously decorated with green marbled basins, chairs inlaid with ivory, copper mirrors and ornate bronze lamp stands. Rare aromatics burned in sconces and the walls were painted with intricate theatrical scenes, still life, rustic images of goatherds and shepherd boys that didn't seem to differentiate between Bulls and Eagles anywhere.

'Where is he?'

Both women jumped. The dog yelped and ran under the couch.

'Who?' they chorused.

'I have neither the patience nor the time to play any more games with you two. Nobilor. Where is he?'

Hermione had gone red. Calypso had turned pale. They both looked at each other. 'He's dead, lovey.'

'Please don't insult my intelligence. Your son staged that accident, choosing a bend where the incline would be too steep to recover a body. Though just to be safe, you had the hillside burned to hide the evidence—'

'Begging your pardon, dear, it was the station master who arranged barrels of burning tar to be rolled down. The stench was putting travellers off.'

'Hector organized it, but only because you suggested it to him. And since it was in your own interests that he took the credit, you cleverly let him think the idea was his.'

'This is very rude of you, Iliona,' Calypso declared. In spite of the panic, the smoke, the fear of the station burning down, her strawberry-blonde hair was immaculately coiffed, her pink robe looked like it had just come out of the chest and her jewels were perfectly in place. 'Barging in unannounced, making horrid accusations! Poor Pookie's scared to bits.'

'Oh, so you're worried about the dog. Never mind my poor old heart might give out at any minute—'

'Stop it, the pair of you.' Most of the time, she'd enjoyed their comic squabbling, found it very entertaining. But now was not the time. 'I won't ask again. Either you tell me where Nobilor and the girl are hiding out, or I go straight to the authorities with this.'

She expected Calypso to be the one to cave in, but it was Hermione who crumpled into a heap on the bed.

Like they say. Confession is good for the soul.

TWENTY-SEVEN

Consciousness didn't come quickly to the gold thief. For one thing, there was a blinding light behind his eyes, when he tried to open them. For another, a vicious pounding inside his head. He tried to move, but his limbs were stiff and refused to budge. It took a moment before he realized he was bound.

Tied to a log in the forest, no less.

He also became aware of a lump on his temple, from the pole that spiralled him into oblivion. The lump was throbbing and hot, and the stiffness on his cheek was probably blood that had dried.

When he eventually managed to focus, he discovered his clothes had been stripped from him and were hanging neatly in the trees, like washing out to dry. The spookiness of it made the hairs on the back of his neck prickle, but when he struggled against the ropes, he found he'd been lashed tightly as well as horizontally. The bark of the tree trunk was rough. It chafed his spine raw. He stopped trying. There was no sense fighting what he could not win. He would need other tactics to escape.

Looking beyond the clothes, he could see the first changes in the leaves. Saw a squirrel scamper through the branches with an acorn wedged in its mouth. He smelled mushrooms and hazelnuts, apples and leaf litter. With a faint hint of leather and wood smoke.

A horse snickered. From the corner of his eye, he could see a tail swishing. Obviously, the means of transporting a comatose body to a nice, quiet and extremely remote spot. At least from his captor's viewpoint.

'What amazes me is that you thought you could get away with it,' a gravel voice rumbled.

From the corner of the other eye, he saw a chest emblazoned with a scarlet lambda. The definitive emblem of Sparta. *Shit.*

'You have balls, I'll give you that,' the voice said.

With the tip of his sword he dangled the tunic of the Cretan banker above the gold thief's face.

Shit, shit, SHIT.

'Where's the best place to hide a pebble?' Lysander's knuckles cracked. 'Among scores of other pebbles, so that one particular stone won't stand out.'

Warriors served two years in the Krypteia, where, among other things, they learned camouflage skills. A test that separated the men from the boys, but more importantly identified future generals. The new commander of the gold train, for example, could hide in the fields, using mud and leaves as camouflage, and never be found. Lysander, on the other hand, would pick up a hoe and get stuck in among the labourers, where he'd gather information and also never be rumbled.

'The bolder the move and the brighter the colours, the less people question or look.' He let the Cretan garb fall. 'I was in plain sight in the yard, and you didn't see me. Yet I saw you.'

His sword tip lightly nudged each of the garments hanging in the trees. The brightly bejewelled turban. Red leather slippers. The Babylonian tunic with its somewhat effeminate fringe.

'But then that is why I'm head of the secret police, Gregos.'

He paused to look into the face of the man he had trusted with this mission. Not just the gold, but his own reputation, as well as Sparta's. How could he have been such a fool?

'Strange as it may seem, I do admire the planning and precision you put into this heist.'

'Bloody brilliant, wasn't it?' Gregos grinned. 'Right back in the spring, when there was only talk about trading horses and iron for Macedonian gold, I began laying the groundwork.'

Newly promoted from platoon leader, and while still serving in the Krypteia, he cultivated a friendship with his boss. Not too difficult. The families were connected, albeit distantly, but with Lysander's wife and kid dead, even a hard-boiled commander needs company sometimes. He'd shown him his secret hideaway, knowing right back then how he would stage his own murder. He made sure it would be a night Lysander remembered. A night they both did, for that matter. They drank, played dice, darts, then drank a lot more. That night was the first time in a long while that Gregos had actually enjoyed himself. Ironically enough, it was the last time, as well.

'I wrote in your record that you were both careful and crafty. It was a compliment,' Lysander said. 'The trouble was, you were too careful, too crafty, and in the end your very arrogance gave you away. This is how it was done,' Lysander continued. 'Right from the start, I'd made it clear that you were the man I wanted guarding that caravan. A soldier with brains, who could outfox any thieves. I sent you on a reconnaissance mission, in which you scouted the terrain but also put it to good use by finding yourself a patsy.'

'The groom wasn't my first choice,' Gregos said ruefully. 'But a man has to do what a man has to do. She fell for my not inconsiderable charms almost at once.'

And so the scene was set. The first gold train comes in, it is ten per cent short. Lysander and Gregos discuss how and where the switch could have been made, but agree the plans to transport it were foolproof.

'A good man died because of you,' Lysander said levelly. 'You shot him, purely to cast him in the role of the villain, with no thought to his family or honour.'

'He died because of you,' Gregos snapped back. 'You're the one who told me to spy on the men of Lynx Squad. You're the one who planted the seed for pinning the blame on to one of our own. I'd have been happy letting clouds of suspicion hang over the posting station.'

'There was nothing to stop you,' Lysander snarled back. 'God knows, there are enough people there for us to have spent weeks – months! – trying to sort through the mess.' He spiked his hands through his long warrior hair. 'But that's what I meant about being too careful and too crafty, because once again, you were too clever by half.'

With a swirl of his wrist, Lysander tossed his dagger into the air and caught it in a nonchalant hand.

'I admit you had me fooled with the hut. Very convincing, that blood-sodden mattress and the drag marks down to the river. What was it, by the way? A pig?'

'Suckling sow. Very messy. I knew you'd examine the scene, asking yourself, was I really dead? So I made it look like the work of a woman. Please tell me you don't think that's too clever by half.'

'No, you arrogant son-of-a-bitch, I do not. In fact, I followed every signpost you left for me. Your affair with the groom. How smitten you were with this girl. I believed everything you wanted me to, even that she was an accomplice. Which was easy enough, since it happened to be true. The difference was –' he tossed the knife up again – 'the poor cow didn't know she was a co-conspirator to murder and theft.'

Well, he could hardly tell her, could he? Instead, he pretended to be madly in love, and for her part she fell like a stone. He swore her to secrecy when he promised to desert the army and elope with her, and she, bless her stupid heart, wouldn't risk betraying the love of her life. He sent her on errands to make it appear as though she'd followed him to Sparta and killed him, then quickly disposed of her when she became redundant. Meeting at a landmark that was easily recognized, not too close to the station, yet not too far away.

'At least the bitch died happy.'

'Hm.' Lysander rested his foot on the log and leaned his arm on his knee. Minutes passed. 'I went to the mines, took a long look around, then backtracked over the route, over the plans, over all the security measures we'd put in place, until I finally realized the more audacious the act, the less it is questioned. There is no such thing as impossible.'

'You're just guessing.'

'All right, let's say I'm you. I'm at the mines,' Lysander said. 'In charge of loading the gold. I'm counting the sacks at the top of my voice as they're loaded on to the donkeys. . . . 29, 30, 31, 33, 34, 35, 37 . . . Easy, isn't it?'

Bloody master stroke, Gregos thought to himself. At the end, there's a full complement, because no one pays attention to numbers. Their minds are on stacking saddlebags, getting home to their kids, what they'll be eating for dinner tonight. While ten per cent of the gold gets set aside, where Gregos had already confided to the mine-owners that this was an extra security precaution. He bore the king's seal, why wouldn't they believe him? Consequently, another donkey slides into the caravan. When it slides out at the posting station, hey presto, there's still a full head count.

'You should have stuck to the first three caravans, Gregos. But no. You got greedy—'

'Materialistic, if you don't mind.'

The army bored him, all that training and discipline, and stifling rules. His wife didn't need him, he didn't like *her* – or the dullness of family life. What was wrong with wanting an endless supply of wine, women and song, far away from trudging and fighting? Zeus, the relief when he hacked off his long warrior hair! The freedom he'd felt, as it fell.

'I had in mind Phoenicia, or maybe Carthage, if that didn't work out.'

Some exotic destination, where he could flout the tedium of convention in comfort. He already thought of himself as Prince Gregos.

'Materialism, greed, it's still thieving, you bastard. How much were you planning to steal this time?'

'More than ten per cent,' Gregos laughed.

That's why he staged his own murder. To throw the investigators off the track, then changing his modus operandi.

'You knew the fourth caravan would have to stop to change animals. You even knew we were on the alert. Yet you honestly believed that if you played this with enough balls, you could just walk up and steal it from under my nose.'

Lysander's sword hooked a different set of clothes from the branches. The Germanic leggings and hood that was to be the next disguise, having shrugged off the Babylonian merchant.

'Over-careful, over-crafty, that's what gave you away. That shot through the warrior's neck, for example. Too clean. As was the execution of the female groom. Those kinds of actions betrayed you, Gregos, but do you know what really let you down? The reason I found you, in fact?'

'You're obviously going to tell me.'

'It was the stupidity of believing you were smarter than me.'

'I still am.'

Lysander's eyebrows shot up. 'How would that be, when you're bound and trussed like a hog for the spit?'

'I know where the gold is.' He'd been planning his escape route from the moment he realized who'd tied these knots. 'I also know how desperately you want it back, because in your book, to lose ten per cent of three caravans is to fail. And you do not, and I mean really do not, want to fail.'

'Damn right.' Lysander's grin was colder than ice. 'I have no intention of returning without the full quota, so why don't we save ourselves a lot of time and, truly, my friend, an awful lot of pain by making this easy.'

The offer was simple. A quick, painless death in return for Gregos telling him where he'd hidden the gold dust.

'I'll be honest, that wasn't the plan I had in mind here.' Gregos saw himself walking away with his life. 'Torture won't get you far, anyway. I've been trained to withstand extremes of pain, and you're the one who taught me, remember?'

'You want to cut a deal?'

'I swear by the River Styx to give you the exact location of the gold in return for walking away.'

A few hours' start was all Gregos needed.

'I make it my policy not to make deals with traitors, and as for persuasion –' he twirled a red slipper on the end of his finger – 'once again, this is why I command the Krypteia. I never reveal all my secrets.'

Gregos swallowed. Overhead, geese honked in noisy migration. A leaf fluttered down from an oak.

'Well?' Lysander asked. 'What's it to be?'

'Fuck you,' Gregos said.

TWENTY-EIGHT

With hindsight, it was obvious Nobilor would be camped out close to where his chariot went over the edge. That way, whenever Calypso or Hermione went up to stare into the ravine, scatter petals, reflect, meditate, or whatever grieving women were supposed to do in such circumstances, he would be able to meet them.

They'd bring him fresh food, to bolster supplies he'd laid down in advance. The nights were warm, and it would not be for long.

Right from the beginning, at the Festival of the Axe God, it had been bothering Iliona why two women who hated each other's guts spent so much time in each other's company. If you don't like someone, you avoid them, it's that simple. You don't engage in insults . . . unless, of course, it's to draw attention to them.

Diversion tactics again. People see what they are expected to see, and the foundations had been laid from the very beginning. Hermione playing up the old bag of a mother-in-law, such a favourite of comic playwrights. Openly calling Calypso a money-grubbing bitch and pretending to bully her, while the new bride played the foil to perfection.

Not quite so empty-headed after all.

Iliona tied her stallion close to some lush mountain grass and tiptoed along the path Hermione had described. Five minutes later, she heard giggling, mock groans, and the unmistakable clack clack-clack of a game of knucklebones.

'That's five hundred thousand drachmas you owe me.' Daphne's voice filtered through the late summer undergrowth. For the first time, she sounded happy.

'Double or quits,' a rough voice chuckled.

'Make it a million, Daddy, or I'm going home.'

'My daughter, the hustler! All right, a million it is. One, two – oh, no! Not three kings. How do you do it?'

'Cadur showed me. It's all in the wrist, see?' She cheered her own luck as she threw yet another winning set. 'Let's play horse in the stable with the bones.'

'What's wrong with eggs in the basket? I usually win that.'

'Yes, but there's no fun if you can't hear them click. How about a game of Thread the Needle – *Iliona*?'

If Nobilor, the most famous wrestler that ever lived, was surprised to see a high priestess walk into his secret glade in the mountains, he was too schooled to show it. He jumped to his feet. Placed his fist against his breast in salute. Then clipped his fifteen-year-old daughter round the ear.

'You call her *my lady*, now then, young woman!'

'Sorry.' The sulky face Iliona knew and loved was back in a flash. 'But it's not fair. How did you find us?'

'When you count the grains of sand on the seashore and measure the drops in the ocean for a living, this was pretty straightforward,' she said.

Nobilor swallowed his grin. 'Go and water the lady's horse, love. There's a stream just over the ridge.'

'But—'

'Run along.'

He was big. Much bigger than Iliona expected. Broken nose, battered eye sockets, nothing left of his ears, it was easy to see how Daphne won every bout throwing jacks. His huge paws were gnarled and misshapen after twenty years of being broken and crushed. Any delicacy of movement was long past.

'I killed them for nothing, then.'

The good humour that underpinned the big man was replaced by a terrible sadness, and suddenly she saw there was no paradox in a man who fought for a living wanting to avoid confrontation in his private life. Nobilor was as soft as bread dough inside.

'My two beautiful, spirited girls, and I killed them. Murdered them.' He sat down, burying his head in his hands. 'It was horrible. The screams . . . The suffering . . .'

He was talking about the horses, of course. The dark bay, and the gold palomino.

'I really loved them, but I hoped that by sacrificing them, we would be able to start a new life.'

'What's stopping you?'

'Huh?'

'Let me tell you a tale of impossible feats.' Iliona settled herself on the rock opposite him, making herself comfortable by crossing her legs. 'In a world where only aristocrats have the luxury of time and money to compete at Olympia, it's a miracle when a penniless youth from the slums finds a backer who nurtures his talent. The youth is a natural at Wrestling School. He wins hands-down at the Games, a dream come true, but the fairy-tale doesn't end there. The youth remains the best wrestler ever to have lived, and after two decades of unrelenting success, his stature has become almost godlike.'

For most champions, fame was ambrosia and nectar rolled into one. A drug they couldn't give up, and why should they?

Free meals in every city state. Best seats at the theatre. Their face painted on wine mugs. The joys of being mobbed, fêted, adored wherever they went.

'With every passing year, though, the pressure grew. It mightn't be this year, it mightn't even be next, but before long one of those eager young bucks lapping at his heels would end up taking his title.'

Nobilor sighed. 'I wanted to retire even before I met Calypso,' he said. 'But twenty years ago, I signed a contract with my sponsor, saying I'd fight whoever he wanted, whenever he wanted, for as long as I retained my crown. So when the King of Thebes invites me to fight and Athens puts up their best wrestler, there's no refusing. He has me by the balls.' He scratched the back of his neck. 'I emerge victorious from the contest, but every time I seem to be more of an animal, less of a man. I had to call a halt, one way or another.'

A woodpecker drummed the side of a holm oak. Lizards basked on the stones.

'You could have thrown the competition.'

'I thought about that,' he said slowly. 'But I don't hold with cheating, it's not right, and look at me. Is this a face you forget? Exactly. I'd be no more anonymous for losing, which means the crowd would be sneering where they used to cheer. Worse, I'd have to live with the fact that I let someone I don't respect take my title.'

'A man has his pride, eh?'

'I don't want my daughter teased. I want her to be proud of me, and proud of my achievements. My fame and my name is her heritage too, and the men seeking the hand of a champion's daughter aren't the same as those seeking the hand of a has-been's.'

Valid point.

'We'd have got away with this, had that banker not been delayed. But we needed confirmation that word's filtered through that Nobilor's dead, and that his estate and his affairs have been wound up.'

Out of sight is out of mind, Billi. Unless you stay in the thick of it, you'll be forgotten by this time next year.

Wise words from a wise woman.

'I don't know what's keeping him,' Nobilor said. 'But for every day we've been kept hanging on, Daphne's crush on that hunk of a groom has grown stronger and stronger. She's asking if she can marry him, now.'

Iliona remembered him leaning against the tree at the funeral, just one point of his shoulder blade touching.

'Not a good idea,' she said slowly.

'I agree, but my daughter's logic is inescapable. *Look at you and Calypso*, she says. *Love comes in all sorts of packets.*'

Nobi always called us Pinkie and Pookie. Don't you think that's absolutely darling?

'Calypso must love you an awful lot, to give up friends, family, everything for a life of anonymity.'

His big, ugly face twisted. It took a moment before Iliona realized it was happiness. 'I never knew I was alone until I met her.' His eyes filled. 'Even when I went off on my chariot, I kept looking round, hoping she'd wave me off. Giving me the strength to go on.'

She couldn't, of course. Partly to keep up the act of the not-so-bereaved widow. Partly because she'd probably have broken down when she saw him trotting out of the yard. Calypso was as straight as a die, Nobilor told her. Honest and faithful. Not domesticated, of course, but that's where his Ma came in. Doing what she'd always done, running the household with ferocious efficiency. Despite the act they put on, all three hit it off at once.

'This whole fake-death thing was Calypso's idea,' he said proudly. 'She chose the Lake of Light, the posting station, planned it from beginning to end. Even found us an island where people won't recognize me, where we can settle down in a country villa.'

I told him, the first thing you do, now you've won that laurel crown, is buy a villa in the posh end of Thebes.

I was thinking more of a place in the country, Ma.

He swallowed. 'I'm so lucky to have them. My three girls, and little Pookie.'

Oh dear. Now Iliona was welling up, too. This big man with a face like a battlefield, going daft over a fluffy rat and his child-like wife.

'I don't want Daphne to think it's her fault that I've been exposed as a fraud.' He blew his nose. 'She's young, and they get impatient at that age, or so my mother tells me. She couldn't wait for the banker. Kept itching to see me, make sure her old dad was all right, and bring him supplies.' He chuckled as he showed her what Daphne had brought. 'What does she think I am, an ox?'

'That note, telling your mother and Calypso she'd gone, certainly set a cat among the pigeons,' Iliona said. 'But, like I said, I haven't come here to scupper your plans. As far as I'm concerned, the dead can stay dead, and I wish all three of you nothing but luck.'

She was going to say *all four*, but she still had the marks in her finger from that bloody dog's teeth. She hoped it pooked every inch of the sea crossing.

'Then begging your pardon, ma'am, why did you come all the way up here?' He dribbled the knucklebones through his knobbly paws. 'I'm guessing it wasn't to admire my good looks.'

'I'll save that treat for next time,' she said. 'Right now, I need your help, and Daphne's.'

There were still loose ends to tie up.

TWENTY-NINE

Darkness settled over the lake and the mountains, enveloping them in a cloak of warm velvet. The Hunter's Moon, swelling visibly, rose in the sky, casting silver light on the rocky coves and white beaches that the Commander of the Krypteia had so eloquently tried to promote. In a few weeks, a thick coating of ice would cover the lakeshore and wolves would howl in the night. But for now, the silence was broken only by the rustle of dry autumn leaves, the sporadic bark of a fox, and the soft chirr of a nightjar in the bushes.

Iliona watched Lysander lead three pack mules into the yard, curtly dismissing offers of help from the grooms. She heard him explain to the men of Lynx Squad that there had been a bout of late trading, resulting in extra Macedonian gold to be transported to Sparta. No one questioned Lysander's authority. Why would they, of course.

He saw her watching and came over. 'You are free to leave.' He wore his army uniform of red kilt and tunic. 'My work here is done.'

He looked tired. And his voice had more gravel than ever. 'What about the gold thief?'

Measureless eyes looked into hers. 'In hell.'

She wanted to ask how, but instead found herself asking, 'Who?'

Time passed. Lips pursed into nothing. 'We leave at daybreak,' he said at length. 'Lynx Squad will act as your escort.'

'Yessir,' she said, with a mock salute, but his expression didn't change, and suddenly the need to be back in her own temple was overwhelming. To be among the wind chimes that danced in the plane grove. Soothed by the voice of the River God, as he gurgled over the rocks. To sleep in her own feather bed.

'How's the wound?' he asked, almost as an afterthought. Except nothing escaped his attention.

'You were right. There's nothing like treachery, murder and ballsing up Sparta's reputation when it comes to convalescing. I feel like a million drachmas after this break.'

In a way it was true. The stitches in her side were itching like crazy, which Jocasta assured her was a good sign. In fact, Iliona had almost forgotten the bastard who'd stabbed her.

A good physician can treat the sick anywhere.

So why did she have a feeling he only brought Jocasta along in order to protect his investment?

'Anyway,' she said. 'Your work might be done, but mine isn't.'

There was still the matter of the curse to undo.

She, too, had pride in her work.

Indoors, the house had been cleaned and purified with incense and herbs, to appease the souls of the dead. Wreaths had been hung, a vigil held over Yvorna's ashes until the sun set, when an urn painted with octopus, fishes and reeds was interred in the cemetery half a mile out on the road heading west.

Not the gruelling ceremony of the funeral pyre. More a serene end to a chaotic beginning, for there is no relief when it comes to grief.

Only the heavy tread of the passage of time.

Which could at least be broken with some impressive theatrics! Of course, once news got out that the Oracle intended to call on the gods to lift the curse, it spread faster than this morning's fire in the stables. Better and better. She really needed a crowd, and decided the ideal time to stage this particular drama was midnight. The traditional witching hour.

'Will you help?' she asked Nobilor.

'Are you kidding?' His battered, gnarled face broke into a smile that showed false teeth held in place with gold wire. 'To make dragons breathe fire and roar through the mountains? My lady, if Medusa turned me to stone on the spot, I'd still do it.'

Good, because all afternoon Sandor had been busy collecting dry brush. By now, this would have been transformed into a line of small bonfires set thirty feet apart, leading from the interior of the cave to its mouth, with a thick trail of oil connecting each pile.

'You will be in charge of the first dragon,' she explained to Nobilor. 'Daphne will be in a second cave, and Sandor will be in a third.'

Amazing how quickly the priest took to trickery, once he saw the power that it bestowed.

'For my part,' she explained, 'I will pore over a black bowl with a film of oil floated over it, making it appear that the water is cloudy. I'll drop into a trance, beseech the gods to stop rivers in full spate, arrest the stars and make the earth groan with their Olympian powers. By magic, the film over my bowl will catch fire, the cue for a blast on the battle trumpet. That will be your signal to light the oil in the caves.'

Each line of flame would then flare up as it reached its next bonfire. The dragons would breathe fire from the bowels of the mountains.

'I've also borrowed three bronze breastplates from the Spartan soldiers. Bang them with a stick, and the dragon will roar as well.'

If that didn't lift the curse and put Sparta's reputation on the map, she didn't know what the hell would.

But first . . .

First there was another job to be done . . .

THIRTY

They were all squashed into the station master's office. Hector, his wife and the warrant officer on one side of the desk. Melisanne and Lisyl holding hands on the other, with Lisyl's fiancé behind her, sporting a huge bruise on the side of his nose and the beginnings of one hell of a shiner. In the corner, Cadur leaned against the wall, his legs crossed at the ankles, his forearms bandaged in gauze. Dierdra stood beside him like Cerberus guarding Hades. She wasn't letting her boy go down without a fight.

Iliona squeezed in, closing the door softly behind her. This was her idea, after all. On her return from talking to Nobilor in the hills, she approached Hector, outlining what she saw as a solution to many of the problems that were seething within the walls of this station.

Sadly, not all the solutions were ideal—

'Right, then.' The master gave his hands a brisk rub. 'I've asked you here this evening because I have an announcement, which affects each of you in one way or another.'

The oil lamps were numerous, lighting every face in the room. Each appeared strained, and Iliona's was no exception.

'Plans are in hand to double the size of the barracks on the far side of the lake. The aim is to step up patrols and therefore render the roads safer.'

Bandits were rife, and the trade routes were still dangerous for those travelling without the luxury of private bodyguards.

'Inevitably, the town of Phaos will grow and prosper as a result. Bath houses, temples, gymnasia and theatres will spring up, attracting dyers, weavers, leather-workers and tanners. There'll be booksellers, smokeries, shield- and harness-makers, and I intend to take advantage of this boom by opening a tavern over there.'

'Really?' Anthea was shocked. 'Where's the money coming from?'

Good question, Iliona thought. Luckily, Hector had been in the trade long enough to find some means of financing this venture.

One step at a time.

'And for heaven's sake, it's not as though you don't have enough to occupy you here.'

'More than, my dear.' He laid a conciliatory hand on his wife's immaculately draped shoulder. 'But by your own admission, the lack of stimulation stifles you here, and you said yourself your talents are wasted. Wouldn't you be happier taking a more active role in the management of this station?'

'Well, I . . . Yes, I suppose I would.'

See, Melisanne thought. Hadn't she seen Anthea taking over the running of this place, while she and Hector ran a tavern elsewhere? Her heart skipped a beat as she remembered standing outside Dierdra's hut, thinking how such an arrangement would make everyone happy. Especially when she could give him all the things Anthea could not. Love. Squeezy cuddles. A baby . . .

Love, warm and spreading, the Oracle said, *like the sun in a hayfield.*

She hadn't told him about the child yet. After Yvorna died, they'd hardly spent more than a few seconds together, and then mostly with her in floods of tears. But she would tell him about the child tonight. Wouldn't he be just overjoyed?

'So that's Anthea's role,' Hector was saying. 'Let me explain how it affects the rest of you. Morin.'

'Sir?'

'First of all, I want to make it clear that I am not in the habit of reversing my decisions, but on this occasion I intend to make an exception.' He glanced at Melisanne. 'This has been a difficult week for everybody, but I have not forgotten that it was you, Morin, who cut down the body of your fiancée's sister while Lisyl was still present at the scene. Frankly, this would be a harrowing enough task for anyone, without having any personal involvement.' He stroked his beard. 'Given the circumstances, I am therefore prepared to overlook the nauseating remarks you made later concerning Yvorna.'

'You mean I'm not fired?'

'You will remain in your post. But in return, I do expect you to buck your ideas up and stop loafing around, as is your wont at the moment. Also, if there is any lapse whatsoever, you will leave at once, without pay or recommendation, do I make myself clear?'

'Yes, sir. Thank you. It won't happen again.' The big groom gingerly felt the side of his nose. 'What about him?'

Hector followed his gaze to the young man watching intently through his fringe. 'Cadur will not be working at this posting station.'

'That's not fair,' Dierdra said. 'He's just as cut up about this business. We all are—'

'You will have your chance to speak later, Dierdra. Let me

continue, please.' He turned to the warrant officer at his side. 'I have been concerned for some time that you don't have sufficient work to keep you occupied, Ballio. Every time I turn round, you seem to be watching, listening, making notes or filing spurious reports, and I find this an unhealthy arrangement.'

Anthea nodded firmly.

'I am therefore recommending that you take responsibility for sanctioning all traffic coming in and out of the station.'

'But that's three times the work!'

'If you feel unequal to the task, I'm sure your superiors will be happy to find a replacement who isn't. Melisanne.'

'Master?'

Hector clasped his hands behind his back, in case Anthea should see them shaking. 'You have proved yourself extremely capable when it comes to managing my wife's personal affairs, and we have found you loyal, trustworthy and honest. I would therefore like you to take on the responsibility for female guests at the tavern.'

Melisanne couldn't hide the blush of joy that seemed to go down to her feet. 'That's just wonderful,' she gushed. 'I don't know what to say!'

Hector didn't want her to say anything. When Iliona had told him Melisanne was with child, he'd gone white. When she'd proposed this solution, he'd almost cried. 'I would also like Lisyl to go with you,' he said quickly. 'Working here would be hard on you both, with tragic reminders wherever you looked. In Phaos, you'll have the same independence and freedom, with the advantage of a fresh start, and still have each other's support.'

Mella would need her sister once the baby arrived.

'To begin with, Lisyl, I'd like you to take charge of the laundry. If, over time, you show aptitude for other aspects of management, I am quite happy to review the situation.'

Anthea's face was set like stone, but Iliona knew it was to mask her relief. With the sisters out of the picture, her guilt at accusing Yvorna of seducing her husband would quickly recede, and with Hector busy setting up a new tavern on top of his work at the station, she didn't see him having time for a mistress.

Iliona swallowed her smile. If Hector wouldn't divorce his

wife, yet was unable to give up Melisanne, there were precious few options left. He'd practically bitten Iliona's hand off when she suggested this double life.

'Didn't you also mention a share of the profits?' she murmured.

'Did you?' Anthea barked.

Hector blinked. Glanced at Melisanne's still mercifully flat stomach, then back to Iliona. 'I may have done,' he said meekly. 'Financial incentives, and all that.'

Iliona nodded. Maybe a second family at the tavern would unclench his tight fists, for he wasn't quite the idealist he liked to portray. By hiring cheap labour, he counterbalanced the luxurious accommodation for VIP guests, which reminded her. Those sumptuous frescoes on her bedroom walls. Pastoral scenes, depicting heroes and gods, in what she'd concluded were very much Bull territory settings. Seeing Calypso's bedroom changed all that, and a quick peer into other rooms proved the artist had chosen his designs for their beauty and tranquillity, with no thought to politics. There are times, she reflected, when you just have to accept facts at face value. Things don't always have hidden meanings. Sometimes a painting is simply a painting. Just as an onion is simply an onion.

When Yvorna came running out of that store room wiping her eyes, it really had been on account of raw onions. Iliona went in to investigate later, and ended up crying herself.

'Which leaves you, young man.' Hector turned to address Cadur. 'What you did today was extremely brave. Stupid,' he said, with a half-smile. 'But brave. Mind telling me why you risked your life to rescue those kittens?'

'If I'd known there was a litter, I'd have drowned them,' Anthea said. 'You know how I feel about cats. Vile things!' She shuddered. 'The odd mouser's unavoidable, but ugh! You should have reported it to me.'

'Precisely why I didn't,' Cadur said levelly.

Iliona could only imagine the challenges of keeping a litter of kittens secret from Ballio and the rest of the grooms.

'Well, I suspect we'll be needing mousers at the tavern,' Hector said, in an effort to lighten the atmosphere. Unlike his wife, he was fond of cats. Especially the little ginger one that fell asleep in the fold of his tunic. 'Which brings me to my next point. Namely, that we shall be needing someone to take charge of the stables.' He looked into Cadur's unblinking eyes. 'I've watched

you with horses. You have an affinity for them. Do you feel up
to the task?'

'If he's so good, why don't you promote him to head groom
at the station?' Dierdra asked indignantly. 'Better pay, better
conditions! He works hard, does my boy.' She linked her arm
through his and squeezed. 'Cadur deserves a reward.'

'This *is* promotion,' Hector reminded her. 'And I already have
a head groom at the station.'

'But Phaos is a long way away,' she protested. 'Twenty miles,
and that's just as the crow flies!'

'I can write,' Cadur said.

'No, no. It's too far, love. You won't be happy in town. You
like the peace of the country—'

'Too late, Dierdra,' Iliona said quietly. 'You've already lost
him.'

Her eyes wandered round the room. At the thin weasel
features of the warrant officer. Morin's smug grin. Unsmiling
Cadur. Melisanne and Lisyl, unable to hide their excitement,
despite the horrific events of the last couple of days. She looked
at Hector's lined face. His unhappy, unfulfilled wife. Then
finally turned back to Dierdra. The ringlets and ribbons, the
kohl and the jewels, the brightly patterned tunic and thrusting,
pert breasts.

'You killed her for nothing,' she said. 'Cadur was never in
love with Yvorna, Dierdra.' She turned to the groom. 'Were you?'

He frowned. 'We were friends—'

'How dare you! I've never so much as wrung a chicken's neck
in my life,' Dierdra barked. 'This was just a prank that went
wrong!'

Iliona had already told the sisters that Yvorna was murdered.
In a strange way, the news came as a comfort, knowing she
hadn't taken her own life – or, worse, done something imma-
ture and stupid that had backfired.

'Oh, this was murder,' she said, 'though for the record, you
killed the wrong person.'

'Excuse me, I didn't kill anyone.' Dierdra planted her hands
on her hips. 'And besides. I knew full well Cad and Yvorna
were only platonic. She was my friend, remember? She confided
in me.'

'I beg to differ. You saw them walking together more and
more often. You heard Yvorna shouting at him, nagging him,

in fact doing all the things you think lovers do, because how would you know? You've never had a man love you.'

Dierdra tossed her dyed ringlets. 'Huh! I've lost count of the men who asked me to marry them—'

'No one's asked you to marry them. Those admirers of yours? All those gifts? You bought them yourself to convince everyone you were popular, but the money came from services rendered.'

'That's a lie!' She turned to the station master for support. 'I'm no tart and I never killed anyone.'

'You don't need to deny it,' Iliona pressed on. 'Cadur was well aware of what went on in that cottage.'

Men grow lonely on the road, a long way from home, and when a pretty girl is willing, they'll happily tumble her. A joyful interlude on both sides, no strings attached, but Dierdra?

'I'm guessing you offered services other girls wouldn't provide. The sort of services men would brag about to the grooms.'

Just been getting me axle greased, mate.

'So what?' Cadur shrugged. 'What Dierdra does in her own time is her business, same as what I do in my time is mine. I don't judge.'

'Exactly why you and Yvorna got on so well. You could share confidences, knowing they'd not be betrayed or judged.'

'She was my friend, too,' Dierdra cut in, 'and I didn't kill her, now then!'

'Well, that's the funny part. She wasn't your friend. You made up how she was beckoning you over, wanting your advice. This was part of the fantasy you spun. A fantasy world, in which you were gorgeous, and popular, and everyone loved you. In reality, it was Yvorna's popularity you were feeding on, but as to the hanging? No, Dierdra. Of course you didn't kill Yvorna.' She turned to Cadur. 'Remind me again where you were the night Yvorna was hanged.'

'Me?' He backed against the wall. 'N–nowhere. Walking. Down by the lake—'

'But it was you who suggested to Morin where to take Lisyl for her special occasion. Somewhere quiet. Romantic.'

'What of it?'

The room had fallen so quiet, you could hear the dust drop.

'Yvorna trusted you. She'd have happily gone there with you, and of course, you had motive.'

'What motive?'

'I'll come back to that in a second, but you're strong, you have no alibi, and most importantly, you knew Lisyl would find the body.' Iliona turned to Ballio. 'Clap him in irons, and don't worry about calling the army. We have Spartan soldiers on site. They will take care of this.'

The meaning was clear. Summary execution.

'Whatever you say, ma'am.' Ballio stepped smartly round the desk.

'Lisyl, I swear—'

'Leave him alone,' Dierdra said. 'He was with me. All night, if you must know.'

Iliona looked at Cadur. 'Is this true?'

'Of course it is,' Dierdra snapped. 'He—'

'Be quiet,' Iliona ordered. 'Cadur? Is it true? Did you spend the night in Dierdra's bed the night Yvorna died?'

She held her breath for what seemed like eternity.

'No,' he said eventually. 'I was by the lake. On my own.'

Praise be to Apollo! Iliona released the air from her lungs. 'See how it would have been?' she asked him. 'See what she would have done?'

He did see. Looking at Dierdra, he saw very clearly . . .

'For gods' sake,' he rasped. 'Why?'

Dierdra opened her mouth in indignation, but Iliona cut in again.

'She doesn't think of you as her long-lost son at all. For a start, there never was a son. Nor a husband. Just year after year of endless disappointment. Too many men who left money but never their names.'

'I didn't care about that. I went to her hut to play chess and drink wine, because I felt sorry for her.'

'Sorry for me? *Sorry* for me?' Of all the insults, that hurt the most. 'After all I've done for you, you ungrateful bastard. And to think I was prepared to give you an alibi, too!'

'On the contrary, you were trapping him into giving you the alibi, Dierdra. Then you'd have had him over a barrel.'

You can't leave, you'd be dead without me.

'Bollocks!'

Iliona met the hard eyes of the masseuse. 'You finally found someone who didn't judge you, and you fell for him. Hard.'

It didn't matter he was twenty years younger. Look at Hector and Anthea! She loved him, that's what counted. Why else would his favourite foods be there when he called? Why else would she fill his water skin before he set out with the horses, packing sweetmeats and pies in his saddlebag? And the wonderful thing was, Cadur sought out her company!

'For once, someone is interested in what you have to say. Who doesn't call to lay coins on the table.' Poignant, really. 'Then you notice he's calling less frequently, while spending more time with Yvorna, and even when he does come, the visits are shorter, and it's you who has to instigate them. You try warning Yvorna off, but she laughs in your face.'

'She called me an old bag,' Dierdra hissed. 'Me! She was the one sleeping around, dirty little whore. At least what I did was business!'

The last straw, Iliona imagined.

'Humiliated, jealous, believing her to be poisoning Cadur's mind against you, your only chance to claw back happiness was to wipe out your rival, making it appear like a suicide, then pretending you were such a good friend you couldn't believe she'd actually done such a thing.'

At the same time, painting her as spiteful and vindictive in playing such a cruel prank on her sister.

'Just as you told Yvorna that Melisanne was in my room, having already stolen the brooch yourself.'

I've multiplied its powers by leaving it on the altar in my room.

'You pinned it on her breast, as though she was flaunting the theft, then hid some of your own jewellery under her pillow. At which point, you cranked up the rumour mill, putting it about that she was a thief, again covering your tracks by supposedly sticking up for her, when all the time you kept blackening her name.'

It seemed everyone in the room was holding their breath.

'No one "ogled your jugs" at the Festival of the Axe God, and that clansman didn't "lose his eyeballs" down your front at the Feast. It was all part of the ploy to make Cadur notice you.'

And possibly make him jealous.

'Every time he stuck up for Yvorna, you jumped in to back him up. *Look at me*, I'm her friend. The trouble was, you were on a loser from the beginning. He'd never have fallen for you.'

'Yes, he would. After he realized she was so weak and cowardly

as to take her own life, he'd have seen who really loved him!
He'd have come back—'

Dierdra stopped short with the sudden realization that she'd
just admitted the killing.

Aware for the first time of the horror and revulsion on
everyone's faces . . .

'It – it was an accident,' she whined.

I have my plans, my lady. Everything's mapped out.

'It was murder.'

Maybe tonight . . . maybe tomorrow . . .

She'd heard Sandor throwing Iliona's words back at her at the
Feast of the Eagles, warning her that *tragedy was coming, trust
me on this* and that, when it came, it would be on her conscience,
not his.

'Pure fluke that Lisyl was at the Blue Goddess that evening.
Your intention was that Sandor should find the corpse in the
morning, to make the prophecy come true.'

Pure bad luck for Yvorna that she'd overheard Lisyl in the
stables, promising Morin her virginity.

Dierdra must have thought the gods were with her that night,
when Yvorna actually did confide in her.

'I did it for you, Cad,' Dierdra bleated, and this time they
were genuine tears streaking her make-up, even if they were
born of self-pity. None of the crocodile tears she'd produced for
the funeral. 'She wasn't good enough for you. I'm the one who
loves you. You do care for me, don't you?'

'His heart is, and always has been, elsewhere,' Iliona said
sternly. She turned to the groom. 'Am I right?'

Cadur slowly lifted his head. 'You count the grains of sand,
you tell me.'

'With pleasure.' She smiled. 'Working in the stables, you naturally saw a lot of Lisyl when she popped in to see Morin, who
of course was skiving more often than not. The more you talked
with her, the more you saw of her, the deeper you fell. Which
is why you spent so much time with Yvorna. To be even closer
to Lisyl, even though you knew she'd never be yours.'

'Yvorna was always telling me Morin was the wrong man for
her. That I should do something to *stop her committing herself
to that oaf.* But the decision was Lisyl's to make. Not mine.'

'Well, I'd have made it a bloody sight quicker, if you'd told
me, you daft sod!' Lisyl was also wiping tears from her eyes,

but for once there was something other than grief shining through.
'I thought it was Morin who'd changed. It was me.'

Iliona had seen it. Yvorna had seen it. The only person who
hadn't was Lisyl.

Even big, burly Morin, biting his lip till it bled, had noticed
his girl cooling off. Passion had died, her heart wasn't in it,
but like a dog cocking its leg, he was desperate to mark his
territory, hoping the loss of her virginity would cement the
relationship.

'You ground those chestnuts for me, just like you waded in
for that tunic,' Lisyl said. 'And stuck up for me when Morin
called Yvorna a coward.'

Cadur looked at her through his long, heavy fringe. Dark as
an adulterous liaison.

'If I went through fire for four tiny kittens, imagine what I'd
go through for you.'

'Oh, for goodness' sake, go outside and kiss the girl,' Hector
said. 'It's what you've both been waiting for.'

No one heard Dierdra's screams for the cheering.

THIRTY-ONE

The hour was late. In the garden, the scent of basil and
lavender mingled with the heady perfume of roses and
honeysuckle and the incense that burned for the gods.
Apollo the Prophet, Demeter the Gentle, and Hermes, who
protected travellers and trade. The station had dipped into
silence. A silence broken by the occasional snore. The odd
snicker of a horse in the pastures. The squeak of a bat taking
moths on the wing.

Iliona stood among the topiary and lilies, her white robes
ungirdled and her blonde hair loose, watching the reflection of
the moon in the fountain.

My work here is done, Lysander had said.

Hers, too, now. The dragons had roared. Quite impressively,
too. Shame they didn't have them in Sparta. By now, Melisanne
would have told Hector what he already knew, and would be
planning her – their – new life at the tavern. Would it end

happy-ever-after? Very doubtful, given the tissue of lies, but for now it was the only solution and at least the child would be taken care of. Cadur and Lisyl would be wrapped up in love, and Morin was already well on his way to getting drunk before the dragons began to breathe fire. In his own way, he loved Lisyl, but deep down some part of him must have known that she'd never be his. You can't lose what you've never had.

And Dierdra? Justice in Phaos was relatively merciful. Murderers, rapists and bandits were forced to drink hemlock, a slow paralysis that eventually led to death, giving them plenty of time to reflect on their crimes.

Gossip's the lifeblood of this posting station.

There would be a little less of it flowing, now Dierdra had stopped tipping lies into the mill.

He's been acting odd lately, must be his age, she'd said of Sandor.

Rubbish. Pure falsehood designed to ingratiate herself with the Spartan priestess, because having sucked the priestess in with her honey, she was free to pave the way for killing Yvorna.

First he came on to me, and when that wouldn't wash, he made a play for Yvorna.

The worst kind of falsehood, staining a man's character whilst bolstering your own, at the same time painting your victim as a weakling who couldn't cope with the pressure of a priest demanding she *purified Zabrina's altar with her love*.

From the first time Iliona saw Yvorna, flirting with the men as she topped up their goblets, she didn't look the sort of girl who'd want advice, much less take it. But Dierdra was convincing, and appearances can be deceptive.

However, the minute Iliona began to question it, she saw how cunning and cold Dierdra was underneath. In the office tonight, she realized the masseuse had no intention of buckling under verbal attack and, without evidence, there was no hope of extracting a confession. Iliona's only chance was to accuse Cadur and trust that his integrity was all she'd believed it to be and that Dierdra would trip herself up.

Suppose, though, he'd snatched at the offer of his friend's alibi. What would have happened then?

The case against him would have been dropped, but the slur would remain and the pariah would have no friend other than Dierdra. For a while, it might work, but what happened when she finally realized he hung around out of pity, not love? Would she poison him with his favourite meal of fresh crab? Stab him while he slept? Or revert to the blunt instrument she was already so familiar with?

Only the murmurings of ghosts would bear witness to the tale, and the truth, Iliona thought, was colder than the statues in this garden, and more elusive than the west wind.

In his room, Lysander was slouched over his couch, clicking the abacus that confirmed the full quota of missing gold had been located and loaded. Just a single lamp burned on the alderwood table next to his bed. The sound of funerary pipes drifted in through the window. The stars in the sky twinkled like the sun on the ocean.

'You're working late,' Iliona said.

'Hm.' A lean and bronzed arm pushed the counting frame to one side. 'Something wrong?'

'You and I have unfinished business,' she said, closing the door.

'Really? And just what might that be at this hour of the night?'

She unclipped the brooches pinning her robe and let the linen pool at her feet. 'Drugged to the eyeballs I may have been, but your arousal that night was for real.'

It's real now, he thought.

'Think carefully, Iliona. There's no future in this.'

'I know.'

Trust no one.

'No matter who it may be, or how close you become, that person will betray you,' he warned. 'Either that, or you will betray them.'

'I don't want a future.' She snuffed the light. 'I just want to forget.'

To obliterate the face of the son she had lost. The monster who stabbed her. The laughter of a girl with red hair.

'In which case, I don't think that's beyond my abilities, ma'am.'

A strong hand drew her down on to him.

Come into my parlour, said the spider to the fly.

√10